Fairy Tales

Fairy Tales

Retold by Bridget Hadaway

octopus

Acknowledgment

The publishers appreciate the cooperation of Mr Baum's estate in allowing them to retell
Dorothy and the Witch from THE WIZARD OF OZ

First published 1974 by Octopus Books Limited, 59 Grosvenor Street, London W1
Reprinted 1976, 1978
ISBN 0 7064 0374 6

Text © 1974 Octopus Books Limited   Illustrations © 1974 L'Esperto S.p.A., Milan – Octopus Books Limited
Printed in Czechoslovakia by Polygrafia, Prague
50334/2

Contents

Jack & the Beanstalk

ONCE upon a time there was a poor woman who lived in a humble cottage in the countryside with her only son, whose name was Jack.

They owned a cow that gave more milk than any other cow in the neighbourhood, and they made butter and cheese with the extra milk and sold it at the market nearby. But one day the cow went dry and there was no milk to make butter and cheese. There was not even milk for them to drink. They ate less every day, but before long they had almost nothing left to eat and no money to buy food. Jack was still too young to work and his mother had fallen ill.

Jack's mother called him to her bedside. "I am too weak to go out myself," she told him, "so you must take the cow to market and sell her there for as much money as you can."

Jack liked going to market, but he was sad that they would have to sell the cow. He set out, walking slowly, and had gone about half the way when an old man stopped him.

"Do you want to sell that cow?" he asked Jack. "I'll buy her from you here and now in exchange for these magic beans."

The beans, which were all different colours, were very beautiful, and the old man *had* said they were magic. So Jack gave him the cow and ran home with the beans.

"Look what I've got, mother!" he cried as he hurried into her room. But his mother was furious when she saw that he had come home without any money for the cow. "What!" she cried. "You've sold our good cow for these worthless beans?" And she threw them out of the window.

That evening Jack and his mother ate their last crust of bread and went to bed very sadly, for they knew that there was nothing left for breakfast. Jack woke up early next morning, still hungry. He was so hungry, in fact, that he jumped out of bed and went into the garden to look for something to eat.

To his amazement he saw that the magic beans had grown into a huge plant that stretched right up over the roof and disappeared into the sky. The stems of the plant were so thickly twisted that he could climb up them as if they were the rungs of a ladder. He began to pull himself up higher . . . and higher . . . and higher.

At last he reached the top of the beanstalk. In front of him was a white road, which led to a great castle, far in the distance. There was no one to be seen, so he started to walk along the road. Maybe someone at the castle would give him something to eat. In any

case, it would certainly be an adventure.

He was hot and tired and hungrier than ever by the time he reached the castle. Its great gate was shut, but Jack knocked on it loudly. After a while it was opened by a huge, ugly old woman, who had only one eye, in the middle of her forehead.

"Ah!" she cried. "I need a boy just like you to clean out the fires for me every day! Come in quickly and hide, or my husband will see you and eat you up!"

Frightened, Jack hurried inside at once and told the giantess he would become her servant in exchange for something to eat. She gave him a piece of bread and a glass of buttermilk. But while he was drinking it the castle walls began to shake with a heavy tread and Jack could hear the giant coming closer.

"Quick, hide behind the cupboard," whispered the giantess, and Jack slipped out of sight as the giant stamped into the room shouting:

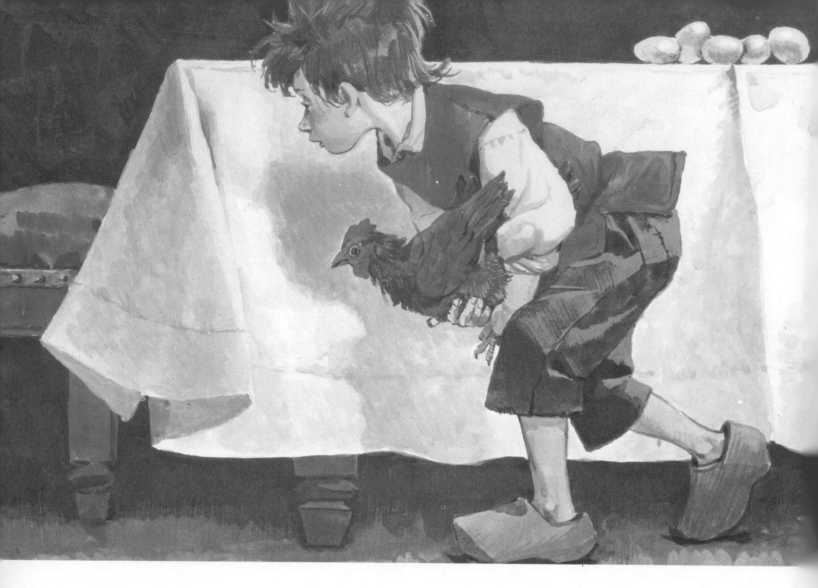

"Fee, fi, fo, fum,
I smell the blood of an Englishman;
Be he alive or be he dead
I'll grind his bones to make my bread."

"Nonsense!" said his wife. "It's only a nice young elephant that I've cooked for your breakfast. Sit down and eat it while it's hot."

So the giant sat down, ate his breakfast, and forgot all about the Englishman who stood watching him from behind the cupboard. When he had finished he called out:

"Wife, bring me my magic hen. I want to see some new golden eggs."

Jack could hardly believe his eyes when he saw what happened next. The giantess brought in a little brown hen and put it on the table in front of her husband.

"Lay!" the giant commanded, and plop! plop! plop! she immediately laid one, two, three golden eggs.

The giant scooped the eggs into his pocket. Then he settled back in his chair and soon was snoring so loudly that the castle walls shook with the noise.

Jack crept out from behind the cupboard, snatched up the magic hen, and ran out of the castle as fast as his legs would carry him. With the hen tucked under his arm, he climbed quickly down the beanstalk and hurried into the cottage and up to his mother's room. She was so happy to see him again that she cried for joy, and then she cried some more, because now they would have as many golden eggs as they wanted and need never be poor again.

But Jack soon began to long for another adventure and it was not long before he set out once more to climb the beanstalk higher . . . and higher . . . and higher. He walked up to the giant's castle again and knocked at the gate as before, but this time he had disguised himself so that the old giantess would not recognize him and had

10

dyed his hair orange. He was lucky. The old woman could not see very well with her one eye and she did not know him again.

"Come in," she said, opening the door. "You can wash our clothes and mend our socks. But mind my husband doesn't see you or he will eat you up."

No sooner had Jack entered the castle than the walls began to shake with the giant's heavy footsteps.

"Hurry, hide behind the milk churn," hissed the giantess, and Jack obeyed. The giant's voice filled the room like the roar of the sea:

"Fee, fi, fo, fum,
I smell the blood of an Englishman;
Be he alive or be he dead
I'll grind his bones to make my bread."

"You've got a cold in your nose and you can't smell anything!" scolded his wife. "And if you can, it's only the bull I've roasted for your supper. Eat it up quickly before it gets cold."

So the giant sat down and his wife served the bull on an enormous wooden platter. The two of them ate and ate until there was nothing left on the platter but the bones. Then Jack, who was still crouching behind the milk churn, heard the giant say to his wife, "Woman, bring me my money bags."

She brought him bag after bag of gold pieces and he scattered them on the table and counted the pieces and then put them back in the sacks, one by one. By the time he had closed up the last bag he was yawning, and almost as soon as he lay back in his chair he was fast asleep.

Jack tiptoed across the room, seized the money bags, and ran out of the castle with them, down the beanstalk and back to his mother. She was so glad to see him return safely that she didn't care about the gold in the sacks at all, and scolded him only for taking such risks.

Although there was now more than money enough, Jack's adventurous spirit still sent him climbing up the beanstalk again and again. Each time he dyed his hair

and fooled the giantess anew, each time he hid at sound of the giant's familiar *"Fee, fi, fo, fum,"* and waited to see what he ordered his wife to bring him once he had polished off the sheep, ox or rhinoceros she had roasted for his breakfast or supper. Then, when the giant had done his gloating and fallen into his snoring slumber, Jack would snatch up his latest prize and scramble down the beanstalk again. And if the giant and his wife never suspected that they were being depleted bit by bit of all their treasure, it was because each thought the other had stored it back where it belonged.

Jack's last haul had been a sackful of priceless emeralds and pearls, but the time came when he hankered for one more adventure for its own sake. So one morning he set out again up the beanstalk, higher . . . and higher . . . and higher, until he reached the top. This time he had dyed his hair black, and yet again the giantess did not recognize him.

"Ha! You're just the boy to help me clean out the chicken run and chase the mice away. Hurry inside, for if my husband sees you he will surely eat you up!"

Jack just had time to dart behind the woodpile as the giant came down from his turret, shouting:

"Fee, fi, fo, fum,
I smell the blood of an Englishman;
Be he alive or be he dead
I'll grind his bones to make my bread."

"You stupid old giant!" his wife shouted back. "It's only a fat sow which I've grilled for you on the spit. Sit down and eat it up quickly, before it gets cold."

The giant was very pleased for, after Englishmen, grilled pork was his favourite dish. By the end of the meal he felt so cheerful that he called to his wife: "Woman, bring me my magic harp!" and the giantess brought in a beautiful harp, inlaid with rubies and diamonds, which he had stolen from the fairies many years before.

"Play!" he said, and the harp played a soft, sad tune about the green hills and the sea.

"Play something merrier than that!" said the giant. So the harp played a happy tune, which children used to dance to.

"Play me a lullaby now," the giant said, yawning. The harp played a sweet lullaby and soon the giant was fast asleep.

Then Jack crept out from behind the woodpile and picked up the harp, intending to run away with it. But as he seized it, it began to shriek, "Master! Master!" and its strings jangled together and filled the castle with noise. The giant woke up to see Jack running out of the door with the harp.

He leaped up with a roar and lumbered after him, along the road that led to the beanstalk. The earth shook with his heavy tread and Jack could tell he was getting closer all the time. He was very frightened, but he clutched the harp closer and ran on as fast as he could.

At last he reached the beanstalk and began climbing down it as fast as he could with the harp under his arm. He could hear the giant's shouts and feel the beanstalk swaying and shaking under his weight.

Jack's mother was out in the yard and he shouted to her from halfway down the beanstalk, "Quick, mother, bring me an axe!" She ran to the woodshed and came back with the biggest axe she could find.

Jack leaped to the ground, thrust the harp into her arms, and began hacking away at the beanstalk with all his might. "Stand clear, mother!" he shouted. The stalk began to crack and sway from side to side as the giant climbed nearer. Then Jack slashed through the last stem and sprang aside, just in time, as the beanstalk came crashing down, bringing with it the giant, who hit the ground with such a thud that he was killed at once.

Jack had had enough adventures to last him the rest of his life and he and his mother lived happily for many years.

Little Red Riding Hood

ONCE upon a time there was a little girl who lived with her mother in a cottage on the edge of a large forest. Her grandmother, who doted on her, had made her for her birthday a red velvet bonnet with a tunic to match to wear over her dresses. The child liked the costume so much that she wore it every day wherever she went, until her real name was altogether forgotten and everyone who knew her called her Little Red Riding Hood instead.

One day when she was playing in the garden her mother called her and told her that she had just baked a cake which she would like Little Red Riding Hood to take with a bottle of wine to her grandmother who had fallen ill and had to stay in bed.

"As your grandmother is all alone in her house in the forest," she said, "she will be glad of your company. And this cake and the wine will do her good. Tell her I shall come myself a little later on when I am less busy." She wrapped the cake in a cloth and laid it carefully beside the bottle of wine in a basket. "Now see to it," she admonished, "that you don't stray off the path. And don't on any account talk to strangers."

Little Red Riding Hood dearly loved her grandmother, so she took the basket and set off eagerly, very proud to be entrusted with such an important errand. She was not often allowed to go so far from her home alone and, heeding what her mother had said, kept close to the path, taking care not to stumble over the sticks and stones as she ran along humming a little tune to herself. She looked very pretty with the ribbons of her red bonnet flying out above her long flaxen hair, and around her waist a blue sash the same colour as the dress that peeped out beneath her beloved red tunic.

She had to slow down when she reached the forest itself, where the trees grew thicker and the path more winding. And it was there that she met the wolf.

She had never heard of a wolf, and certainly never seen one and, having no notion of his evil cunning, was not the least bit frightened of him. It didn't enter her head that anyone would want to harm such a little thing as herself anyway.

"Good morning," said the wolf. "What a pretty red riding hood you're wearing."

The child was so pleased to hear this that she immediately forgot what her mother had said about not talking to strangers. She had always been a friendly little girl.

"Yes, isn't it," she replied. "My granny made it for my birthday. She is ill in bed and I am on my way to visit her."

"And what have you got in your basket, Little Red Riding Hood?" the wolf inquired politely.

"A cake my mother baked and some wine that we hope will make granny feel better." She held out the basket so that the wolf could have a peep inside.

"Where does your grandmother live, Little Red Riding Hood?" asked the wolf.

"She lives in the cottage next to the three oak trees in the middle of the forest."

"What a tasty little creature she does look," the wolf thought to himself, unable to keep his hungry eyes off the child. "How I'd like to eat her up this very minute. But if I'm clever I shall be able to have both her *and* her grandmother for my lunch today."

So he walked along beside Little Red Riding Hood, making amiable conversation about the beautiful morning and what a lucky little girl she was to be visiting her grandmother, while what he was really up to was trying to think of a way of delaying her so that he could reach the grandmother's

house before Little Red Riding Hood did.

Suddenly an idea came to him and he said, "Look at those lovely ripe strawberries over there and all those flowers growing under the trees. Wouldn't it be nice if you picked some to take to your grandmother?"

Little Red Riding Hood needed no persuading. She was usually an obedient little girl, but she at once forgot her other promise to her mother not to leave the path. The sunlight filtering through the trees seemed to beckon to her, and all the berries and the flowers looked so tempting that she simply *had* to pick some. Waving goodbye to the wolf, she disappeared into the forest.

Meanwhile the wolf wasted no time. With a leap and a bound he made straight off for the grandmother's cottage by a short cut and was soon knocking at the door.

"Who is there?" the old lady called out feebly from her bed.

"It's Little Red Riding Hood, granny dear, I've brought you a cake and some wine," said the wolf, trying to imitate the little girl's high-pitched squeaky voice.

"Let yourself in, my dear," replied the grandmother. "I am too weak to get up. Just lift the latch."

The wolf quickly opened the door and took a stealthy look around the room. Then in one great spring he leaped up onto the grandmother's bed and before she could let out so much as a whimper gobbled her up, nightclothes and all, in a few greedy swallows. Feeling somewhat less ravenous, he bounded across to a chest in the corner where he rummaged until he found another of the old lady's neatly folded nightgowns and caps. Slipping these on, he hastily drew the curtains to make the room a shade darker, scrambled back into the bed, and crouched down low between the sheets.

Little Red Riding Hood lost all thought of the time as she darted about picking flowers and berries. The ripe strawberries, red as her bonnet, looked so enticing that she popped almost as many into her mouth as she did into her basket. As for the flowers, there were so many that she scarcely knew which to choose, so she ran from one spot to another, trying to pick as many different colours as possible. It was only when she had gathered as many as her basket and hands could hold that she remembered her errand.

By now she had wandered so deep into the forest that she had to heed her step through the tangled bushes a little more carefully on the way back. And there were still things to distract her. A bushy-tailed squirrel didn't seem to mind such a little girl watching him bury a nut, then smooth the earth over his hiding place with his skilful paws. And what child could have resisted chasing the prettiest orange-speckled yellow butterfly until it had fluttered out of reach, or not stopped to cock an eye and an ear at a woodpecker tapping its sharp bill against the bark of a tree?

Even when she was back once more on the familiar path she still couldn't help dawdling a little, to watch a bird flapping its wings overhead or hopping about underfoot, to sniff at her posy of white, yellow, blue, red and purple wildflowers.

But eventually she reached her grandmother's cottage and knocked at the door.

"Who is there?" called the wolf, trying

hard this time to imitate the old lady's voice.

"It's Little Red Riding Hood, granny dear. I've brought you a cake my mother baked for you and some wine to make you better. And I picked some flowers and berries for you in the forest."

"Lift the latch and come right in, dear," the wolf called back as gently as he could. He had become rather impatient and cross as he waited, thinking that perhaps he had been altogether too wily for his own good and that the little girl was going to cheat him of the juiciest part of his lunch by not coming.

Little Red Riding Hood did as she was told and easily lifted the simple latch. She always enjoyed coming to see her grandmother, but now as she crossed the threshold into the cottage she suddenly felt disquiet without really knowing why. Hesitating a moment, she squinted her eyes around the darkened room, surprised that her grandmother should want to keep the curtains closed and shut out the sparkling sunshine which would surely cheer her up if she wasn't feeling well. Setting down her basket and the flowers, she tiptoed gingerly over to the large bed and was just about to give her grandmother a kiss as usual when she drew back a step with an uneasy start.

"Why, granny," she exclaimed wonderingly, "what big ears you have!"

"All the better to hear you with, my dear," came the reply. The old lady's voice sounded rather croaky, but Little Red Riding Hood thought she must have a cold. It was something much stranger about her grandmother that made her peer even more anxiously at the bed.

"Why, granny, what big eyes you have!"

"All the better to see you with, my dear."

The child's own eyes were by now almost as round as a small owl's.

"Why, granny, what enormous big hands you have!"

"All the better to hold you with, my dear."

"And, oh granny! What terribly big teeth you have."

"ALL THE BETTER TO EAT YOU WITH, MY DEAR!"

And with these ominous words the wolf reached out his great claws, grabbed hold of Little Red Riding Hood and gobbled her up in no time at all, licking his thick lips after each tender mouthful. Feeling very bloated indeed after such a sumptuous meal, he then stretched himself out to his full length on the bed, settled his head comfortably back on the pillow and was soon sound asleep, snoring loudly enough to shake the rafters.

A short while afterwards a huntsman, gun swinging from his shoulder, happened to pass that way. Thinking that something must be seriously wrong with the old lady to make her snore so raucously, he rapped on the door in case she should be in need of help. And when there was no answer, he too lifted the latch and let himself into the cottage. A few long strides brought him to the foot of the bed where he was nearly startled out of his wits to discover the wolf lying there in the old lady's stead.

"You old rogue," he muttered to himself, "so I've got you at last! I've been on your trail long enough!" and he whipped the gun off his shoulder and shot the wolf dead.

It was only then that the huntsman noticed not only that the wolf was wearing the old lady's nightclothes, but how fat he looked bulging there under the counterpane.

"So that's where she is!" he guessed out loud, and there being no sign of the old lady anywhere else, he pulled his hunting knife from his satchel and slit open the wolf's stomach from end to end. And out tumbled the old lady and Little Red Riding Hood, both of them still alive, although stiff from being so cramped, and obviously shaken by their frightening experience.

It wasn't long, however, before the two of them recovered. The huntsman sat the old

lady in an armchair and wrapped a blanket around her, but once she had eaten two slices of the cake and drunk a glassful of the wine, she declared she didn't need fussing over any more and was well enough to get dressed. And dress herself she did in her best pink dress, as if she were giving a party.

"And it really *is* like a party," Little Red Riding Hood thought, nibbling at the cake she was sharing with her grandmother and the huntsman. The porch of the cottage bloomed gaily with flowers, none gayer than her own posies arranged in a handsome pink bowl. No one had scolded her and when the huntsman slung the wolf over his shoulder and waved goodbye, she felt she had made a new friend.

But you can be sure that she never left the path or spoke to a stranger again.

Hansel & Gretel

ONCE upon a time a poor woodcutter lived on the edge of a forest with his wife and two children. The boy was called Hansel and the girl Gretel. They never had enough to eat, and as time went by, the whole country ran short of food and the family began to starve. At last, all they had to eat were a few shrivelled apples. There was not even so much as a crumb of bread left in the house.

That night, when the woodcutter went to bed, he said to his wife, who was the children's stepmother:

"What is to become of us all? How can we live without food?"

"We can't," she said. "Tomorrow morning we must take the children into the farthest part of the forest and leave them there while we go and collect wood to sell. They will never be able to find their way home again and we shall only have ourselves to find food for."

"*No*, wife!" protested the woodcutter. "I can't leave my own children in the forest to be eaten by wild beasts."

"If you don't all four of us will die of hunger, and you may just as well go and start making our coffins now." And being a mean and nagging woman, she went on arguing until at last he reluctantly agreed to her heartless plan.

Now Hansel and Gretel had not been able to go to sleep because they were still so hungry, and they overheard what their stepmother said. Gretel was very frightened and began to cry. "We're going to die, Hansel!" she wept.

"Don't cry, Gretel, I'll find a way to help us," Hansel reassured her.

He waited until his father and stepmother had gone to sleep and then he got out of bed, put on his clothes, opened the door, and slipped out of the house. The moon was shining brightly and the white pebbles that lay in front of the house glittered like pieces of silver. Hansel bent down and filled his coat and trouser pockets with them. Then he went back to Gretel, who was still awake.

"Don't worry, little sister," he said, hugging her tight. "I'll see to it that we don't get lost in the forest." And they went to sleep with their arms around each other.

At dawn the stepmother came in and shook them awake. "Get up, you lazybones —we are all going into the forest to fetch wood."

She gave each of them two apples. "That's for your lunch," she said sourly. "It's all you get today."

Gretel carried the apples in her apron, for Hansel had his pockets full of the pebbles. After they had walked a little while Hansel began to lag behind and kept looking back at the house.

His father noticed this. "Why are you always looking behind you?" he asked Hansel. "You'll stumble and fall if you don't take more care."

"I'm just looking at my white kitten, father," said Hansel quickly. "It's sitting on the roof and waving goodbye to me like it always does."

"You fool!" scolded his stepmother. "That isn't your kitten, that's the sun shining on the chimney."

But in fact Hansel was laying a trail of pebbles on the path behind them.

When they had reached the middle of the forest the father said, "We shall light a big fire here. You can keep it alight with the dry sticks on the ground." And when they had collected a large heap of these and the flames began to take a good hold, he told them:

"Now lie down by the fire, children, and

rest. Your mother and I are going farther into the forest to cut more wood. When we have finished, we shall come back and fetch you."

So Hansel and Gretel sat down near the fire and waited. They stoked it and waited. At lunchtime they ate their apples. They could hear the sound of an axe in the distance and thought it was their father felling trees. But it was not an axe that they heard; it was a branch the wind was blowing against a tree. They talked a little at first to cheer each other up, but after they had waited a very long time their eyelids grew heavier and heavier. Finally, huddled together side by side, they both fell fast asleep.

When they woke up it was completely dark and the fire had gone out completely.

"We shall never find our way out of this wood again," cried Gretel, beginning to weep.

"Wait," said Hansel. "The moon will be up soon and then we shall be able to see again."

Once the moon had risen he took his sister by the hand and followed the track of pebbles, which shone like silver coins in the moonlight, leading them all the way back to their parents' house. They knocked at the door, and when the woman opened it and saw Hansel and Gretel, she pretended that she had been expecting to see them.

"You naughty children," she scolded, "why did you sleep so long in the forest?

23

We began to think you were never coming home."

But their father was really glad to see them and hugged them close, for he had bitterly regretted leaving them behind.

Not long afterwards there was another great famine in the country, and once again there was no more food in the woodcutter's house. That night the hungry children heard their stepmother say:

"It's no good—the children will have to go. There's not enough food left to feed all of us."

Again the father argued and pleaded with her and again she insisted on getting her way in the end.

When his parents had gone to sleep, Hansel got out of bed and tried, as he had done before, to fill his pockets with pebbles. But this time his stepmother had bolted the door and he could not get out. So he returned to Gretel and tried to comfort her. "Don't worry," he reassured her. "Sleep well now for God will take care of us later."

Next morning the woman woke the children at dawn, gave them each a crust of bread for lunch, and told them they were going to collect wood in the forest again.

On the way there Hansel kept looking back at the house, and his father asked him why he was so slow.

"I'm looking at my little pigeon sitting on the roof," he answered.

"That isn't your pigeon, idiot—that's the sun shining on the chimney," said the woman.

But in reality Hansel was crumbling up the bread in his pocket and dropping it on the ground to mark the trail.

This time they went even deeper into the forest than before. Again the parents lit a big fire and told the children to sit by it and wait while they went to cut wood. "In the evening we shall come back and fetch you," the stepmother told Hansel and Gretel.

At midday Gretel shared her bread with Hansel, for he had strewn all his along the trail. Then they fell asleep, and the sun set while they were still sleeping. When they awoke it was quite dark. Gretel began to cry, and Hansel comforted her by saying:

"The moon will be up soon, Gretel, and then we shall see the breadcrumbs I scattered on the path. They will show us the way back to the house like the pebbles did before."

But when the moon had risen there were no breadcrumbs to be seen, because the birds and insects in the forest had eaten them all up.

"Never mind," Hansel said bravely to Gretel. "We shall just have to find our own way out."

By the third morning they realized that they were completely lost. They seemed to be wandering in circles that led deeper and deeper into the forest. Feeling tired and hungry and frightened, they sat down on a log and wondered what to do next. Suddenly they realized that a beautiful little snow-white bird was sitting on a branch above their heads, singing most sweetly. It seemed to be singing to them, encouraging them not to despair. Then it fluttered a little way off and seemed to be waiting for them. They rose and kept following it through the trees until they came to a little house in a clearing. It was no ordinary house, for its walls were built of honey bread and nuts, its roof was tiled with sugar cakes, and its windows were made of peppermint sticks.

"Now we can eat all we want," shouted Hansel, and he and Gretel began pulling off pieces of the roof and walls, and stuffing them into their mouths.

Then a voice called from inside:

"Nibble, nibble, little mouse,
Who is nibbling at my house?"

"The wind, the wind,
The heaven-born wind,"

the children called back gaily with their mouths crammed full.

They had eaten a big chunk of the roof and were pulling out the windowpanes so that they could lick them more easily when suddenly the door of the house opened and

an old woman came hobbling out, leaning heavily on a crutch. The children shrank back in terror, but instead of scolding them, she smiled at them and said sweetly:

"My dears, however did you find your way here? Come inside and I will give you better food than this. Don't be afraid—no harm will come to you."

She took the children's hands and led them into the kitchen, where a wonderful meal had already been prepared. On the table stood steaming hot pancakes, with syrup and apples and nuts. When they had eaten their fill, the old woman led them to a room with two cosy little white beds in it. Hansel and Gretel fell asleep that night thinking they must surely have reached heaven.

But the old woman was only pretending to be friendly. In reality she was an evil witch, whose favourite food was little children. She had built the house of sugar and spice to entice children to visit her, and once they were in her power she killed them, cooked them, and ate them. The witch had red eyes and could hardly see at all, but she could smell as well as a dog or a wolf. When she had smelled Hansel and Gretel a long way off, she had laughed to herself at the prospect of such a tasty dish.

At daybreak next day she went to the

room where the children were sleeping peacefully, snatched up Hansel, and carried him, kicking and struggling, to the yard outside, where she locked him in a cage. Then she shook Gretel awake.

"Get up, you lazy girl!" she shouted. "Fetch some water from the well in the yard to cook your brother something good. I am going to fatten him up, and when he is fat enough, I shall eat him."

Gretel was terrified, but she had to do as she was told. Every day she cleaned the house and helped the witch cook huge meals for Hansel, while she herself was only allowed to eat the scrapings from the bottom of the pot.

Every morning the old witch hobbled out to the yard and cried out shrilly, "Hansel, stick your little finger through the bars so that I can feel how very nice and fat you're getting."

But Hansel always slipped a chicken bone through the bars instead, and the witch, who could hardly see at all, pinched it and couldn't understand why Hansel never grew any fatter.

When a month had gone by and Hansel was still as thin as ever, despite all the good food she had given him, the old witch could wait no longer.

"Go to the well," she ordered Gretel, "and fetch me a bucket of water. Whether Hansel is fat or thin, I'm going to boil him in a pot and eat him for my lunch tomorrow."

Poor Gretel wept and begged the witch not to do it. "If only the wild beasts in the forest had eaten us, then at least we would have died together. Dear God, help us!" she cried.

"Hold your tongue!" shouted the witch. "Crying won't help you."

Early the next morning Gretel had to go out and gather wood for the fire and set the big pot of water on the stove to boil. She began to cry again when she thought what the water was to be used for.

"First we'll bake the bread," said the witch. "I have kneaded the dough and put it on the shelf to rise. Open the oven door and tell me if it's hot enough for me to put the bread in to bake."

And she pushed Gretel towards the oven, intending to push her into it and bake her so that she could eat her as well as Hansel. But Gretel had guessed her plan.

"I don't know how to tell if the oven is hot enough. Will you show me, please?" she asked.

"You silly goose, *this* is how you do it," said the witch impatiently, and she opened the oven door wide and bent over to feel the heat. Gretel gave her a push that toppled her right into the oven. Then she slammed the door shut and bolted it. The witch yelled and screamed, but she could not get out and was soon roasted to cinders.

Gretel ran out to the yard and opened Hansel's cage, crying out: "Hansel, we're free! The old witch is dead!"

Hansel jumped out into the yard and they hugged one another and danced about, crying for joy. Then they went into the witch's house where they found sacks and chests full of pearls and gold and precious stones.

"These are much better than pebbles," said Hansel, stuffing the pockets in his jerkin and his knickerbockers with them.

"I'll take some too," said Gretel, and she filled her apron full.

"Now let's get away from here as fast as we can," said Hansel.

When they had wandered a while they came to a river too broad for them to swim across. While they were wondering what to do a white duck came swimming by and Gretel asked it to carry them to the other bank, which it kindly did, taking first Gretel and then Hansel.

On the far side of the river the forest was less thick and the children soon began to see trees and streams that they recognized. At

last they caught sight of their father's house in the distance, and although they were very tired by now, they started to run. They ran all the way home, and straight into their father's arms. The poor man had regretted his act a thousand times over and had grown thin and grey worrying about them. Their evil stepmother, fortunately, had died.

"Look, father, what we've brought home!" cried the children, and they heaped the witch's treasure onto the table so that pearls and precious stones spilled in all directions. From that day onwards all their troubles were over and they lived happily together for many years.

Ali Baba
& the Forty Thieves

ONCE there lived in a Persian city two brothers named Kassim and Ali Baba. Kassim, who was the elder, married a rich girl, and with her money he bought a big house with plenty of slaves and horses. Ali Baba, however, married a girl as poor as himself; all they owned were three donkeys and three sacks. He used these to pick up firewood which he would sell in the city streets.

One day, as Ali Baba was out collecting wood to fill his sacks, he saw a big cloud of dust on the horizon. As he watched he realized that it was coming towards him, and the earth began to shake under his feet. "The sand out there is being shaken up by a horde of galloping horses," Ali Baba said to himself. "Whoever is on them is in a hurry and won't want me standing in the way." So he climbed up into the nearest tree and hid himself.

Soon a band of robbers came riding up at high speed. Under Ali Baba's tree they drew rein and then dismounted and tethered their

horses. First they fed the horses. Then they unloaded their booty from the horses' backs, piling sacks and sacks of gold and silver in a heap in front of a nearby rock. Then the captain of the band cried out, "Open, Sesamé!" and immediately the stone slid to one side, revealing a cave. The thieves went into the cave one by one, carrying their sacks with them. Ali Baba counted forty of them going in, and forty coming out again. Then their captain said, "Shut, Sesamé" and the rock slid back to its former position. The thieves galloped away, leaving behind them only a cloud of dust.

Ali Baba climbed down the tree as fast as he could, to see for himself what was inside the cave. "Open, Sesamé" he repeated, and waited. The rock slid back, and he stepped into the cave.

He was amazed to see that it was a well-lit vault dug out of the rock and filled to the ceiling with treasure. There were leather bags full of money, rolls of rich brocade and valuable carpets, and chests full of rubies, pearls, and emeralds. Ali Baba heard the door slide closed behind him, but he was not afraid because he knew the password to get out. He carried a few sacks of gold coins to the entrance and said, "Open, Sesamé!" The rock opened as before, and he loaded the sacks onto his donkeys and went back to the city.

When his wife saw the gold she at first thought that he had stolen it, and began scolding him, but when he told her his story she was pleased beyond measure. She began counting the coins one by one, but there were so many that she lost count. So she went to her sister-in-law to borrow her scales to weigh the sacks instead.

"What do you want them for?" asked Kassim's wife suspiciously.

"I can't tell you that!" her sister-in-law replied. Then Kassim and his wife secretly put some wax onto the bottom of the scales, so that whatever was put in the pan would stick.

Having measured the gold, Ali Baba's wife returned the scales without noticing that a piece of gold had stuck to the wax. But when Kassim and his wife saw the coin, they were filled with jealousy.

"Where did you get all that money?" Kassim demanded.

Ali Baba, who was an honest man and a good-natured one too, told his brother everything, even the password into the cave. No sooner had Kassim learned this than he was filled with greed to possess the treasure himself. He saddled ten mules, piled sacks on

their backs, and set off as fast as he could to the place where the cave was hidden. "Open, Sesamé!" he cried, and the walls of the rock slid apart before his eyes. He entered, and the walls closed behind him again.

Kassim was overcome with the sight of so much treasure. He went from one pile to the next, trying to decide which to take first. At last he filled all his sacks and returned to the entrance. But in his greed for the treasure, he had forgotten the password. All he could remember was that it was the name of some kind of seed.

"Open, barley!" he cried, but the doors remained shut. He tried various other grains, but none would work for him. At length he heard the noise of the robbers dismounting outside the cave, and tried to hide in one of the chests. But they had already discovered his mule and it did not take them long to find him too. The thieves killed Kassim and cut his body into four pieces, which they

placed near the door to frighten away anyone else who might find his way in. Then they rode off again to find some more caravans that they could rob.

When Kassim had not returned by nightfall his wife became anxious and begged Ali Baba to find him. Ali Baba guessed where he was, and set out at once for the cave. He saw blood on the rock, and soon found his brother's body inside the cave. In sorrow he wrapped the four pieces together in a sack,

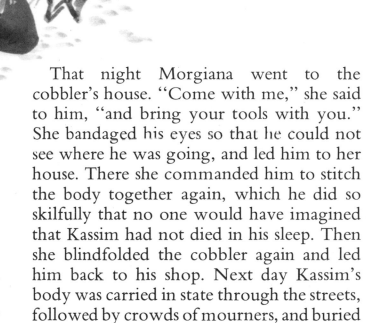

filled two more sacks with gold, and carried all three back to his sister-in-law.

Kassim's widow wept when she saw her husband's body but she was comforted by her slave Morgiana, a beautiful and intelligent girl. Because they were still afraid of the robbers' revenge, they did not want word to get round that Kassim had been murdered. The slave girl hit upon the plan of getting the most skilled cobbler in the city to come secretly and sew Kassim's body together again so that the corpse could receive a public funeral befitting a man of such enormous wealth.

That night Morgiana went to the cobbler's house. "Come with me," she said to him, "and bring your tools with you." She bandaged his eyes so that he could not see where he was going, and led him to her house. There she commanded him to stitch the body together again, which he did so skilfully that no one would have imagined that Kassim had not died in his sleep. Then she blindfolded the cobbler again and led him back to his shop. Next day Kassim's body was carried in state through the streets, followed by crowds of mourners, and buried in a grave outside the city walls.

"I will move into my brother's house and take over his estate," Ali Baba told Kassim's weeping widow, "if you will become my second wife." She dried her eyes and agreed, for it was common practice in those days for families to keep together in this way.

Meanwhile the forty thieves returned to the cave in the forest, and saw to their fury that another man had found out the secret of the cave. Without delay they dispatched one of the band into the city, to find out who it was. The first man the thief spoke to was Mustapha, the cobbler.

"Has anything extraordinary happened in this city recently?" the thief asked him, and Mustapha replied, "I can't speak for anyone else, but the other night I had to sew a dead man together again, whose body had been cut into four pieces." The thief begged Mustapha to lead him to the house where this had happened, and for the price of a gold coin and a few hides of leather the cobbler agreed to be blindfolded again and successfully led the thief to Kassim's house. The thief marked the door of the house with a white chalk cross, and returned to tell his comrades that he had found out who had stolen their treasure.

Soon afterwards the slave girl Morgiana returned from the market and noticed the strange sign on her master's door. She did not know what it meant, but decided that it would be safest if every door in the street were marked in the same way. So she chalked crosses on all the houses around.

When the thieves came to the street and saw so many white crosses they realized that they had been tricked, and in their fury they stabbed their companion to death. Another thief was sent to find Kassim's house, and again he was led to it by Mustapha in the night. This time he chalked a red circle on the door, and returned to fetch the rest of the band. In the morning, however, Morgiana was up early to fetch the milk, and she noticed the sign on the door. Again she marked all the other houses in the street in the same way, so that the robbers did not know which was the right one, and in their anger they cut off the head of the thief who had led them there.

Then the leader of the band of robbers himself visited Mustapha and was led by him to Kassim's house. Instead of marking the door, however, he made a different plan. He disguised himself as a travelling merchant, selling oil in large jars, and knocked on Ali Baba's door at sunset. Ali Baba did not recognize the robber chief, dressed as he was in a long cloak and leading nineteen mules, each with two large oil jars strapped to its sides. He could not guess that only one of these jars was filled with oil, nor that thirty-seven robbers were hidden in the other jars, each one ready to kill him when their leader gave the word.

"It is late, and I have come far," the robber chief said. "Will you give me shelter for the night and allow me to store my oil jars in your yard?" And Ali Baba, following the custom of Persia, welcomed the traveller to his house, and invited him to eat at his table that night.

As Morgiana began cooking their meal in the kitchen, her oil lamp suddenly ran dry. So she took the empty lamp into the yard to fill it with oil from one of the jars. When she approached the first jar, the robber concealed inside it mistook her for his chief and called out, "Is it time?" Morgiana was startled by the voice but she was a very quick-witted girl. "Not yet!" she replied in as deep a voice as she could. She went to every jar in turn and gave the same answer. Then she filled her biggest kettle with oil from the last jar, and set it on her stove to heat. When the oil was boiling, she carried it back to the yard and tipped some into each jar, scalding the thieves inside to death.

Her master meanwhile was eating and drinking with his guest, and Morgiana continued to wait on them as if nothing had happened. When the meal was over, Ali Baba called to Morgiana to dance for them. She came in wearing a veil and carrying a drum and a jewelled dagger. So well did she dance to the beat of her drum that the robber chief was hypnotized by her sinuous movements. Closer and closer she circled around him—then, suddenly, she stabbed him through the heart.

"What have you done?" cried Ali Baba, rising in horror. Morgiana showed him the hidden knife with which the robber chief was intending to murder his host, and when she led Ali Baba into the yard where the oil jars stood with dead thieves inside them, her master realized how well she had served him and his family.

In gratitude he gave Morgiana her freedom, and soon afterwards his son asked her to become his wife. As a wedding present, Ali Baba told the young couple the password to the cave, so they and their children were able to live in great comfort and happiness for the rest of their days.

The Magic Kettle

ONCE upon a time there lived in Japan an old man who was very poor. He lived all alone in a small house halfway up a mountain, and he had made himself a beautiful garden around his house. He was too poor to buy plants for it so he went up and down the mountain digging up the most beautiful wild flowers he could find to replant in his garden. Soon he had such a wonderful collection of flowers, trees, and shrubs that people travelled miles just to look at them.

One evening the old man was sitting in his house, resting after the day's work. He had slid back the paper walls of his room because it was so warm and because he wanted to smell his trees and flowers. Suddenly he heard a kind of rustling noise behind him. He turned round and was surprised to see a dusty old iron kettle in a corner which had been empty just a moment before. The kettle was one of those very heavy brown ones that his grandmother used to boil the water in when he was a little boy—so you can imagine how old it must have been. He had no idea how it came to be in his house, for he had never set eyes on it before. He picked the kettle up, blew the dust off it, and carried it into the kitchen.

"This is a piece of luck," he said to himself. "A good kettle costs money, and my old one is thin and cracked—in fact, it's beginning to leak."

He poured water into the kettle and put it on the fire to boil.

Soon the water in the kettle began to warm up and to sing in the way that water does when it's heating. Then a strange thing happened—so strange that the old man had to rub his eyes to make sure he wasn't dreaming.

First the handle of the kettle began to change shape. It became a head, and when it had become the size it wanted to be, the spout began to move and grow into a tail. Then the body grew four paws and a lot of fur, so that it began to look like a kind of badger called a tanuki.

The little animal jumped off the fire and ran around the room like a kitten, climbing up the paper walls and over the ceiling and then down a screen, so that the old man began to fear that it would tear his room to pieces. He ran out to ask his neighbour for help, and between them they managed to catch the tanuki and lock it up safely in a wooden chest. Then, feeling quite exhausted, they sat down and tried to decide what to do next.

"If I were you," said the neighbour, "I would sell it."

So the old man called to a child who was passing the house to go and fetch Jimmu the trader.

When Jimmu arrived the old man said to him:

"I have something I want to get rid of." With that he carefully lifted the lid of the wooden chest in which he had shut up the tanuki. But to his surprise the animal had vanished, and in its place was the kettle.

"Well, that's very odd—it's disappeared. But I can sell you this kettle instead. How much will you give me for it?" the old man asked Jimmu.

Jimmu thought the kettle wasn't worth much, but he agreed to buy it for a few yen.

He was walking down the mountain with the kettle under his arm when he noticed that it was getting heavier and heavier. By the time he reached his house he was feeling so tired that he went straight to bed and fell asleep at once. In the middle

of the night he was woken by a loud noise in the corner where he had put the kettle. He sat up to see what it could be, but there was only the kettle by the wall and so he lay back again. He had just dozed off when he was woken again by a loud crash. He jumped up, picked up a lamp, and went over to the corner. To his amazement he saw that the kettle had become a small furry tanuki, which was running round and round, chasing its tail.

Then it ran out onto the balcony and turned a few somersaults. Jimmu scratched his head and wondered what he should do with the animal. He decided to let the problem rest until morning, and went back to bed. But when he opened his eyes next day there was no tanuki, only the old kettle that he had set in the corner the night before.

As soon as he had had breakfast Jimmu went off to tell his neighbour, a wise old man who listened carefully and said:

"I am not surprised at what you tell me. I remember when I was a boy that someone in the valley had a magic kettle. If I were you I'd go and travel with it and show it to people for three yen a time—and you'll become rich."

"I must ask the tanuki's permission to do that," said Jimmu, and he thanked his friend for his advice.

The tanuki agreed gladly, for it liked to show people how it could chase its tail and turn somersaults. Jimmu built a handsome booth for it and wrote out a handbill describing the wonder, and he painted a picture of it for those who could not read the handbill.

People came in great numbers to see the show and Jimmu's fame spread far and wide. At every performance the kettle would be passed from hand to hand, looked at carefully inside and out, and handed back to Jimmu. He would then set it on a platform and command it to become a tanuki. Immediately the handle began to change into a head, the spout into a tail, and four

paws appeared, two from each side.

"Dance," said Jimmu, and the tanuki stretched itself and began to move from side to side, so gracefully that people could not stop themselves from joining in and dancing too. The tanuki led them into one dance after another until Jimmu told it to stop. Then the booth would be closed and the people would leave to make room for those who had been waiting outside to watch the next performance.

So many people came to see the strange act that Jimmu soon became rich. But he kept thinking of the simple old man who had sold him the kettle. He knew how poor he was, and it seemed to him unjust that the gains had been so unevenly divided between them.

One morning he put a hundred gold pieces into the kettle, hung it on his arm, and once more climbed the mountain to see the old man.

"I have earned as much as a man needs for the rest of his life from this kettle," he told the old man. "Now I have brought it back

to you so that you can enjoy the wealth that it brings too."

The old man thanked Jimmu and praised his honesty. Thanks to the magic kettle they both were able to live in comfort to the end of their lives, and were beloved and respected by all who knew them.

Aniello & His Little Speckled Hen

THERE was once a poor boy called Aniello who had a speckled hen. The hen died and two wizards tried to buy its body from him, but Aniello was warned just in time that his hen had a magic stone which was embedded in its head.

He cut the bird open and found the stone, and at once wished that the hen was alive again and could speak. Immediately it was so. There stood the hen, perkily ruffling her feathers and asking Aniello what he would like to wish for now. The boy, who had eaten nothing all day and was very hungry, wished right off for some food. Almost before the wish was out of his mouth, a table appeared groaning under a platter of sizzling roast beef, a heaped dish of apples and grapes, an outsize jar of strawberry jam, and a tall pitcher of lemonade.

When he had tucked happily into as much of the feast as he could possibly manage, Aniello turned to the hen and asked her, "What shall I ask for next?" And she replied, "To be a handsome lord and have a fine castle and marry a princess."

Immediately it was so and Aniello found himself sitting in his castle with his hen on his knee. He wrote to the king, asking for his daughter's hand in marriage, and the hen delivered the letter. The king was amazed that the hen could speak, and when he heard of the riches of Lord Aniello, he gladly gave him his daughter.

The pair had everything they wished for until one day the wizards managed to trick the princess into giving them the magic stone. As soon as they had it, they wished that everything was as it had been before. Aniello became a rough peasant again and was thrown out of the king's palace, and the princess hated living in a hovel so much that she ran straight back to her father.

Aniello and his hen set out to look for the wizards. They passed through the land of cats and came to the land of mice. Here one very old mouse told them he had seen the wizards and led Aniello and the hen to their castle. Once there, the old mouse slipped into the wizards' room and stole the magic stone from them while they were asleep.

Aniello immediately wished that the wizards were donkeys—and there they were, with long ears and tails. Then he wished for food for himself and the hen and the mouse, and then that he was back in his castle once more. And immediately it was just so.

But he didn't want his foolish princess back again. So he wished that he was married to somebody else, and then, almost without thinking, he wished that his hen was a girl.

And then and there, to his utter astonishment and delight, she turned before his eyes into the most beautiful girl imaginable.

"Thank you for disenchanting me," she said, for she was really a bewitched princess, and they married and—of course—lived happily ever after.

The Princess & the Pea

THERE was once a prince who wanted to get married. Being a prince, of course he had to marry a princess, but he had been brought up by his mother, the queen, to be very particular. She must be a real princess, he insisted; nothing less would do. There were no princesses in his own kingdom, so he travelled all over the world searching for one. But every princess who was introduced to him seemed to have some fault. Either her feet were too big or her nose was too long or her voice was too squeaky. He just couldn't find a real princess anywhere. So he returned to his kingdom very disappointed and thinking he would have to give up the idea of marrying altogether.

One night soon after he got back the rain began to fall in torrents and lightning and thunder shook the sky. Everyone was crouched around their fires listening to the wind when a knock was heard at the palace gate. The old king put on his boots and went to open it.

There, standing in the rain, was a princess. But what a sight she looked! Her golden hair stuck to her graceful neck and the rain was running out of her silk shoes. Yet she said she was a real princess. She said she was on her way home to her own country from a visit to a neighbouring kingdom when she was caught by the rain.

"We'll soon see about that," thought the queen when the princess was brought inside and introduced to everyone. "That's the most unlikely story I've ever heard. No real princess could ever look so bedraggled."

Guarding against being watched, the cunning old queen thereupon took a dried pea from a kitchen jar, went cautiously up to the guest room and put it in the centre of the princess's bed. Next she smuggled twenty mattresses out of the linen closets and laid them one after another on top of the pea. You never saw such an assortment of mattresses!

They were all of the finest quality of

course; in this, as in all else, only the best would have found a place in the fussy queen's household. So out came a mattress of goose feathers stitched into quilted pale pink satin, another of lustrous purple silk enfolding the fleeciest lamb's wool, a third of the purest white muslin encasing a billow of swansdown. There were striped mattresses, sprigged mattresses, brocade, linen and lawn mattresses. And yet to come were mattresses of the supplest cloth of gold interwoven with the royal initials and the royal coat of arms. Finally, the queen topped off all these accumulated layers with twenty feather quilts.

"There!" she murmured at last, huffing and puffing a bit by now after so much unwonted effort. "*Now* we'll see whether she's a real princess or not!"

In the morning the princess came down to breakfast look-ing very tired. "Did you sleep well?" asked the old queen.

"No I didn't," replied the princess. "I don't know what was in the bed. Something as hard as a rock and as big as a cannonball. In fact I think it *was* a cannonball—I'm bruised black and blue all over."

Then everyone smiled with delight, for now they knew that she was a real princess: no one else could have such delicate skin. The prince immediately took her for his wife. As for the pea, it was taken out of the bed and put in the royal museum, where it probably remains to this day.

Snow White & the Seven Dwarfs

ONCE upon a time a queen sat sewing by her window. The snow was falling outside, and she watched the flakes settle on her black ebony window sill. As she sewed, she pricked her finger with the needle and a drop of red blood fell onto the snow. She thought to herself:

"I wish I had a daughter with skin as white as this snow, with lips as red as this blood, and with hair as black as this ebony."

By and by her wish came true and she gave birth to a baby girl whom she called Snow White. But the queen died when her baby was born and not long afterwards the king married again. The new queen was very beautiful, but she was an evil woman and could not bear the idea that anyone might be lovelier than she.

A magic mirror hung in her room and each day she would look in it and ask:

"Mirror, mirror on the wall,
  Who is the fairest of us all?"

And the mirror would reply:

"You, O queen, are fairer than all."

The years went by and each day Snow White grew more beautiful until one morning, when the queen looked yet again into her mirror and asked:

"Mirror, mirror on the wall,
  Who is the fairest of us all?"

it replied:

"You are fair, O queen, it's true
  But Snow White is fairer far than you!"

The queen was beside herself with hatred and jealousy, and resolved to get rid of her stepdaughter at once. She sent for a huntsman and ordered him to take the girl deep into the forest and kill her—and bring back her heart as proof that she was dead.

The huntsman rode with Snow White into the deepest part of the forest, but when he took out his knife to kill her he was so touched by the girl's beauty and gentleness that he could not plunge its blade through her heart.

"I cannot kill you myself," he said, "but I cannot take you back to the palace, and I fear the wild beasts of the forest will soon eat you up."

He left Snow White in the forest, and on his way back he killed a deer instead and gave its heart to the queen, who believed that it was Snow White's.

Poor Snow White, meanwhile, was wandering in the dark forest, terrified. The wild beasts watched her as she stumbled through the trees, but they did not touch her. At nightfall she came to a clearing in the wood, where there was a little house. She tapped on the shutters, but no one answered. She tapped on the door, and then opened it and went inside.

She found herself in a low room with a wooden table and benches stretching the length of it. On the table were seven bowls, seven spoons, and seven cups. For this was the home of the seven dwarfs, who worked in the mountains digging for gold.

Snow White was so hungry that she sat down and ate a little of the pudding in each bowl and sipped some milk from each cup. Then she went upstairs, where there was a

room just large enough to hold seven small beds. She slipped into one of them and was soon fast asleep.

As the moon came up in the sky the seven dwarfs returned. Each carried his shovel and pickaxe on his back and his bags of gold tied to his waist with a leather strap. As soon as they set their lanterns on the table, they saw someone had been in their house.

"Who has been eating our food?" they cried. Then they climbed upstairs to the bedroom and found Snow White asleep on a bed.

"And who is this beautiful child?" they asked each other in delight and amazement. Then Snow White awoke and told them her story, and the dwarfs felt so sorry for her that they invited her to stay with them and be their housekeeper. They warned her that she must never open the door to anyone while they were away digging in the mountains, for they feared that the wicked queen would find out she was alive and try to kill her.

So Snow White stayed with the dwarfs, and made their beds and swept their rooms and cooked supper for them. She was very happy with the dwarfs and before long she had forgotten all about her wicked step-mother.

One day, however, the queen again asked her magic mirror:

"Mirror, mirror on the wall,
Who is the fairest of us all?"

and the mirror replied:

"You are fair, O queen, it's true
But Snow White is fairer far than you.
Deep within the forest glade
She her home with dwarfs has made."

The queen's face turned black with rage at these words. Realizing the huntsman had tricked her, she resolved to kill Snow White with her own hands. She disguised herself as a pedlar woman and made her way to the dwarfs' house in the forest. Snow White was sitting by the window, patching a jacket belonging to one of the dwarfs. The queen called out to her in a rough countrywoman's voice:

"Buy my buttons, ribbons, lace,
Every one will suit your face."

Delighted at the chance of buying something pretty, Snow White quite forgot the dwarfs' warning. She ran to open the door.

"The laces on your bodice are loose, my dear," said the disguised queen. "Let me tie them up for you!"

And with that she laced Snow White up so swiftly and so tightly that the girl could not breathe and fell to the ground as if she were dead. Laughing, the wicked queen hurried back to her palace, feeling certain she had got rid of Snow White for good.

When the dwarfs came home that night, they found Snow White lying in the doorway. As soon as they lifted her up, they could see what had happened. They cut the laces on her bodice with a knife and at once the air rushed back into Snow White's lungs and she began breathing again. She told them what had happened, and the dwarfs realized that the pedlar woman was the wicked queen in disguise, still determined to kill her.

"Never open the door to *anyone* again," they begged her, and Snow White promised she would not.

That night the queen went to her mirror again.

"Mirror, mirror on the wall,
Who is the fairest of us all?"

she asked, and the mirror replied:

"You are fair, O queen, it's true
But Snow White is fairer far than you."

The evil queen's blood ran cold as she heard this, and she could not rest until she had made a new plan to kill Snow White. Again she disguised herself as a pedlar woman, but this time she looked completely different and much younger. When she came to the dwarfs' house she tapped on the door and Snow White came to the window and looked out. Delighted by the combs and jewellery the pedlar woman carried on her tray, she opened the window so that she could see better.

"You have such pretty things," she said, "but I can't come out to buy anything, for I have promised I won't open the door to strangers."

"Take a look at this, my dear," urged the queen, holding up a beautiful comb made of tortoiseshell and gold.

Snow White was so interested in the comb that she forgot all about her promise and came out of the house to look at it more closely.

"Let me comb your hair with it," coaxed the queen, and she started to draw the comb through Snow White's shining black hair. But it had been dipped into a deadly poison and its teeth had only to graze Snow White's scalp for the poison to take effect. She fell to the ground in a dead faint, and the queen went away smiling with hatred.

That day the seam of gold that the dwarfs were mining ended sooner than they had expected and they came home unusually early. There they found Snow White lying as if she were dead with the poisoned comb still in her hair. They snatched it out, and as they did so she opened her eyes and smiled at them. When they heard what had happened, they warned her that the pedlar had been her stepmother and begged her never to open the door to anyone again.

The queen, meanwhile, had returned to the palace in triumph. She went straight to her mirror and asked:

"Mirror, mirror on the wall,
Who is the fairest of us all?"

But the mirror, which could only speak the
truth, replied:

*"Your poison was in vain, O queen,
Snow White's beauty reigns supreme."*

At this the enraged queen rushed to her
cellar in the castle where she kept her secret
potions. There she made a poisoned apple.
One side was bright red, the other green.
The green side could safely be eaten, but one
bite of the red side would kill in a second.

Yet again the queen disguised herself.
This time she dressed as a countrywoman in
ragged clothes with a basket of apples over
her arm. On top of the pile she placed the

beautifully coloured poisoned apple.

She arrived at the dwarfs' house just as Snow White was drawing water from the well. But as soon as the girl saw her coming she grew frightened and ran indoors, bolting the door behind her.

Then she heard the voice of the country-woman calling:

"Apples, fresh and sweet,
Apples!"

and she longed to taste them. If she opened the window and kept the door shut, there could be no danger. So she opened the shutter and leaned out.

"Let me see your apples," she called down.

"Taste this one, my pretty, it's one of the best," replied the queen, holding up the poisoned apple. Then, as the girl hesitated, she went on, "Don't be afraid to eat it. See, I'll cut it in two halves, one for you and one for me."

She began to eat the green half and threw

the red one up to Snow White, who could not resist taking a bite. But she had no sooner put the apple into her mouth than she fell to the ground, dead.

That night the queen polished and stroked the mirror as she asked:

"Mirror, mirror in my hand,
Who is the fairest in the land?"

and the mirror replied:

"Queen of beauty, you are she,
None can now your rival be!"

When the dwarfs came home and found Snow White dead beyond reviving, they built a glass coffin which they set among flowers nearby so they could watch over her day and night.

One day a young prince came riding by with huntsmen. Seeing the glass coffin, he dismounted from his horse, curious for a look at the girl inside. She seemed to be in a deep sleep, for her skin was still as white as snow, her lips as red as blood, and her hair as black as ebony. Her beauty en-enchanted him.

"Let me carry the coffin away with me," he begged the dwarfs. "I will give you greater riches than you can ever hope to dig out of these mountains."

"No," the dwarfs replied. "She is worth more to us than all the gold in the world."

But at last, when they saw that the prince had fallen in love with their dear Snow White, they took pity on him and gave him the coffin as a present.

The prince told his huntsmen to carry the glass case carefully to his palace, but as they were lifting it up one of them stumbled over a root, and the jarring made the piece of apple fall from between Snow White's lips. She awoke and sat up, looking about her in

the banquet she asked the mirror:

"Mirror, mirror on the wall
Who is the fairest of us all?"

and the mirror replied:

"Fairer than you was rarely seen,
But Snow White too is now a queen;
Your fairness, then, is nothing worth
Now Snow White's radiance fills the
earth!"

When she heard this the queen smashed the mirror in pieces to the ground, and she was so filled with a jealous rage that her heart burst and she fell down dead. But Snow White and her prince lived happily ever after.

amazement. The prince told her everything that had happened, and then asked her to become his wife. And Snow White, who had loved him the moment she set eyes on him, happily agreed.

A great feast was held in honour of their marriage and one of the guests invited was the wicked queen. As she robed herself for

Puss in Boots

THERE was once a poor miller whose only possessions were his mill, a donkey, and a cat. When he died his three sons shared them out as follows: the eldest son took the mill, the middle son the donkey, and the youngest son the cat. The youngest boy was quite dejected at the way their father's property had been divided and felt that he had received a very poor share.

"My brothers can go into partnership and use the donkey to help work the mill, but what use is a cat?" he said to himself. "I could make it into a pie and sell its skin for a muff, but I don't want to kill it."

The cat happened to have overheard his words and spoke up at once. "Don't be

sad, my good master," he said, "just give me a sack and have a pair of boots made up for me, and you will soon see that you had a better bargain than either of your brothers."

The boy was so surprised to hear the cat talk that he was quite ready to believe him. So he went to the best shoemaker in the village and ordered a pair of boots in the softest leather. The cat was so pleased with them that he wore them all the time—which is how he got his name Puss in Boots.

Then the boy gave him the sack he had asked for and Puss in Boots slung it over his shoulder and made for the woods to hunt rabbits. He put some bran and some lettuce into the sack and stretched himself out beside it, pretending to be dead.

He had barely closed his eyes when things began to happen exactly as he had planned. A plump young rabbit hopped out of the bushes, sniffed all round the sack, and then crawled inside it. In a flash the cat drew the string tightly round the top, caught the rabbit, and killed it.

Feeling very pleased that his trick had succeeded so quickly, Puss slung the sack over his shoulder again and set out for the king's palace. Once there, he demanded to see the king without delay, and the flunkeys escorted him to the throne room.

"Sire," he said, bowing, low to the king, I have brought you a young rabbit which my noble lord, the Marquis of Carabas"—for that was the title he had just invented for the miller's son—"has commanded me to present to your majesty."

"Thank your master," the king said graciously, "and tell him I am very pleased with his present."

Another time the cat hid himself in the wheatfields and held his sack wide open. When a couple of partridges fluttered into it, he pulled the string tight and caught them fast. These too he presented to the king, who rewarded Puss suitably.

One day he overheard the courtiers saying that the king was planning to go for a drive along the river with his daughter, who was the most beautiful princess in the world. The cat ran back to his master and said, "If you do as I say, your fortune is made. All you have to do is to go bathing in the river at the exact time and in the exact spot that I tell you. Leave the rest to me."

The young man was very puzzled at this, but he decided to follow the cat's instructions because it was a hot sunny day and he liked swimming in the river anyway. While he was splashing about the king came by in his carriage. At once the cat began to

cry out, "Help! Help! The Marquis of Carabas is drowning! Help! Help!"

As soon as the king heard this name he ordered the carriage to be stopped and commanded his flunkeys to run immediately to rescue the Marquis of Carabas. While they were dragging the boy out of the river, Puss in Boots came up to the carriage and told the king that while his master was bathing, some thieves had come and taken all his clothes away. In fact, the cunning cat had hidden them under a rock.

The king immediately sent an officer off to the palace to fetch one of his best suits for the Marquis of Carabas. Once he was dressed in these new clothes the miller's son was transformed into such a handsome, noble-looking young man that the princess instantly fell in love with him. She persuaded her father to invite him into the royal carriage to accompany them on their drive.

Puss in Boots, who had watched all this with the greatest satisfaction, hurried off ahead of the royal party. Soon he came across some peasants mowing a meadow and said to them, "The king will be driving past soon. When he stops and asks you who owns this meadow that you are mowing, you had better say it belongs to my lord the Marquis of Carabas—for if you don't, you will be chopped into little pieces."

Sure enough, the king ordered his carriage to stop, and asked the mowers to whom the meadows belonged.

"To my lord the Marquis of Carabas," the mowers answered with one voice, for the cat had almost scared them silly.

The king turned to the young man and congratulated him on his fine fertile lands.

Meanwhile the cat ran on ahead once again, and soon came across some reapers reaping a field. Again he told them to say the fields around belonged to the Marquis of Carabas, and again he threatened them with the chopper if they did not. When the king came by a moment later and asked the men who owned the land, they chorused obediently, "To my lord the Marquis of Carabas," and the king once again complimented the young man by his side.

Puss kept running ahead of the royal carriage, and as the king drove on through the countryside he kept hearing the same story.

Finally Puss in Boots came to a stately castle which was owned by an ogre. In fact, it was he who owned all the lands that the king had been riding through. The cat asked to speak to him, saying that his fame had spread far and wide.

The ogre was very flattered at this and invited Puss in Boots to sit down.

"I have heard much about your great skills," the cat went on, "and have been told that you are able to turn yourself into whatever you like. I have heard, for instance, that you can turn yourself into a lion or an elephant or some such wild animal."

"Indeed I can," said the ogre proudly, "and to prove it, I shall show you now." With these words he transformed himself into a lion and let out a great roar which shook the castle walls. Puss in Boots was so frightened that he leaped up onto the roof, which was a dangerous thing to do in his boots. Eventually, when the ogre had resumed his natural form, Puss jumped down again.

"You really scared me," he told the ogre, "but I have also heard it said that you can take on the shape of a tiny creature such as, say, a mouse or a rat. I think *that* would be quite impossible."

"Impossible? Nothing is impossible for me!" exclaimed the ogre, and with that he changed himself into a fieldmouse and began scampering around the floor. With one pounce the cat caught him and ate him up.

Meanwhile the king had seen the castle in the distance and decided to pay a call on its owner. As the carriage rattled over the drawbridge Puss hurried towards it.

"Welcome to the castle of the Marquis of Carabas!" he called, and the king was delighted to hear that his friend lived in such a splendid place.

The young man invited the king and princess into the great hall, where a feast had already been prepared by the ogre for his friends, who were now too scared to come in. When they had finished eating and drinking everything on the tables, the king proposed to the marquis that since he and the princess had obviously fallen in love, they ought to get married. This they promptly did, and lived happily ever after. As for Puss in Boots, he became a great lord and never chased mice again, except for fun.

Dick Whittington & His Cat

ONCE upon a time when the world seemed a much larger place because people had to go nearly everywhere on foot, a boy called Dick Whittington lived in a village in England. His father and mother were both dead and there was no

one to look after him. The people of the village used to give him food when they could spare it, but Dick was always hungry.

In those days the great city of London seemed like a fairyland to country folk who would never visit it in their lives, and Dick heard many strange things about London. Its streets, people said, were paved with gold. This interested Dick, who had always been poor, and he decided to go to London and see for himself.

It was a very long walk to London and Dick Whittington would never have found his way there if it had not been for a waggoner who let him walk beside his cart. After journeying many days they came to the great river Thames and could see the city of London with its tall church spires across the water. The waggoner paid a toll, and then they were allowed to cross London Bridge and pass through a large gate into the city.

"Now you're on your own," the waggoner said to Dick, and the boy set off bravely, hoping soon to find the streets that were paved with gold. But instead of gold he found mud in the streets and streams of dirty water running down the middle of them.

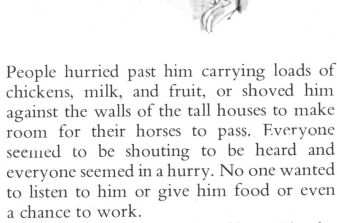

People hurried past him carrying loads of chickens, milk, and fruit, or shoved him against the walls of the tall houses to make room for their horses to pass. Everyone seemed to be shouting to be heard and everyone seemed in a hurry. No one wanted to listen to him or give him food or even a chance to work.

Presently he found himself outside the gate of a large house. He could see into the big courtyard, which was piled with sacks of corn and barrels of food. Servants were carrying them up into the attics and down into the cellars. With so much going on in the household, Dick thought there might be some work for him there too. A delicious smell of roast pork and baked apples came floating over to him from the kitchen, and so he decided to ask the cook for a job as kitchen boy.

Unfortunately, the cook was a very cross woman with a temper as hot as the ovens she stoked. She gave Dick Whittington several cuffs around the

ears as he told her his story, and then she said that he could stay and clean out the pots for her and eat the scrapings inside them if he was hungry. The pots were all made of iron and very heavy, and some of them were almost as large as Dick himself. They were always covered with soot from hanging over the open fire, and the cook was forever scolding Dick for not getting them clean.

As a punishment she made him sleep in a small attic under the roof. The only light was what came through the cracks in the tiles. All he had to lie on was a bale of hay, and he had to share this with the mice and rats who nested in it. He could not sleep at night because they were constantly fighting and scratching for food.

One Sunday morning when he had a little time off, Dick Whittington went down to the river to see the big ships lying at anchor there. He was walking over the cobblestones when he saw something bright shining in the sunlight at his feet. He bent down and picked up a small gold coin!

Eagerly, he hurried to the nearest fish stall and asked the woman there if he could buy her cat. She agreed and he took the cat home, where it soon caught all the rats and mice that had made him so miserable.

The house belonged to a wealthy merchant named Fitzwarren, and soon after this he called all his family and his servants together. One of his big ships was about to set sail on a trading voyage, and he told them that each of them could send something on it to be sold or exchanged for rich goods in foreign lands. Everyone had something to send save Dick Whittington, who owned nothing but his cat. But he finally let them persuade him to send it with the captain on the forthcoming voyage.

For many months nothing was heard of the ship and the cook began to bully Dick more and more. She threw things at him if he was late and hit him if he got in her way. She shouted at him whatever he did. Dick was so unhappy that at last he decided to run away. Early one morning he wrapped his spare shirt in a red spotted handkerchief, tied it to a stick, and left the house without waking anyone.

He had no idea which direction he should take. But when he had trudged the deserted streets for a while, he found himself at the top of Highgate Hill and sat down on a stone to have a last look at the city of London and consider what he should do next.

Just then Bow Bells began to ring.

"Turn again Whittington
Lord Mayor of London."

they seemed to call. And they rang it again

and again, echoing loud and clear across the hushed early morning air until Dick jumped up, his heart pounding with excitement.

"Lord Mayor of London!" he exulted to the sky. "Me, Dick Whittington! It's worth putting up with that mean cook and her dirty pots and pans if I can drive around the city in a fine coach when I grow up. I was wrong to try to run away—I must go back again right away."

And so Dick Whittington hurried back to the merchant's house by the river, and managed to creep into the kitchen before anyone had noticed his absence.

Meanwhile, Mr Fitzwarren's ship with the cat on board was having a rough voyage and a long one. At last it was driven by the wind onto a part of the Moorish coast which no traders had ever visited before. The Moors were delighted to see the captain and his crew, and their king ordered a big feast to be prepared for them. However, before anyone had a chance to eat more than a mouthful or two of the food, a swarm of rats and mice burst into the room, ran all over the table, and ate up everything on the richly laden plates.

The Moorish king explained that the

country was infested with these vermin and that he would give anything to be rid of them.

At this the captain saw a chance of striking an even better bargain with the king.

"Your majesty," he announced, "your troubles are ended. You need not be starved of your food any more. I carry with me on my ship a great and terrible creature, the enemy of all rats and mice. So greatly do these vermin fear it that the smell of it alone will keep them away from your kitchens and granaries."

The king was amazed to hear of such a creature and asked to see it at once. The captain hurried back to his ship and returned with Dick's cat under his arm. He set it down on the carpet in front of the king and queen, and immediately its whiskers began to twitch. Then its tail flicked from side to side and its eyes narrowed to two yellow slits. Suddenly it pounced under the queen's throne and pulled out a big rat that had been hiding there. It killed the rat, and then another, and then another until, within a surprisingly short time, almost all the vermin had been killed. The king ordered another great feast to be held and this time everyone had as much to eat as they liked.

After a few days of feasting the captain began to make ready to sail. The king wanted to buy the whole ship's cargo and offered him, in addition, half the treasures in his kingdom in exchange for the cat. Instead of Dick's cat, however, the captain let him have five of her kittens, and the grateful king ordered his treasury to be opened and half its contents carried to the boat.

Heavily loaded, the ship sailed away and after many weeks it anchored safely in the river Thames, close to Mr Fitzwarren's house. There was great excitment as the caskets and barrels full of jewels and gold, cloth and spices were carried into his courtyard. Dick ran out to meet his cat, which was very pleased to see him and kept rubbing its head against his legs.

The captain told Mr Fitzwarren the story of the cat and the rats and at the end of it the merchant said:

"Why, then half of this treasure is Dick's and may God's blessing be on it. You are all to call him Master Whittington now, and the cook is to cook him the best dinner she can to celebrate his good fortune."

From then on Dick Whittington's fortunes changed. Instead of being cuffed by the cook all day long he began to read books and study maps and talk with wise people. He bought ships of his own and travelled around the world with them, always taking his cat wherever he went. He had grown into a handsome man, and there wasn't a girl in London who would not have been glad to marry him. But of all the girls Dick had seen, Mr Fitzwarren's daughter Alice, who had been a pretty little girl when he was still a kitchen boy, was the one he loved the best.

So they married and lived happily ever after. But Dick Whittington never forgot the poor. He gave money to hospitals and churches, and to schools, and at length the king knighted him for his services. Three times Sir Richard Whittington served as Lord Mayor of London, and you can see his name to this day in the city's records.

The Pied Piper of Hamelin

L ONG, long ago the town of Hamelin in Germany was suddenly overrun by thousands of rats.

They fought the dogs and killed the cats,
And bit the babies in the cradles,
And ate the cheeses out of the vats,
And licked the soup from the cooks' own
  ladles,
Made nests inside men's Sunday hats,
And even spoiled the women's chats
By drowning their speaking
With shrieking and squeaking
In fifty different sharps and flats.

The people of Hamelin were not prepared to sit quietly by while the rats gobbled the food off their tables. They chased them out of their houses with brushes and brooms and pokers and pails—but the rats just whisked their tails and scurried back in again. Soon every scrap of food had vanished. The people gathered outside the town hall and demanded that the mayor do something about ridding the town of these vermin.

Their angry shouts quite frightened the mayor. He came out onto the steps and said in a shaky voice:

"As mayor of this historic town I declare that it is a great pity that our law-abiding citizens are troubled by rats. . . ."

But the people weren't satisfied with words—they wanted action. And this was just what the mayor couldn't offer. Instead,

he held a bag of gold up in his hand and promised to give it as a reward to anyone who could clear the town of the rats.

Suddenly a voice was heard above the noise in the square. "I'll rid your town of rats," it called. Everyone stopped shouting and turned round to see who was speaking.

A stranger stood there. He was barefooted and wore a tunic of yellow and red, and a high pointed hat with a long feather in it. Around his neck hung a pipe; his name, he told them, was the Pied Piper. The people all laughed at him because he looked so strange, but he paid no attention to them.

"If I can rid your town of rats, will you give me the gold?" he asked.

"Of course," said the mayor.

So the Piper stepped back and put his pipe to his mouth. He puffed out his cheeks and blew a long, silvery note, and then another.

And ere three shrill notes the pipe uttered
You heard as if an army muttered;
And the muttering grew to a mighty rumbling;
And out of the houses the rats came tumbling.
Great rats, small rats, lean rats, brawny rats,
Brown rats, black rats, grey rats, tawny rats,
Fathers, mothers, uncles, cousins,
Families by tens and dozens,
Brothers, sisters, husbands, wives—
Followed the Piper for their lives.

The mayor himself helped to pull wide the huge town gate, and out the flood of rats

poured into the open countryside, with the Piper at their head, still playing.

At length they reached a distant valley where the largest Swiss cheese they had ever seen stood waiting for them. With one accord they ran up to it and in at its thousands of holes, until the tail of the last rat had disappeared inside. Then the holes in the cheese closed up and it slowly faded away until no more than a golden mist remained.

The Piper hurried gaily back to the town of Hamelin to collect his reward. The people were still crowding the city walls, and when they caught sight of the Piper returning they cheered him loudly. It was only the mayor who frowned.

"Give this barefoot wanderer a bag of gold?" he grumbled. "Why, all he's done is pipe a tune and go for a walk in the country." So, instead of the money bag he had promised, he tossed the Piper just one gold coin. The people, who were as mean as the mayor and did not want their gold to go to a stranger, quickly forgot the service the Piper had done.

"All you did was play a tune!" they shouted and jeered.

The Pied Piper began to frown. "How dishonest and ungrateful they are," he thought, "and their children will grow up to be the same. I can save them from that."

Once more he stepped up to the town gate. Once more he raised the pipe to his lips and blew three notes of great sweetness on it. The people stopped jeering and watched in troubled silence. The piper's tune became gay and joyful. He began to dance up and down, as if he were giving an invitation to all the children in the town to come out and join him.

Then all the doors in the town popped open and out the children of Hamelin came running. Children of all ages, even little ones scarcely able to toddle, tumbled into the streets. To the sound of the Piper's sweet and merry tune they began to dance towards the town gate, skipping and turning cartwheels as they went. The gate opened in

front of them and hands linked in a long chain, out they skipped into the country.

They followed the Piper down the road, never once looking back at the town of Hamelin. With him they danced over the hills and far away, to a new land where people were kind and generous and always kept their promises.

The Voyages of Sindbad the Sailor

THERE once lived in the city of Baghdad a poor porter named Hindbad. One day, when he was carrying a heavy load from one end of the city to the other and the sun was beating down on him, he happened to walk into a street where the stones were sprinkled with rose water and a gentle breeze cooled the air. He rested for a moment, looking around him, and saw that he was standing outside a grand villa, with colonnades and courtyards, fountains and shaded gardens. He knew who owned it—Sindbad the sailor.

Hindbad the porter stood looking at the home of Sindbad, growing more and more jealous of the other man's riches. "By the prophet Mohammed!" he shouted, waving his stick in the air. "This Sindbad the sailor is no better a man than I am, yet he seems to enjoy every pleasure in life while I suffer a thousand ills!"

It so happened that the shutters were open in the porch where Sindbad was sitting, and the sailor, sitting behind some hanging beads that kept the flies out, heard Hindbad's bitter words quite clearly. He sent his servants out to bring the porter into the house, and said to him, "I do not blame you for your angry words, brother Hindbad, and I am truly sorry for the hardships in your life. But you are wrong to think I have come by all this wealth without labour. I have in fact suffered many hardships, and have faced death more often and more horribly than any other man in Baghdad. Let me tell you some of my adventures, so that you can judge which one of us has had the more difficult life."

He made the porter sit down beside him, gave him some excellent wine and a dish full of tasty food, and began:

"As a young man I wasted most of my father's money until at length, bored by living in luxury, I went on a trading voyage with some merchants. After a few weeks at sea our ship was caught in a fast current off some islands in the East Indies. The ship was dashed against the rocks, where it split into pieces. But we managed to scramble ashore with some of our cargo. We had been wrecked at the foot of a large mountain, which was entirely composed of rubies, crystals, and other precious stones. Because there was no vegetation nor fresh water, however, my companions quickly died and I was forced to bury them one by one. Then, weak as I was, I noticed that a vast river of black water flowed into the mountain, and I had just enough strength left to build myself a raft from the ship's timbers and embark on it.

"The current quickly carried me underground, but not before I had laden my raft with a cargo of rubies, emeralds, crystals, and gems of all kinds. As the waters swept me into the mountain I fell into a deep sleep, which must have lasted for many days. When I awoke I was surprised to find myself lying on the ground in open country and surrounded by black men, who had tied my raft to the bank of the river. I greeted them courteously, and one of them addressed me in Arabic:

"'Brother, we beg you to tell us how you came to our country and who you are.' After I had eaten some of the food they offered me,

I gave them an account of all that had happened since I left Baghdad. Then they took me to their king, and he, too, was struck with amazement and admiration at my adventures. He said that the rubies and emeralds that I had brought from the mountain were larger than any he had seen, and invited me to stay in his palace as long as I wished.

"During my stay in the city of Serendib, for that was its name, I visited all the places of interest in the country, including the high mountain on whose summit Adam had been placed by the Angel after being banished from Paradise. I also visited the pearl fisheries on the coast, and brought back pearls as big as pomegranates.

"In the palace itself I spent, I admit, an indulged interlude—the only such one in the course of my otherwise cruel misadventures. Attendants came at my bidding, or hovered discreetly, anticipating my every wish, so skilled were they in divining a man's desires before he was even aware of them himself. Spacious hours were given to engaging converse in the languorous pleasure gardens of the palace where peacocks strutted the sweeping lawns and gazelles nibbled out of one's hand. By night there was feasting, the platters fragrant with the choicest of delicacies and the goblets filled with the rarest of wines. The king enjoyed his riches, but was possessed of a wisdom that does not always come with wealth or majesty. Much I learned from him of the precepts of old, the ancient truths that can guide and strengthen along the way and have since stood me in good stead; not least, for all that they near bowed me under, during some of the perils I was yet to endure.

"Though my stay with the king of Serendib was so agreeable, I longed to see Baghdad again, and begged my host to arrange for my return. Regretfully, the king agreed, and gave me a rich present from his treasury, along with a letter to the caliph of Baghdad, which read as follows:

"*From the king of Serendib, who is carried aloft by a thousand elephants, who lives in a palace built of a hundred thousand rubies and who possesses in his treasury twenty thousand crowns cut out of diamonds, to the caliph of Baghdad.*

"We send you, through your loyal servant Sindbad the sailor, a small present of a vase cut out of a single ruby, filled with pearls, and wrapped in the skin of a serpent that can cure anyone of any illness by the touch of its scales. This humble present is no more than a token of our friendship to you. In return, we ask for your friendship, and salute you as a brother.

"I thanked the king by falling at his feet and kissing them. Then the ship set sail, and after many weeks we arrived in Baghdad, where I presented the caliph with the king's letter and gifts, and was made very welcome.

"Several years passed, during which I made seven more voyages and suffered seven more shipwrecks accompanied by unbearable hardships. It was my destiny to see my companions drowned, or roasted by one-eyed monsters, or devoured by serpents, or cooked by cannibals. I alone among them lived to tell the tale, and was lucky to return to Baghdad after each voyage laden with rich merchandise of aloes and sandalwood, camphor, nutmegs, cloves, pepper, and ginger. But the storms and my narrow escapes from death had turned my hair white before its time, so that I became old and bent with the weight of knowledge. I made up my mind that I would never again risk my life at sea, but would stay at home and enjoy the pleasant fountains and pools in my garden, while musicians played and sang around me.

"One day, however, while I was entertaining my friends, the caliph sent for me. 'Sindbad,' he told me, 'I want you to go once more to the king of Serendib, to bring him my thanks and some presents in return for the honour he has shown me.' I protested that I was too old and worn to undertake such a dangerous journey, but the caliph insisted, and gave me a thousand gold pieces to pay for hiring a ship and a crew.

"I had no choice but to obey the caliph's command, and set off once more for Serendib. After a pleasant voyage I arrived at the island and went at once to visit the

king. He was delighted with the caliph's presents and sent him in return a bed made of gold, fifty robes of crimson satin and a hundred more of the finest white linen, two more beds of ivory richly inlaid, an agate bowl, and a table made of camphorwood and pearls, which he said had belonged to the great King Solomon.

"As soon as these gifts had been loaded on board, I set sail for Baghdad, but within a few days we were attacked by pirates. They killed anyone who tried to resist, and took prisoner all the others, including myself. They stripped us of our fine clothes and dressed us in rags. Then they set sail for a distant island, where they sold us as slaves in the market.

"I was bought by a rich merchant who took me to his house, gave me a bow and some arrows, and ordered me to join him on an elephant hunt. After several hours' journey we came to a forest full of elephants. My master ordered me to climb into a tree and shoot as many of them as I could.

"I killed so many of these poor beasts that my master was very pleased with me, because he was able to sell the elephants' ivory tusks for large sums of money to foreign merchants. I went on hunting and shooting in the forest until, one day, the elephants became filled with a terrible rage and set out to destroy me. I had heard them trumpeting as they trampled through the forest looking for me, and had climbed high up into a tree. They surrounded the tree, pounding the earth with their huge feet until

the whole forest seemed to shake. Then the largest of them twisted his trunk round the body of the tree and shook it so violently that he tore it up by the roots.

"To my surprise, the elephant did not kill me, but instead lifted me from the tree and carried me to an open place, where he put me down. Then the whole herd turned and went back to the forest. Looking around me I saw they had placed me on top of a huge mound of elephants' bones and tusks—I think in order to show me how evil it was to kill them just to take their ivory tusks. I made my way back to the city, a wiser and a humbler man.

"My master was so amazed at my escape that he set me free and gave me money to return to Baghdad. The monsoon winds filled the sails of my ship once more, and carried me safely home. As soon as I arrived I visited the caliph, and recounted my adventures. He said he would not have believed the story of the elephants had he not known I was an honest man. Then he ordered his secretaries to write the tale down in letters of gold and store it away in his library. I came home laden with his presents, and made up my mind I would never leave this city again."

Here Sindbad paused, and then he offered Hindbad the pipe from which he had been smoking. "Well, my friend," he said, "have you heard of anyone who has suffered more unhappiness or been through so many misfortunes?"

"No, sir," said the porter, "and my own small discomforts are nothing in comparison with yours."

Then Sindbad offered him a hundred gold pieces, and invited him to be a regular guest at his table. From that day on Hindbad never had to carry another load, and the two old men continued to live together in friendship until the hour of their deaths.

The Snake Prince

ONCE upon a time there was an old woman who lived by herself in a city in India. She was very poor. One day she went down to the river as usual to wash, taking with her a small brass pot which she used to carry water back to her hut. She set the pot down on the river bank while she washed, but when she lifted the lid off to fill it there was a glittering, deadly snake inside. She thought, "I will take this snake home with me and let it kill me there, for I am poor and alone and I long for death."

When she reached her hut she tipped the pot over onto the floor but to her surprise, instead of the snake, a magnificent necklace fell out. She picked it up and hurried to the palace to offer it to the king. When the king saw the necklace he bought it from the old woman at once to give to his queen, whose days were filled with sadness because she had no children.

The queen was delighted with the beautiful necklace and locked it away in her jewel chest. Some time later she wanted to look at it again, but when she opened the door she found to her amazement that the necklace had disappeared and in its place was a baby boy, who sat on the silk cushion

smiling and beaming happily at her.

"Oh!" she gasped. "I've always longed for a baby. This child is a lovelier jewel than any necklace that ever was made!"

The years went by and the boy grew into a young man whose beauty and wisdom were praised by all. His parents started looking for a bride for their son, and eventually it was arranged that he should marry a beautiful princess from a neighbouring state.

Now the old woman who had sold the necklace to the king had been given the position of nurse to the young prince. She loved the boy dearly, and in her foolish pride she could not help boasting a little to the other servants that there had been magic in his birth. This rumour spread until by and by it reached the ears of the prince's bride. Filled with curiosity, she resolved to find out the secret as soon as she became his wife.

When the feasting was over and night had fallen and the scent of flowers filled the air, the prince spoke tenderly to his bride, but she did not answer him. She was silent for a long time, while the prince pleaded with her to speak. At last she said, "Tell me the story of your birth."

The prince was filled with dismay at her request. "If I tell you," he said, "you will be sorry that you ever asked me."

For many months their lives continued in this way, each one growing sadder and paler because of the secret that lay between them. At last the prince could bear it no longer and said to his bride, "At midnight tonight I promise to tell you my secret, but you will repent it all your life."

The princess was so happy to hear this that she paid no heed to his warning. That night the prince ordered their horses to be saddled and a little before midnight he rode

79

with the princess down to the river. By its bank he stopped and asked in an infinitely sad voice, "Do you still wish me to tell you my secret?"

"Yes," she answered.

"Then," said the prince, "know that I am the son of the king of a far country and that I was turned by a wicked spell into a snake."

No sooner had he spoken the last word than he sank to the ground and disappeared. The princess heard a rustle and saw in the moonlight a snake gliding into the river. She called to her love to return and searched everywhere for him. But the night held its secret. The wind mourned through the trees and the river flowed silently past, and her prince did not return.

When the king and queen found her in the morning, she was weeping and her long hair was flowing loose. Her feet were cut and bleeding from the stones that she had stumbled on in the night, searching for her husband. All she asked was that they build a temple of black stone on the river bank where she could live alone and mourn for the prince.

Years passed, and still the princess waited for her husband to return. She never left the temple and the guards who watched over her never allowed anyone to come inside.

Then, one morning when she awoke she found a stain of fresh mud on the pillow beside her. She asked the guards if anyone had entered the room while she was asleep. But they had seen no one.

The next morning she again found fresh mud on the pillow. Again she asked the guards and again they assured her that no one could have entered her room. The third night the princess determined to stay awake and watch, so she cut her finger with a knife so that the pain would keep her from sleeping.

At midnight she saw a snake come gliding along the floor, with mud from the river still clinging to its skin. It came up to her bed, raised its head, and then sank down on the pillow beside her.

"Who are you, and what do you want?" she whispered, terrified.

"I am the prince, your husband," replied the snake, "and I have come to see you again."

The princess began to weep and as he

watched her the snake went on, "Alas! Didn't I tell you that you would repent your curiosity all your life?"

"Oh, yes!" cried the poor princess. "I have repented it all these years that I have been alone. Is there nothing I can do to bring you back again?"

And the snake answered, "Yes, there is one thing, if you are brave enough to do it. You must put a bowl of milk and honey in each of the corners of this room. All the snakes in the river will come and drink the milk, and the one that leads the way will be the Queen of the Snakes. You must stand in front of her and say, 'O Queen of Snakes, Queen of Snakes, give me back my husband!' But if you are frightened and do not stop her, she

will keep me in her power for ever, and you will never see me again."

With these words the snake glided away and disappeared into the river.

The following night the princess took four bowls of milk and honey and put one in each corner of the room. Then she stood in the doorway, waiting. At midnight there was a great hissing and rustling from the river and presently the ground was covered with the writhing forms of snakes, their eyes glittering and their forked tongues quivering and reaching forward as they moved towards the princess. They were led by a huge, hideous creature who was the Queen of the Snakes.

The guards were so frightened that they ran away and left the princess alone, standing in the doorway. She was deathly white, but determined that she would not run away. As the snakes came closer they rose up and began swaying to and fro, flicking their forked tongues in the air. But the princess still stood firm, and when the

leading snake came within reach of her, she cried, "O Queen of Snakes, Queen of Snakes, give me back my husband!" And all the swaying band of snakes seemed to whisper to the night, "Her husband, her husband."

But the Queen of the Snakes moved forward until her head was almost touching the princess's face and her small, evil eyes seemed to flash fire. Still the princess stood in the doorway and again she cried:

"O Queen of Snakes, Queen of Snakes, give me back my husband!"

Then the snake fell back and hissed:

"Tomorrow you shall have him!"

When she heard these words the princess sank fainting onto her bed. As if in a dream she saw the room filled with snakes sliding over and under each other to reach the bowls of milk. And then they went away.

The next morning the princess took off her mourning dress and put on beautiful clothes again. She filled the temple with flowers and when night came she lit the garden with lanterns and the temple with

candles. At midnight the prince
came to her from out of the river.
She ran to meet him, and they
embraced with greater joy and love
than they had ever felt before.

The old king and queen wept for joy too,
and commanded that the feasting and
rejoicing begin. The old woman who had
been the prince's nurse became in due course
his children's nurse too—at least, she was
called that, but in fact she was far too old to
do anything for the children but love them.
And the prince and princess ruled the land
for many years with love and wisdom in
their hearts.

Cannetella & the Wizard

THERE was once in Sicily a proud princess called Cannetella, who found fault with all her suitors. One, she maintained, was too fat, one too short, one was too dark, one squinted, one was too miserly. Nor did Cannetella fancy the most eligible one of all because, although he was rich and handsome, he had a very domineering, imperious mother, and the spoiled strong-willed young girl said with a toss of her head that she would never marry a man who could be ordered about by anyone but herself.

When her father finally grew very angry indeed, Cannetella retorted naughtily that she would only marry a man with a gold head and gold teeth. A wizard called Sciorovante heard this and made himself a gold head with gold teeth, and then came to pay court to her. He was huge and ugly, but the princess had given her word. So she accepted him, and he rode away with her on his great black horse.

When they reached his castle, Sciorovante locked her in the stable with six white horses and the black one. Then he went away for a year, saying she could eat and drink what the horses left, but she must never leave the stable.

Months passed. Then one day, through a crack in the stable wall, Cannetella saw a lovely garden full of plum trees and grape vines, all heavy with fruit. She was so hungry that she slipped out of the stable and gathered some.

Then she hid all the plum stones under the straw in the manger. The very next day Sciorovante came back after his year's

absence and the black horse told him to look in the manger.

He was furious and beat the princess unmercifully, but next day he went away again. Fortunately for Cannetella, a barrel-maker soon came by and rescued her by

hiding her in one of his barrels until they reached her father's palace.

The princess ordered seven iron doors to be put on her room to protect her from Sciorovante, who had found out by magic where she was. Then the wizard bribed an old woman to hide under the princess's pillow a piece of paper which said, "While everyone sleeps, Cannetella shall stay awake."

When they were all asleep, Sciorovante smashed the iron doors down one by one and snatched Cannetella up, bed and all, to take her back with him. But he stumbled over one of the broken doors, the magic paper slipped out from under the pillow, and everyone woke up and hurried to Cannetella's rescue.

Sciorovante changed himself into a lion and was slashed by swords. He changed himself into a hare and was set on by dogs. Then he changed himself into a gnat and the king quickly swatted him to death.

After this the princess willingly married the first prince her father introduced her to, and they all lived happily together. The black horse went back to Sciorovante's stable and kicked it down, and then all the horses were free to roam again.

The Little Mermaid

FAR out to sea, where the water is as blue as a cornflower and so deep that many church steeples would have to be heaped on top of each other to reach from the bottom of the sea to the surface, live the sea people.

Beautiful trees and plants grow there, which stir at the slightest movement of the water. Fishes swim in and out of the branches just like birds in the sky. In the deepest part of the ocean is the sea king's palace. Its walls are made of coral and the windows of clear amber, but the roof is made of oyster shells that open and close with the flow of the water. Each shell in this roof holds a gleaming pearl more beautiful than any queen's.

The sea king was old, but he was very fond of the sea princesses, his grandchildren. There were six of them, and the youngest was the loveliest of all. Her skin was as clear and delicate as a rose petal, her eyes were sea blue, but like her sisters she had no feet, only a mermaid's tail.

The princesses used to play in the great halls of the palace where flowers grew in the walls, or outside in the garden. Here the trees were deep blue or red as coral, the fruit shone like gold, and the flowers were like a trail of fire. The soil was the finest blue sand and sometimes the water above was so calm that you could see the sun through it like a purple flower pouring out light from its cup.

The youngest of the princesses was a strange child, silent and thoughtful. She had found a marble statue of a beautiful boy, which had sunk to the bottom of the sea from a wrecked ship, and she liked nothing better than to play with it. She asked her old grandmother to tell her everything she knew about ships and towns, people and animals above the sea. She was surprised to hear that flowers had a smell and that the fishes in the trees—for that was what they called the birds—could sing.

"As soon as you are fifteen," the grandmother told the princesses, "you will be allowed to rise to the surface of the sea and sit in the pale

moonlight on the rocks and watch the great ships sailing past."

The youngest princess still had five years to wait, and she was filled with longing. At night she would look up at the moon and the stars through the dark blue water; they looked much larger than they do to us, and every now and then a dark shadow would pass between her and their light, and she knew that a ship was moving overhead. The people on it certainly never imagined that a lovely little mermaid beneath them was stretching out her arms to their ship.

When the eldest princess was fifteen she was allowed to go up to the surface. When she returned she told the others how she had lain on a sandbank and seen a big town where lights twinkled like a thousand stars, and music and the ringing of church bells filled the air.

The next year the second sister was allowed to swim to the surface. She came up just as the sun was setting and found the sight most beautiful. The whole sky looked like gold and crimson and violet clouds sailed overhead. Then the sun set and the glow disappeared.

The year after that the third sister went up. She swam up a wide river and saw green slopes with fruit trees, castles, and farms. She heard the birds singing in the trees, and saw some little children swimming in the water—although they had no tail.

The fourth sister was frightened of the land. She stayed out in the ocean, and told them how the sky hung above her like a big glass bell and the whales spouted water up in the air like fountains.

Now it was the turn of the fifth sister. She came up in the winter and saw huge icebergs floating in the sea, sparkling like diamonds. Then the sky became overcast and the wind

and waves roared. She sat on one of the icebergs, her long hair streaming in the wind, while the ships sailed in terror through the storm.

At last the youngest sister was fifteen. At last she was old enough to be allowed to go up to the surface and see the world above the sea. "Goodbye," she said, and swam up through the water as lightly as a bubble.

The sun had just set and the evening star shone clear and beautiful above her. The sea was calm and the air sweet and fresh. Ahead of her lay a large ship. Music and singing came from it and hundreds of lanterns shone from its rigging.

The mermaid swam up to the porthole of the cabin. Through the glass she could see a crowd of splendidly dressed people, but the handsomest of them all was a young prince with dark eyes. It was his birthday too, and as he came out on deck the sailors shot a hundred rockets into the sky, which broke in myriads of stars over the sea.

The little mermaid couldn't take her eyes

off the ship and the handsome prince, but deep down in the sea there was a mumbling and a rumbling. The waters swelled, heavy clouds blew up, and lightning flashed in the distance. A terrible storm broke. The waves rose like huge black mountains and pounded the ship until it cracked and its mast snapped in half like a stick. The water rushed in through the cracks and the ship broke up. Just then there was a flash of lightning and the mermaid saw the young prince sink into the depths of the sea. She remembered that human beings can't live under the water, and that the prince would die before he reached her father's palace. So she lifted his head above the water and let the waves carry her along with him.

In the morning the sun rose red and glowing out of the water and the mermaid kissed the prince's forehead and his eyes, which were still shut, and wished that he might live.

Presently she saw land in front of her. By the shore stood a large white building surrounded by trees. She swam to the shore with the prince and laid him gently on the sand. Then she hid herself in the sea foam to see who found him.

Soon a young girl came along, and the prince woke up and smiled at her. He did not smile at the little mermaid out at sea, for he did not know that it was she who had rescued him. Then the girl fetched her friends to carry him away—and the mermaid dived into the sea and swam sorrowfully home.

She had always been silent and thoughtful, and now she grew still more so. Her sisters asked her what she had seen on her visit, but she would not tell.

Again and again she rose to where she had left the prince. She saw the fruits in the garden ripen and be picked, she saw the snow fall on the blue mountains and then melt, but she never saw him. At home, the sea flowers in her garden grew so tall and wild that their long stalks and branches shut out the light. All the little mermaid wanted to do was fold her arms around the statue that looked so like the prince.

At last she could keep her sorrow to herself no longer. She told one of her sisters, and immediately all the others learned about it, and a few other mermaids too. One of them knew who the prince was and where he came from.

"Come, little sister!" said the princesses, and with their arms around each other they rose in a line out of the sea in front of the prince's palace. It was built of glittering pale yellow stone, with great flights of marble steps, one of which led down to the sea. Splendid domes of gold rose into the sky, and through the clear glass windows they could see into the magnificent rooms, lit by sparkling chandeliers alight with candles.

Now that she knew where he lived the little mermaid came to look at him every morning and every night. She swam close to the shore and even went up the narrow canal under the marble balcony that stretched over the water. Here she sat and gazed at the young prince, who imagined he was quite alone.

She used to watch him sail out to sea in his splendid ship, with musicians playing around him and coloured lanterns swaying in the breeze. When the wind caught her long fair hair the people on board imagined it was a swan spreading its wings. On other nights she would swim up close to the fishermen at sea casting their nets by torchlight. Listening to them speak well of the prince, she was glad again that she had saved his life. She remembered how closely his head had rested on her breast and how lovingly she had kissed him. But he knew nothing about that, of course—he never even dreamed she existed. She became fonder and fonder of human beings and

longed to be part of their world, which seemed to her so much more real than her own.

"If human beings don't drown," she asked her grandmother, "do they never die, as we do down here in the sea?"

"Yes, they too have to die," replied the old lady. "Their lifetime is even shorter than ours. We can live for three hundred years, and when we die we turn into foam on the water. We have no immortal soul. We shall never have another life. But human beings have a soul which lives for ever, and goes on living even after their

bodies have turned to dust. The soul climbs up through the clean air, until it reaches the stars. Just as we rise up out of the sea and look at the regions, so they rise up to beautiful regions unknown to us—ones we shall never see."

"I would give all three hundred years of my life to become a human being for one day and share in that lovely world after death," said the little mermaid sadly. "Isn't there anything at all I can do to win an immortal soul?"

"No," said the old lady, "only if a human being loved you so much that you were dearer to him than his father or mother—if he let the priest put his hand in yours and promised to be faithful and true to you now and for ever—then his soul would flow into your body, and you too would be filled with human happiness. He would give you a soul and still keep his own. But that has never happened. The fish's tail which is so beautiful here at sea seems ugly to people on earth. They have to have two clumsy stumps called legs to take them around, and they imagine these are lovelier than our fins."

The little mermaid sighed and looked sadly at her tail.

"Be content with what you have," said her grandmother. "Dance and be gay for the three hundred years you have to live—then you can float as foam on the sea all the

more peacefully afterwards. Tonight we're having a court ball."

The ball was more magnificent than anyone has ever held on earth. Mermaids sat on the backs of seahorses and spun round and round with them to the music of the seashells. The mermaids sang to the music of the shells, in voices lovelier than those of any human being. The little mermaid sang the most sweetly of all, and they praised the magic in her voice that had bewitched them. For a moment she was joyful, for she knew that she had the most beautiful voice of any creature on earth or at sea.

But then her thoughts returned to the world above her. She could not forget the handsome prince nor the sorrow she felt at not possessing an immortal soul. So she crept out of her father's palace, away from the song and laughter, to sit grieving by the side of the statue in her garden. She suddenly heard the sound of the prince's horn echoing through the water. "Ah, there he is," she thought, "I will dare anything to win him and have an immortal soul. I will go to the sea witch—I have always been dreadfully afraid of her, but perhaps she can help me and tell me what to do."

So the little mermaid left her father's garden and set off for the place where the witch lived, on the far side of the roaring whirlpools. She had to pass over volcanoes

and eddies and hot bubbling mud—these the witch called her garden. Her cave lay behind in the middle of an extraordinary wood. All the trees and bushes were polyps, half animal and half plant, whose writhing arms would grasp at everything they touched and never let it go.

The little mermaid was terribly frightened as she paused at the entrance to this wood. She nearly turned back, but then she remembered the prince and the immortal soul that human beings have, and that gave her courage. She wound her long hair tightly around her head so that the polyps could not catch her by it, and then she folded both her hands across her breast and darted through the forest just as a fish darts through water.

Now she came to a large slimy open space in the wood, where fat water snakes were circling about and showing their bloated whitish-yellow bellies. In the middle was a pile of bones of human beings who had been drowned. The sea witch had made a hole under them and was sitting there, letting a toad feed out of her mouth.

"I know well enough what you're after," she said to the princess. "You want to get rid of your beautiful fish's tail and walk on stumps like a human being, so that the young prince will fall in love with you and you can win both him and an immortal soul. I can give you a drink that will make your tail split in two and shrink into what humans call 'pretty legs.' But it'll hurt—it'll be like a sharp sword going through you. Everyone who sees you will say you are the loveliest, the most graceful creature they have ever seen. But every step you take will feel as if you were treading on a sharp knife, enough to make your feet bleed. And once you've got human form, you can never become a mermaid again—and if you don't win the prince's love, then you won't get an immortal soul. The first morning after the prince marries someone else, your heart will break and you will become foam on the water. Are you ready to bear all that?"

"I'm ready," said the little mermaid, pale

as death, and shaking and trembling with fear.

"Don't think you get my help for nothing," the witch went on. "You have the loveliest voice of all creatures, and with it you probably think you can enchant him. But you must give it to me. I need the best that you have so that I can make another spell. You see, I have to give of my own blood in order that the drink may be as sharp as a sword that cuts through you."

"But if you take my voice," said the little mermaid, "what shall I have left to make him love me?"

"Your lovely shape," replied the witch, "and your graceful movements, and your eyes that speak better than words. With these you can enchant a human heart. Well, where's your courage? Put out your little tongue and let me cut it off in payment. Then I will mix you the spell."

"Go on, then," said the little mermaid, and the witch put on the cauldron to brew the magic drink. "Cleanliness before everything," she said, scouring out the cauldron with a bundle of snakes she had knotted into a mop. Next, she scratched her breast and let her black blood drip down into the liquid; the steam hissed up into a grotesque shape, terrifying to look at.

But that was only the beginning. The little mermaid, hovering nearby, watched all but hypnotized with dismay as the grinning old crone kept adding ever more and weirder ingredients to the concoction, chuckling and mouthing strange incantations over each fresh item her falcon-like fingers clawed out of the air to toss into the greedy pot. From here came a viper's fang, a newt's toe, the sting of a hornet, from there a shark's eye, the tail of a water rat, a lizard's tongue, the juice of a flamboyant sea anemone, until as the brew started to bubble and boil, it sounded like the wailing of all life itself since the creation.

There was still more stirring to be done, with an alligator's tail for a spoon, still an octopus claw to come, an asp's venom for seasoning, but at last the spell was ready. It looked as clear as spring water from a sparkling mountain stream.

"There you are!" crooned the witch, squinting triumphantly at the phial into which she had poured the liquid, turning it this way and that the better to admire her handiwork. "Now for your side of the bargain!" And while the little mermaid shut her eyes tight against the pain, the witch in one swift stroke cut out her tongue so that she was all of a sudden completely dumb, unable either to sing or even to speak.

"And don't come back blaming me if it doesn't bring you all your heart's desire," the witch flung after her, not altogether unkindly, once she had handed over the spell and was gloating over her own prize.

But the little mermaid was by then beyond her hearing. Swimming bravely, the phial clutched firmly in one small fist, she was already well on her ardent way towards the prince's palace.

Up from the sea bed she swam, up through the schools of playful fish, the waving fronds of tapering ferns, up and on past jutting rocks and narrow inlets, past rolling meadows and golden beaches until, rounding a rugged cliff rising steep from the sea that sheltered her objective briefly from view, she swam unerringly up to the marble steps of the palace immediately before her and came to rest at last on the sandy strip of shore at their foot.

There she uncorked the phial and, with scarce another glance at the ocean home stretching deep and far into the distance that she was leaving for ever, drank the potion in one eager swallow. The pain that pierced

her through and through the moment the liquid touched her throat was like the sudden thrust of countless daggers, so keen and searing in intensity that she swooned.

She did not know how long she lay there at the edge of the lapping waters, nor could she have told of the monstrous images that might have leaped straight out of the witch's cauldron to trouble her sleeping vision. But when she awoke, it was to the healing sight of the prince who, happening to catch a glimpse of her through one of the palace windows, had at once made for the steps and was now gazing down at her with something of ravished astonishment. Only then did she realize that her mermaid's tail had vanished, to be replaced by a pair of slender mortal legs.

The prince murmured some endearing words to her, asked her what miracle had brought her to this secluded shore. But all she could do was give him a gently wistful look in answer. Impulsively he tore off his gold-trimmed scarlet jacket and wrapped it

like a cloak about her slim body, then led her by the hand up the marble stairway and so into the palace. Each step she took scored her feet as though she trod on fresh-sharpened knives, but with the prince assuringly by her side she felt as light as a bubble, while he, guiding her, marvelled at the charm of her graceful movements.

He dressed her in silks and muslins, and she danced for him, gliding across the floor with an exquisite, almost ethereal grace. Yet every time her feet touched the ground it still felt as though they were slashed by knives. The prince pampered and petted her, said she must never leave him and she slept on a velvet cushion outside his door. But when he was asleep she would steal down the steps to cool her burning feet, and see her sisters swimming far out at sea, searching for her.

Day by day she became ever dearer to the prince, but he didn't dream of making her his future queen. He kissed her forehead and told her she was the loveliest creature and

had the kindest heart, that he cherished her and they must never be parted.

Had he been left to his own choice, he may well have acted otherwise. But he was still young enough to be much influenced by his father the king, and the queen his mother. She was quite a pretty little thing to have about the court, they agreed—the king especially was quite taken with her— and if their adored and indulged only son enjoyed her as an undeniably winning play- mate, all very well. But to make her his consort was something else again. For that, nothing short of a princess would do. True, the girl had the prettiest manners, but, besides not being able to talk, heaven alone knew where she came from!

The little mermaid could have told them, had she but had a tongue with which to speak, that she was herself a princess. But that would only have baffled the king and queen, and even the young prince, the more. What changeling was this, they would have fussed, who claimed to be the daughter of the king of the sea who ruled over so mysterious an underwater world?

"Little does he know that I saved his life and carried him back to land, and that I would give up my life for him," thought the little mermaid.

But people said that the prince was to be married to the pretty daughter of a neigh-bouring king. A splendid ship was fitted out to take him to visit her. "I shall have to go, to please my parents," the prince told the little mermaid, "but I shall not bring her back with me as my wife. If I am to marry, I would rather have you as a bride than she," he added, and he kissed her and laid his head against her heart, so that she dreamed of human happiness and an immortal soul.

The prince's ship sailed into the harbour of the neighbouring king's capital. The princess was waiting to greet him and her beauty filled the prince with happiness. Perhaps it was natural that he should by now be attracted to a girl who could talk to him

with more than just a tenderly loving look. "Yes, she will be my wife," he told the little mermaid. "I know my happiness will give you pleasure, because you love me," and the mermaid kissed his hand and felt her heart begin to break.

The priest joined the young couple's hands together as man and wife, and they went on board the ship that would take them across the sea. A luxurious royal tent had been put up on deck where the prince and princess were to sleep that night. The little mermaid held the bride's train and knew that this was her last night on earth. As she laughed and danced with the rest, she thought of death.

She had gone to the railing, looking eastwards for the sun to rise, when suddenly she saw her sisters rising out of the sea. "We have a knife," they cried. "You must stab it deep into the prince's heart and his warm blood will flow over you and turn you into a mermaid once more. Kill the prince before the sun rises, and come back to us!" And with that they sank beneath the waves.

The little mermaid drew aside the curtain of the tent and saw the girl and the man sleeping peacefully with their arms around each other. She bent and softly kissed the prince's closed eyes, and he stirred and murmured his bride's name in his sleep. Yet the little mermaid loved him too much to kill him. She flung the knife far out into the waves and threw herself after it.

As she touched the water she felt her body dissolve into foam, while a brightness shone all around her. Hundreds of lovely creatures came to her and lifted her up into the air.

"We are the spirits of the air," they said to her in voices full of music. "By good deeds we can win ourselves immortal souls and share in eternal happiness. By your suffering and your goodness you have been changed from the foam of the sea into the light of the air. Now you can win yourself an immortal soul."

And the little mermaid raised her arms towards God's sun and sang of the light that was all around her.

The Gingerbread Man

ONCE upon a time there was an old man and an old woman and a little boy. One day the woman made a Gingerbread Man and put it in the oven to bake. She said to the little boy, "Your father and I are going out to work in the fields. Keep an eye on the Gingerbread Man."

Suddenly the little boy saw the oven door burst open and out jumped the Gingerbread Man and ran off down the garden path. The boy chased after him, shouting, "The Gingerbread Man is running away! Help! Help!" The old man and the old woman threw down their tools and joined in the chase. But the Gingerbread Man shouted back, "Run! Run! As fast as you can! You can't catch me, I'm the Gingerbread Man!"

Next three mowers in a field called out, "Where are you going, Gingerbread Man?"

"I've outrun an old man and an old woman and a little boy," he replied, "and I can outrun you too!"

"You can, can you?" cried the mowers, and they started to run after him. "Run!

Run!" laughed the Gingerbread Man, "as fast as you can! You can't catch me, I'm the Gingerbread Man!" And he ran so fast that he soon disappeared and the mowers flopped down exhausted under a tree.

On ran the Gingerbread Man, and presently he came across a brown bear lying in the sand. "Where are you going to, Gingerbread Man?" the bear asked.

"I've outrun an old man and an old woman and a little boy and three mowers, and I can outrun you too," he replied.

"You can, can you?" growled the bear, and began to chase after him. "Run! Run!" laughed the Gingerbread Man, "as fast as you can! You can't catch me, I'm the Gingerbread Man!" And he ran so fast that he left the bear far behind him.

After a while he came across a fox curled up under some bushes by the roadside. "Where are you running to?" called the fox.

"I've outrun an old man and an old woman and a little boy and three mowers and a bear," he hollered back, "and I'm

quite sure that I can outrun you *too*." The fox whispered, "I can't hear you. Come closer." So the Gingerbread Man went closer and shouted, "*I've outrun an old man and an old woman and a little boy and three mowers and a bear, and I can outrun you too!*"

"You can, can you?" smiled the fox, and snapped him up and swallowed him whole. And that was the end of the poor boastful Gingerbread Man.

Goldilocks & the Three Bears

ONCE there was a pretty little girl who was called Goldilocks because her head was covered in golden curls. She liked to walk by herself in the woods; when she was hungry she would eat the wild strawberries there, and when she was tired she would sleep on the dry moss.

Three bears lived in the woods: Father

Bear, who was big and had a deep voice, and Mother Bear, who was smaller and rounder and had a middling-deep voice, and Baby Bear, who was like a ball of fur and had a squeaky voice. Because they were all such different sizes, each one of them had his own chair, own bed and own porridge bowl.

Every evening Mother Bear used to put the porridge to soak in a saucepan on the oven, and every morning she boiled it up and poured it into the three bowls for the bears' breakfast. On the morning that this story happened, the sun was shining in the window and the birds were singing outside, and Father Bear and Baby Bear were splashing around in the stream behind the house, having their morning wash. Mother Bear called to them that breakfast was ready, and they all sat down in front of their bowls of steaming hot porridge.

"Oh! My porridge is too hot!" exclaimed Father Bear in his deep, gruff voice.

"Oh! My porridge is too hot too!" said Mother Bear in her softer voice.

"Oh! My porridge is too hot too!" said Baby Bear in his squeaky voice.

So they all decided to go out for a walk until their porridge had cooled down. No sooner had they left their cottage than Goldilocks came along. She was hungry and tired because she had been walking for a long time, and she decided to stop for a while at this strange little cottage.

She looked in through the window and saw a well-scrubbed wooden table with three bowls of porridge laid out on it, and around it three chairs to sit on. "Is anybody home?" she called out, but nobody answered her. The bears had left the door ajar, so Goldilocks walked through the door into

the bears' living room. Since there was no one there she sat down in Father Bear's chair to rest. But it was much too big for her, and her feet could not even reach the ground. So she climbed down and into Mother Bear's chair, and wriggled around in it to get comfortable. In the end she decided that it was too big for her too, so she hopped off and sat down in Baby Bear's chair which broke because it was too small.

Goldilocks walked around the table again, and the smell of the porridge made her hungry. She dipped a spoon into Father Bear's bowl, but the porridge in it was too hot, and she dropped it again. Then she tried some from Mother Bear's bowl, but that was too cold. The porridge in Baby Bear's bowl was just right, and Goldilocks ate it all up.

By now she was very sleepy, and when

she caught sight of a large bed in the next room she decided she would have a short rest before returning home. So she climbed up into Father Bear's bed, but when she lay down on it, it was so big that she felt quite uncomfortable. So she climbed off it quickly and went to lie in Mother Bear's bed. But that one was so soft that she still felt quite uncomfortable, so she scrambled out of it again quickly. Then she tried Baby Bear's bed, which was so comfortable that she immediately fell fast asleep.

106

Soon afterwards the three bears returned. "Somebody's been eating my porridge!" Father Bear thundered when he saw the wooden spoon in it.

"Somebody's been eating *my* porridge!" Mother Bear cried when she saw her bowl.

"Somebody's been eating my porridge and has finished it all up!" wailed Baby Bear and burst into tears.

Then Father Bear said, "Somebody's been sitting in my chair!"

And Mother Bear said, "Somebody's been sitting in *my* chair *too*!"

And Baby Bear squeaked, "Somebody's been sitting in my chair and has broken it all to *pieces*!"

Then the three bears began to look around for what else they could find.

"Somebody's been sleeping in my bed!" Father Bear growled.

"Somebody's been sleeping in *my* bed *too*!" Mother Bear said.

"Somebody's been sleeping in my bed and here she is *right now*!" cried Baby Bear.

At that, Goldilocks woke up and opened her eyes. When she saw the three bears looking down at her she got such a fright that she jumped off the bed and ran out of the house as fast as she could go. She ran all the way home, and never went into the woods alone again.

The Sleeping Beauty

ONCE upon a time there were a king and a queen who were unhappy because they had no children. They had been married a long time and had almost given up hope when at last their dearest wish came true with the birth of a most beautiful baby girl. Their joy was so great that no cost was spared in the preparations for the splendid christening to which the king and queen invited all the fairies in the kingdom. All, that is, except one. There were thirteen fairies in the domain, but actually only twelve had been invited because no one knew exactly where the thirteenth was to be found; when last heard of some time ago she was living alone in an isolated hamlet in some distant part of the realm. Not that any great pains had been taken to look for her. Nobody liked her very much anyway; she was always inclined to be crochety and quarrelsome and was always picking on the other fairies, probably because they were all younger and prettier than she was.

Since the custom, then as now, was to make gifts to the baby on its christening day, the twelve fairies were asked to be godmothers, with no doubt in anyone's mind that they would bestow every manner of good fortune on the little princess.

After the christening ceremony, all the guests proceeded to the king's castle where a great feast awaited them in the magnificent banqueting hall. Each fairy's place was set

with elaborate plates and tableware of the finest gold, with goblets of the purest crystal, made especially in their honour. But just as everyone was about to be seated, the thirteenth fairy appeared in a rush of rage at having been overlooked. The king at once ordered a place to be set for her, but to his embarrassment there were golden appointments only for the invited fairies, so the new arrival had to be served from the same dishes as the rest of the company, which only made her glower all the more with menace.

Fearing some mischief was brewing, the youngest fairy hid herself behind the tapestry hangings so that she would be the last to announce her gift and could undo whatever harm the old fairy was plotting.

Then the fairies began to make their gifts to the little princess. The first gave her beauty, the second goodness, the third gracefulness, the fourth made her a perfect dancer, the fifth gave her a lovely singing voice, and the sixth, the skill to play every musical instrument in the world perfectly. In short, they gave her everything one could wish for in life.

Then came the old fairy's turn. Angrily, she stepped up to the princess's cradle and cried out with jealous spite, "When you are fifteen you will prick your finger with a spindle and fall lifeless to the ground!"

Then she turned around and left the hall.

At this terrible curse everyone trembled and began to weep. But at that instant the youngest fairy stepped out of her hiding place.

"Take heart," she said to the king and queen, "your daughter shall not die. It is true that I have not the power to undo the envious fairy's spell completely. The princess will indeed prick her finger with a spindle when she is fifteen. But instead of dying, she will only fall into a deep sleep that will last a hundred years, and when that time has passed, a king's son will come and waken her."

The king, hoping to save his daughter from the old fairy's spell, immediately ordered that every spindle and every spinning wheel in the country should be burned.

All the good wishes of the first fairies came true. The princess grew into a young girl of such beauty, goodness, and grace as had never been seen before. She had just become fifteen when one afternoon she was playing a game of hide-and-seek with the other boys and girls in the castle. It was her turn to hide, and she ran into the farthest end of the courtyard, where there were several doors that led into a cluster of towers which had been shut up for many years. She found herself in front of a little door she had never noticed before, and pushed it open. She climbed the winding stairs, up and up, into a narrow tower. At length she reached a little room at the top, and there she found an old woman sitting at a spinning wheel, with the wheel whirring round and the flax twirling on the spindle.

"What are you doing?" asked the princess, who had never, of course, seen such a sight before.

"I am spinning," replied the old woman, who obviously had not heard of the king's

decree that every spinning wheel in the land should be destroyed, and did not know who her visitor was. "Sometimes I spin flax into linen, sometimes I spin a sheep's fleece into wool. Sometimes I even spin gold into thread for fine ladies to sew with."

"Is it difficult?" asked the princess.

"Yes, at first it is," the old woman replied.

"Let me try, please!" the princess begged, and the old woman handed her the spindle and the thread. No sooner had she taken the spindle than its point pricked her hand and she immediately fell to the ground in a swoon. The curse of the wicked old fairy had come true.

The old woman, terrified, cried out for help, and people came running from all parts of the castle. They tried to bring the princess round by throwing water on her face, loosening her gown, and holding smelling salts under her nose, but nothing worked.

Realizing that the spell had begun and must run its course, the king ordered his daughter to be carried to her bedchamber and laid on a bedspread embroidered with gold and silver, to sleep in peace until the appointed hundred years had passed.

When the accident happened the good fairy who had saved the princess's life by changing the curse from one of death to one of deep sleep, was in the kingdom of Matakin, twelve thousand leagues away. She was told about it instantly by a dwarf who had a pair of seven-league boots—which enabled him to cover seven leagues in each stride. The fairy left immediately in a chariot of fire drawn by six dragons, and arrived at the king's palace in less than an hour.

As she walked through the palace she brushed every living thing in it with her

wand, except the king and queen. As she touched them, they fell asleep—ministers, governesses, clerks, maids of honour, soldiers, cowherds, footmen, pages. She also touched the horses in the stable, the cows and the chickens, the doves and the mice, and Puff, the princess's puppy, who had curled up beside her on her bed. The spits in the fireplace stopped turning and the cook, who was about to box the kitchen boy's ears for tasting the gravy, fell asleep with his arm still raised. The kitchenmaid, who was plucking a fowl held firmly on her lap, slumbered with her hands still among its feathers. Outside in the courtyard the wind stopped blowing and in the gardens the flowers closed their petals and prepared for their long night.

Then the king and queen kissed their beloved daughter and sadly left the castle for ever.

Within a quarter of an hour a forest of trees and briars had grown up around its walls, so thickly intertwined that no one could pass through them and disturb the princess as she slept. The topmost turrets of the castle could barely be seen above the mass of greenery. The fairy had done her work quickly and well.

Ninety-nine summers and ninety-nine winters had passed when one fine day the son of the reigning king—who was of quite another family from that of the sleeping princess—was hunting in the forest. He caught sight of the distant turrets and asked his men what they were. Some told him that they believed it was a ruin haunted by spirits, others that witches and sorcerers used it at nights. Most of them seemed to think it was a castle that belonged to an ogre, who was the only creature who was able to make his way through the tough, dense, impenetrable forest.

Finally, an old peasant stepped forward and said:

"May it please your highness, more than fifty years ago I heard my father say that *his* grandfather told him there was a castle in this forest in which the most beautiful princess ever born was lying asleep. She was under a spell and it is said that she could be awakened only by a king's son."

The prince's heart was set on fire by these words. Impatient to discover the truth for himself, he drew his sword and advanced towards the briars. The metal flashed in the sunlight as he struck it into the deepest knot of thorns. To his surprise it gave way easily— he had only to touch the branches for them to fall apart and allow a passage large enough to let him and his horse through. What surprised him even more was that as soon as he had passed through the briars they closed again behind him, cutting his followers off.

Alone, he advanced through the first courtyard, which was filled with horses and men whom at first he thought were dead. Then he realized that they were all asleep and breathing peacefully. The clatter of his horse's hoofs echoed in the stillness, but the pigeons on the battlements slept as soundly

as the guards leaning on their weapons.

He entered another marble courtyard, where he left his horse while he climbed the great staircase lined with snoring guards. He passed through several chambers filled with lords and ladies all fast asleep, some sitting, others standing up. Finally, he came to a room where the pale light filtered through draperies finespun as maidenhair onto a bedecked bed on which lay a sleeping girl more ravishing than any he had ever beheld.

Trembling, the prince approached the bed and fell on his knees beside it, gazing at the princess. The tapering fingers of her hand rested lightly on a puppy curled up sleeping in the crook of her arm. A faint smile played about her lips as if a sweet dream contented her as she slept. At last the prince bent over the princess and kissed her gently on the forehead. And now the enchantment was at an end. At the touch of his lips the princess awoke. "I have waited for you so long," she said, smiling at the prince.

Together they walked through the castle and wherever they went the people woke up around them. The spits in the fireplace began to turn again, the kitchenmaid began plucking the fowl in her lap, while the cook at last gave the kitchen boy the box on the ears that had waited a hundred years. All the court awoke and everyone set about their duties again.

The prince and the princess went into the great hall, where a delicious supper was served to them. While they ate, the princess's minstrels played from the gallery above, and the prince noticed that they were using instruments that had long ceased to be played everywhere else. However, their tunes gave great pleasure, although none of them had been heard for a hundred years.

The prince and the princess, who were falling more deeply in love with every minute that passed, were married as soon as supper was over. And then the merriment and rejoicing, the feasting and music-making began all over again, for after so long a sleep the time seemed short indeed.

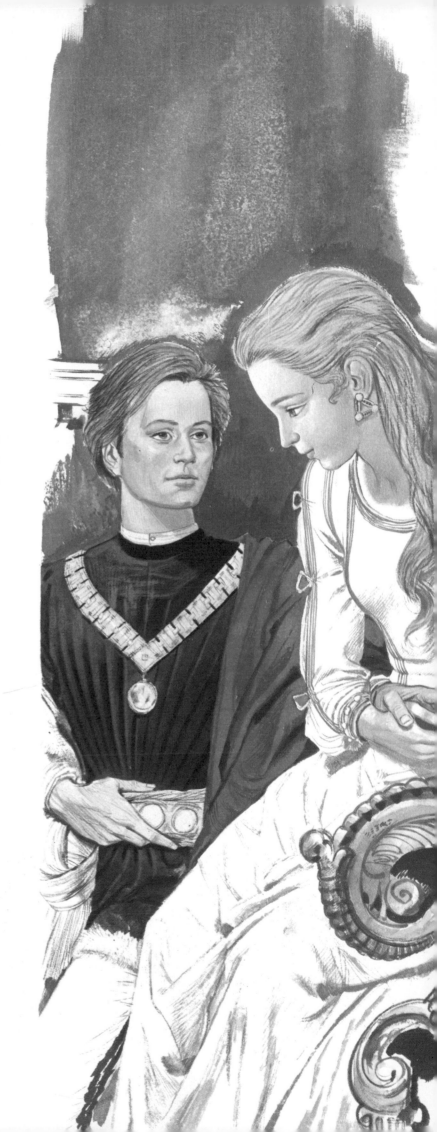

Rapunzel

ONCE upon a time a man and his wife lived in a small house which lay close to a splendid garden that belonged to a witch. From their windows they could see rare herbs and flowers growing in the garden, but they never dared to pick any for they knew that if they did they would fall into the witch's power.

One day, however, the wife fell ill with a fever and it seemed certain that she would die. In her sickness she longed for one thing only: the leaves of a herb called rampion, which grew in the witch's garden. Her husband, who loved her dearly, was ready to risk anything to save his wife and so, at dusk, he climbed over the witch's garden wall. He picked some of the leaves and returned safely with them to his wife, who ate them and recovered her strength. It was not long, however, before she fell ill again, and this time it was the root of the herb she wanted.

At dusk the husband again climbed over the wall, and tried to pull the herb up by its roots. Suddenly he felt a burning pain in his hands, and looking up, he saw the witch standing in front of him.

"A curse on you," she cried, "for stealing the rampion from my garden!"

"My wife is ill, and will die without your

herb!" pleaded the man, but the witch had no mercy.

"Go," she said, "but in exchange for the rampion you have stolen, I shall take your first-born child. I shall come and collect it on the day that it is born."

Not long afterwards a daughter was born to the couple, and no sooner had she opened her eyes to the world than the witch appeared to claim her as she had declared she would. In their rejoicing at the birth of the child they had so ardently awaited, the couple had pushed to the back of their minds the harsh demand the witch had made of the husband, and they begged her now to let them keep their small daughter. But neither tears nor entreaty had any effect on the merciless witch who, impatient to be off, picked up the child and carried her ruthlessly away. From the start she called her Rapunzel, which is another name for rampion.

Years passed and Rapunzel grew up to be the loveliest creature in the world. When she was twelve the witch locked her into a tower in the depths of a forest surrounded by mountains. The tower had neither stairs nor door, and the only way into it was through Rapunzel's window, high up in the wall. When the witch wanted to visit her she would call up:

"*Rapunzel, Rapunzel,*
Let down your hair."

The girl had wonderfully long golden hair which she would twist into a thick plait and wind around the window bar, so that it dropped clear down to the ground and the witch could use it as a rope to climb up.

A prince who had lost his way in the forest came riding past the tower one evening. As he drew near he heard the loveliest voice he had ever heard singing, and he stopped to listen. It was Rapunzel, singing to herself in her loneliness. Then he heard the witch's voice call up:

"Rapunzel, Rapunzel,
Let down your hair."

He saw thick coils of golden hair let down from the tiny window. The witch climbed up and disappeared from view. The prince

was determined to see the girl who sang so sweetly, so he waited until the witch had gone, and then he called up:

"Rapunzel, Rapunzel,
Let down your hair."

At once the golden rope swung down the tower wall to him, and he climbed up it. As soon as he saw Rapunzel's beauty he fell in love with her, and he asked her to become his wife. Rapunzel, who had never seen anyone but the old witch, was delighted by this handsome young man, and agreed to escape with him. She said:

"Every time you come to see me you must bring a skein of silk and I will plait it into a ladder as thick as my hair and then we can climb down and ride away together."

The prince came to see her every evening because the witch visited her during the daytime. The day of their escape was drawing near when Rapunzel, who could think of nothing but her prince, said dreamily to the witch:

"Why is it, good dame, that you are so much heavier to pull up than my prince?"

Thus the witch learned that Rapunzel had deceived her, and she flew into a rage. She cut off Rapunzel's long hair and tied it to the window bars. Then she carried the girl to a distant valley and left her there alone to live in misery.

That evening, the prince came and called to his beloved as usual. Her hair came tumbling down to him, and he climbed up into the tower. But this time it was the witch who pulled him in, cursing him as she did so.

"She is gone!" she cried. "You will never see her again!" With that she threw the young man out of the window, into the forest below. He fell into a thicket of briars, and the thorns scratched his eyes and blinded him. He wandered, blind and sad, through the forests and over the mountains, weeping for his beloved.

One day at last he came to the valley where Rapunzel was living. As soon as she saw him she ran to him, weeping, and her tears fell on his eyes and healed them, so that he could see again, as well as ever.

Then the prince took Rapunzel to his kingdom, where they married and lived the rest of their lives in complete happiness.

The Firebird

ONCE upon a time there was a tsar of Russia who had a golden apple tree. Every night the tree blossomed and bore fruit, but every morning the apples were gone and no one could discover who was the thief.

At last the tsar said to his three sons, "Whichever one of you succeeds in capturing the thief will receive half my kingdom now and the whole of it after my death."

That night the eldest son undertook to stand watch over the apples, but as the moon rose he fell asleep and by the time he woke again the tree had been stripped bare.

The next night the second son stood watch, but when the moon rose he too fell asleep and again the tree was stripped bare.

The third night it was the turn of Ivan, the youngest son, to guard the tree. When the moon rose the golden apples began shining so brightly that they lit up the whole garden, and Ivan marvelled at their beauty. At that moment a magic bird with glittering golden

came to a wide green meadow. In it stood a stone on which these words were written:

He who goes straight on will hunger and thirst; he who goes to the right will prosper, but his horse will die; he who goes to the left will die, but his horse will prosper.

Ivan spurred his horse along the road to the right, but it was not long before he met a big grey wolf who at once attacked his horse, devoured it, and ran away. Ivan walked on, sorrowing at the loss of his companion, until suddenly the grey wolf appeared again.

"Forgive me for eating your horse, Ivan," he said. "To make up for it I will carry you to the palace where the Firebird lives." With these words he took Ivan on his back and sped over steppes and seas to a garden surrounding a great palace.

"Inside this garden," the wolf told Ivan, "you will find the Firebird hanging in its golden cage. Take the bird out, but don't touch the cage itself, or you will be captured."

feathers alighted on the tree. In no time at all it had eaten all the apples and was just about to fly away when Ivan seized its tail in his hands. But the bird managed to shake itself free and fly off, leaving only a single gold feather in Ivan's hand.

When the king saw the feather he said, "I will not rest content until the Firebird itself is mine." He promised his three sons that whichever one of them captured the magic bird would receive his whole kingdom without delay.

The brothers set out at once in different directions, and soon Ivan, the youngest,

Ivan did as the wolf told him, but when he was hurrying back across the garden with the Firebird, he suddenly thought, "The bird will surely fly away from me—I must take its golden cage." But he had no sooner touched the cage than hidden bells rang an alarm throughout the garden, and he was captured by its guards. They brought him before the king, who said when he had told his story:

"I would have given you the Firebird if you had asked for it honourably, but now I shall tell the whole world you are a thief—unless you can bring me the golden horse that runs even faster than the wind."

Ivan returned sadly to the grey wolf and told him what had happened. "You don't deserve my help," the wolf said. "Nevertheless, mount on my back and I will take you wherever you want to go." And they rode swiftly for many, many miles to the stables where the golden horse was tethered.

"Go into the stables," said the wolf, "and lead out the golden horse, but don't touch its bridle, or you will be captured." The young prince did as he was told, but he was just leading the magic horse away when he suddenly thought, "How can I ride the horse without its bridle?" and reached out to take it. At once the alarm bells rang out and Ivan was led, a prisoner, before the king.

"I would have given you the horse if you had come and asked for it like an honourable man," exclaimed the king when he heard Ivan's story. "Now I will tell everyone what a thief you are unless you can bring me back the beautiful Princess Elena, whom I have loved for years but cannot win as my bride."

"Why didn't you listen to me?" the wolf said to Ivan when he returned. "Never mind, mount on my back and I will take you to the princess."

The animal sped like an arrow through the night until they arrived in the land where the princess lived. The wolf told Ivan to wait in a garden of orange and almond trees, for here the beautiful princess would walk with her ladies every evening. No sooner had the princess appeared than the wolf leaped forward, picked her up gently, and made off with her to the place where Ivan was waiting. They settled themselves on the wolf's back and hurried away, leaving their pursuers far behind.

As they rode along Ivan and the princess fell deeply in love, and when they reached the king's palace Ivan began to weep.

"Why do you weep, my friend?" asked the wolf. "Alas!" Ivan replied, "I am in love with the princess and she with me, and yet she must become the bride of the king!"

"I have served you well, Ivan," the wolf said, "and I will help you again. When you go to the king to give him the princess and receive the golden horse in exchange, I will go with you in the form of the princess and stay with the king. Meanwhile, you can ride away with the real princess behind you."

Ivan thanked the wolf, and everything happened exactly as the animal had foretold. The wolf stayed only a day or two with the king and then disappeared to rejoin Ivan.

When they arrived at the palace where the Firebird was kept, Ivan begged the wolf to turn himself into a golden horse because he wanted to keep the real one. The wolf did as the prince asked and turned himself into a golden horse exactly like the first, and the king unwittingly gave Ivan the Firebird in exchange for the wolf.

By the time Ivan and the princess had reached the borders of his father's kingdom they were overcome by sleepiness. They dismounted, hung the Firebird in its cage on the branch of a tree, and lay down.

At this moment Ivan's two brothers came by, returning from their quests. They were furious because they had been unsuccessful and when they caught sight of their sleeping brother and his treasures, they stabbed him to death without a moment's hesitation. Then they took the fair princess, the golden horse, and the Firebird to their father's palace, where they pretended they had captured them themselves.

For ninety days Ivan's body lay rotting under the tree, until the grey wolf chanced to come past. A mother crow had just perched on the body with two of her young ones, intending to dine on the flesh. The wolf promptly seized one of the young birds and pretended he was going to rip him in two.

"Grey wolf!" cried the old crow. "Spare my child!" The wolf replied, "Only if you will fly to the end of the world and bring me back the waters of life and death."

The crow flew swiftly away and soon returned, carrying two flasks. The wolf sprinkled the waters over the dead prince and in no time at all Ivan came to life again.

He thanked the wolf, and together they set out for his father's palace, where one of his evil brothers was planning to marry the Princess Elena that very day. When the princess saw her true love she gave a cry of joy.

"This is my true betrothed!" she cried. "His brothers are thieves and murderers!" And with that she told the whole story. The tsar angrily commanded that his two elder sons be cast into a deep dungeon, and he

gave Ivan the princess and his kingdom.

After the wedding feast the grey wolf appeared once more and spoke to Ivan. "I have served you well and I ask for one favour in return: cut off my head and feet and bury them under the golden apple tree."

The prince wept at his friend's request, but finally did as he was asked and killed the wolf. No sooner had he done this than a young man rose from the ground.

"Princess Elena is my sister," he said to the astonished Ivan, "and you have released us both from a wicked spell."

And so they all lived in happiness for many years, and peace and prosperity spread throughout the land.

The Knights of the Fish

A MAN and his wife once lived by the sea in Spain. One evening the man had gone fishing to catch something for their supper when he felt a strong tug on his line, and pulled out of the water the most beautiful fish he had ever seen. He was even more amazed when the fish opened its mouth and spoke to him.

"Do not eat me," said the fish, "but bury me in your garden and plant two olive trees over me, one at my head and one at my tail."

The man thought it best to obey, and in due course the two small trees grew into big ones. One morning his wife went into the garden and found, under each olive tree, a fine baby boy lying in a basket. She carried them in and fed them and looked after them as if they had been her own children.

The day came when the two boys, who still looked exactly alike, grew into young men and left their humble home to seek adventure in the world. Each of them was mounted on a black horse, wore silver armour that resembled scales, and carried as his banner the sign of a fish.

Presently one of the brothers, riding alone through a mountainous region, came across a beautiful princess tied to a tree and weeping bitterly. When the knight asked why she had been so cruelly tied up she replied very sadly, "Every year a maiden is chosen to be

sacrificed to a monstrous dragon, and this year he must take me, the king's daughter. So fly! Please fly while you have time before the dragon sees you here."

The knight galloped away, only to return a short while later carrying a huge mirror across his horse's neck. Quickly, he untied the princess from the tree and told her to hide behind the mirror while he lay in wait for the dragon behind the tree.

No sooner had the princess done as he bid her than the dragon appeared, breathing fire and brimstone. When he looked into the mirror he was so angry to see another dragon there that he smashed it into a million pieces, thinking he was killing his rival. But instead of one reflection he now saw a million reflections of himself in the pieces of broken mirror that surrounded him, and before he could decide what to do next, the Knight of the Fish had come out from behind the tree and killed him.

Then the knight made the princess mount in front of him on his horse and they rode to her father's castle together. The king was so overjoyed that his daughter was safe and the dragon slain that he gave the knight her hand in marriage.

For a while they lived together in great happiness. Then one day the knight was out riding when he noticed a castle in the distance which towered black and sinister into the sky. He turned his horse towards it, and soon was knocking at its gate.

A very old woman—so old that she could hardly hobble around—came at his knock. Besides her great age, she was also extremely ugly. But she beckoned him inside and he ·found himself standing in a vast anteroom, its walls draped with rich tapestries, its pillars of marble hung with splendid shields and coats of arms, and two wide staircases winding up from each side.

As she stood watching the knight looking about him with astonishment, the old woman croaked, "I see you are surprised at first sight of what my castle holds. I am proud that so noble a knight should visit

me. Follow me and I shall show you my real treasures."

She then led him through all the many chambers of the castle. Some were filled with costly clothes, encrusted with diamonds and pearls. Others were lined with elaborate chests brimming over with gold and silver and even with crowns studded with gleaming rubies and emeralds.

The knight had never beheld such a display of riches, not even in the king's palace, where he lived with the princess.

At last, while he was still marvelling at all he had seen, the old crone turned to him and said, "You have come to my castle, which is called the Castle of Albatroz. I have bid you welcome and shown you all my treasures. Now you must marry me!"

"Marry you?" exclaimed the knight, aghast. "Why, you must be over a hundred years old! Besides, I love my wife."

For a long moment the old woman gave him a hideously evil look. Then she said," "Very well. Now I will show you the finest of all my treasures."

With these words she led him down into the depths of the castle. Just as they reached the bottom step, the woman stepped aside and the knight put his foot on a hidden trap door which opened under his weight, pitching him into a deep, dark dungeon where he landed on the bones of many other unfortunate knights who, like him, had refused to marry the ugly witch and had

therefore fallen to such horrible deaths.

A few days later the knight's twin brother rode by the Castle of Albatroz with his banner of the fish fluttering proudly in the wind. He too was overcome with curiosity at sight of the castle's dark and sinister aspect, and he too knocked at the gate and asked to be let in.

When the old woman looked out through the bars and saw him standing there, she nearly fainted from fright, for she thought he was the ghost of the youth whom she had thrown to his death in the dungeon. Still shaking from head to foot, she at last opened the door to his repeated knocking, fell on her knees and begged for mercy.

The knight could at first make no head or tail of what the old woman was talking about through her chattering teeth, but by and by he was able to piece together the story of his brother's disappearance.

"If you will leave me alone, I will tell you how you can restore his body to life again," she pleaded, and told him there was a magic well in her garden whose water would bring the dead back to life.

Thereupon she guided him down the steep stairway to the deepest part of the castle, and in the dark stooped over and lifted up the trap door. Fumbling in her apron pocket, she drew out a candle and lit it, pointing out the steps that led into the dungeon.

So the knight brought up his brother's body and bathed him in the magic well until he came to life again. Then together they went back to the dungeon and carried the bones of the other victims to the well and washed them. The moment the last youth emerged alive from the water the old witch's spell was broken forever. The Castle of Albatroz crumbled in dust and all the knights rode joyfully away to their homes.

The Little Tin Soldier

THERE were once twenty-one tin soldiers, all brothers, who had been made out of the same old tin spoon. They wore splendid blue tunics with red trousers and stood stiffly at attention—*Shoulder arms! Eyes front!*—that's how they were. The very first words they ever heard when the lid was taken off the box in which they were lying, were "Tin soldiers!" It was a little boy who shouted this, for he had been given them for his birthday, and now he put them all on the table in a row.

Each soldier looked exactly like the others, except for one who was a little bit different. He had only one leg, because he was the last to be made and there was not enough tin for his second leg. Still, he stood up just as straight as the rest, and as it happens, it's this soldier that my story is about.

There were a lot of other toys on the table with the tin soldiers, because the small boy's little sister had a birthday on the same day and there were all kinds of presents for both of them from their mother and father, their grandparents, and all their aunts, uncles and cousins.

There was a round-eyed pink elephant with great white tusks jutting out over its drooping trunk, there was a teddy bear, a rabbit, a fluffy panda, a long-necked giraffe. A clown with bobbles dangling from his baggy costume and pointed hat was turning a somersault to amuse a dainty milkmaid who, carrying a pail and three-legged stool,

130

seemed morc interested in ogling a dashing harlequin in his glittering tights of all the colours in the rainbow. A driver in goggles sat bolt upright at the wheel of a clockwork motor car. There was a bus, a fire engine and a miniature train. There was even a cardboard railway station, its signalman in his box holding a red flag to stop the train for the tiny passengers waiting on the platform.

But among more toys than the tin soldier had ever dreamed existed, the handsomest of all was a beautiful paper castle. You could see right into the rooms through some of its open windows. In front of it were some small trees dotted about a little lake made out of a gilt-framed mirror with three graceful swans swimming on its gleaming surface. Everything about it was pretty, but the prettiest of all was an enchanting little lady standing at the edge of the lake. She too

was cut out of paper, but she was wearing a billowing short dress of the finest muslin and a blue ribbon draped over her shoulder, with a glistening clasp at the centre nearly as big as her face. She was a ballet dancer, and had one arm outstretched and the other curved close to her head, and she had kicked one leg so far out behind her that the tin soldier didn't see it at first and could almost pretend that she had only one leg, like himself.

"That's the wife for me," he thought to himself. "She's so beautiful, poised on one foot. But she's very grand—she lives in a castle. I've got only a box that I share with all my brothers, and that's not good enough for her. Nevertheless, I must get to know her."

Later that evening all the tin soldiers went back into their box, except this one, who had hidden behind a snuffbox. After the people in the house had gone to bed the toys began to play games. They visited, they fought, they danced, and they made such a noise that the canary woke up and began singing. But the tin soldier just stood staunchly on his one leg. His eyes never left the little dancer for a moment.

Suddenly the clock struck midnight. Click! The lid of the snuffbox flew open and a little black goblin jumped up, like a Jack-in-the-box.

"Tin soldier!" cried the goblin. "Will you please keep your eyes to yourself!" But the tin soldier did not answer. He just went on looking at the little dancer.

"All right—you wait until tomorrow!" the goblin exclaimed.

When tomorrow came the children put the tin soldier on the window sill, and whether it was the goblin or the wind that did it, the soldier fell out headlong through the open window, landing upside down on his helmet, with his leg sticking straight up in the air and his bayonet jammed in between the paving stones.

The little boy came down to look for him, but although he very nearly trod on him, he never saw him. If only the tin soldier had called out, "Here I am!" the boy would have found him. But he did not think a soldier in uniform ought to shout.

Then it began to rain, more and more heavily. People hurried past sheltering under umbrellas and with no one giving so much as a thought to the little tin soldier jammed upside down on the pavement with the rain beating relentlessly against his face and un-protected uniform.

When the rain stopped, leaving the street full of puddles, two little boys came by. "Oh, look!" said one of them. "There's a tin soldier. Let's send him for a sail." So they made a boat out of some paper, put the tin soldier in it, and away he sailed down the gutter, with the two boys running beside him and shouting. The paper boat bobbed up and down and whirled around so fast that the tin soldier became quite giddy. But

he kept upright and never moved a muscle. He looked straight ahead, still shouldering arms.

Suddenly the boat drifted into a broad drain, and it became quite dark. "I wonder where I'm going now," thought the soldier. "If only the little lady was here with me, I wouldn't mind if it were twice as dark!"

Just then a large water rat appeared, who lived in the drain. "Where's your passport?" asked the rat. "Now then, show me your passport!"

But the tin soldier just went on looking straight ahead, clutching his gun tightly. The boat rushed on and the rat hurried after it shouting, "Stop him! Stop him!" to the sticks and straws.

The current grew stronger and stronger and the tin soldier could already see daylight ahead, where the drain ended. But he could also hear a roaring sound that brought terror into his heart. Just imagine—where the drain ended it plunged straight out into a large canal. That was as dangerous for him as plunging over Niagara Falls would be for us.

By now he was going so fast that there was no stopping the boat. It dashed out, with the tin soldier holding himself as stiffly as he could, spun round three or four times, and filled with water. The tin soldier was up to his neck in it. The boat sank deeper and deeper as its paper grew more and more soaked. At last the water closed over the tin soldier's head. He thought of the pretty little dancer he would never see again, and an old song rang in his ears:

"Go onward, brave soldier!
Face death without fear!"

At this moment the paper fell to pieces and the tin soldier sank straight through—but was instantly swallowed by a large fish. It was even darker inside the fish's stomach than it had been inside the drain, and terribly cramped.

The fish darted about, twisting and turn-

ing in a most terrifying manner. Then at last
it lay quite still, and broad daylight flashed
through it. Someone called out, "A tin
soldier!" For the fish had been caught, taken
to market and sold, and brought into this
kitchen, where the cook cut it open with a
big knife. She picked up the soldier and
carried him into the nursery, where everyone wanted to see this extraordinary man
who had been travelling about inside a fish.
They set him up on the table, and there—
well, what wonderful things can happen!

The tin soldier found himself in exactly
the same room he had been in before. There
they were—the same children, the same toys
on the table, the same beautiful paper castle
with the pretty little dancer who still stood
on one leg and kept the other one high in the
air. She too had never moved. This touched
the tin soldier, who could have wept for
love of her, except that he felt soldiers ought
not to weep. He looked at her and she looked
at him, but neither of them so much as
murmured a single word.

Suddenly one of the small boys picked up
the soldier and threw him straight into the
fire. He had no real reason for doing this—
of course the bad goblin was behind it all.

The tin soldier stood completely wrapped
in flames. The heat that he felt was tremen-
dous, but whether it came from the fire or
from the love in his heart he did not know.
His bright blue and red colours were gone,
but no one could tell whether this was as a
result of his rough voyage or his grief. He
looked at the little lady, she looked at him,
and he could feel that he was melting, but he
stood stiffly upright, still shouldering arms.

Then someone opened the nursery door.
The draught caught the dancer and she flew
like a bird right into the fire to the tin
soldier. She flared up for a second and was
gone. The tin soldier was melted down to a
lump and when the maid cleared out the
ashes next morning, she found him in the
shape of a little tin heart. And all that was
left of the dancer was a little tin clasp that
was burned as black as coal.

134

Foolish Jim & Clever James

ONCE there was a fellow whom every-one called Foolish Jim because he was so contrary. In the middle of summer he would light a big fire in the house and in the winter he would shiver over a cold grate.

He would cook a chicken and give it to his horse to eat, and then eat oats for his own dinner. He would water his vegetable patch when it was raining and leave it to shrivel under the sun. At night he would spread a

mattress over the bed and lie down to sleep on the hard floor. Everything he did in fact was just plain topsy-turvy. The king heard about his curious ways and thought he would have some fun. So Jim was sent for.

"Can you answer riddles?" asked the king.

"Yes," said Foolish Jim.

"If you can answer this one, you can marry my daughter," said the king, who didn't think Jim could possibly answer a riddle. "But you have only three guesses, and if you fail your head will be chopped off. Fifty men have lost their lives already."

"I can answer it," said Foolish Jim.

"What begins on four legs, proceeds on

two legs, and ends up with three legs?" asked the king. Jim said he would have to go home to think up the answer.

Now Jim had an evil neighbour who wanted Jim's horse, which was a good one. He left a basket of poisoned pies on the bridge that Jim would cross on his way back from the palace, and went away feeling sure Jim would eat the pies and die so that he could take his horse.

When Jim saw the pies he got down from his horse intending to eat them. Then he began to wonder why anyone would leave such good pies there and go away, instead of eating them himself. So he gave the pies to his horse, who immediately dropped dead.

"What a good thing I didn't eat them," he thought. He threw the horse's body into the river, and as it floated downstream, three crows alighted on it and began to peck at the flesh.

Jim went straight back to the king. "The answer," he said, "is that a man first crawls on all fours, then walks on two legs when he's grown up, and leans on a stick when he is old—which makes three."

The king was astonished. "My daughter is yours," he said.

"May I ask you a riddle now?" said Jim. Now the king thought himself so clever that he could answer any riddle, so he replied, "If I cannot answer it, my whole kingdom is yours."

"Here it is," said Jim. "A dead being passes along with three live ones riding it and feeding on it. It does not touch the land, neither is it in the sky."

The king puzzled and puzzled. He answered this and that, but in the end he had to give up.

Jim said, "My horse died as I was coming here, and I threw it in the river. Three crows sat on it and began to eat it. It didn't touch the land, neither was it in the sky."

The king was even more amazed at Foolish Jim's cleverness, and had to give him his crown and kingdom. And from then on, Foolish Jim was known as Clever James.

The Three Little Pigs

ONCE upon a time there was an old sow who lived with her three piglets in a large, comfortable, old-fashioned farmyard. The eldest little pig was called Curly, because he had such a curly tail, the second was called Tusker, because he was always rooting around with his nose, and the third one's name was Porker, because he knew exactly where he was going.

Now Curly was a very dirty little pig who

loved nothing better than rolling about in the mud. Tusker was quite an intelligent pig, but he was greedy. As soon as the pigs' food was poured into the trough he would push his two brothers out of the way and snatch the best bits for himself. Porker was a good and thoughtful little pig. His skin was always pink and his manners were excellent. His mother used to say that he would be a prize pig when he grew up.

The little pigs lived happily with their mother in the farmyard until the old sow fell ill. Weaker and weaker she grew until it was obvious she was soon going to die. She called her three sons to her and said to them:

"I am growing so weak and feeble that I know I shall not live long. Then the farmer will give this house where we have lived happily for so long to a new family of pigs, and you will be turned out. You must leave this farmyard and go into the world and build new houses for yourselves there."

So the three little pigs rubbed their snouts up against their mother for the last time and set off into the world to seek their fortunes. Before long, Curly came across a stack of straw and decided to make a house out of it. He found a nice big patch of mud; then he rolled the straw in the mud and built a house with four walls and a roof. It looked just like a mud pie, but Curly liked it that way. He curled up inside it and went to sleep.

As for Tusker, he made his way to the nearest cabbage field. He collected a big bundle of sticks from a nearby wood, and stacked them up to make his house. Then he lined the floor and the roof with the cabbage leaves, and lay down to eat them in comfort.

Porker meanwhile had gone farther than his brothers and found some men at work in a brickyard. He watched them load the newly baked bricks on to waggons and take

them away to build men's houses. In a corner of the yard was a pile of bricks which could not be used because they were chipped. Porker carefully chose the best of these and carried them off to build his own house.

When he had finished, he had a nice, solid little house, just right for a prize pig.

Now the old sow used to tell her sons about the big, bad wolf who lived in the woods and was always hungry. He liked nothing better than a dish of fat, juicy piglet for his supper. And sure enough, no sooner had Curly gone to sleep in his new house than the wolf came knocking at the door.

"Little pig, little pig, let me come in!" called the wolf.

"Not by the hair of my chinny chin chin!"

squealed Curly in a shrill voice.

"Then I'll huff and I'll puff and I'll blow your house in!" growled the wolf, and he puffed and he huffed, and in no time at all Curly's house of straw had blown away in the wind. He himself managed to escape just in time, and ran as fast as he could to Tusker's house, to seek shelter there.

The wolf, however, had seen where Curly went. Soon he appeared in the cabbage field and knocked at the door of Tusker's house.

"Little pig, little pig, let me come in!" he called.

"Not by the hair of my chinny chin chin!" squealed Tusker. "You're the big, bad wolf and I'll never let you in."

"Then I'll huff and I'll puff and I'll blow your house in!" snarled the wolf, and took a deep breath. He huffed and he puffed and he puffed and he huffed and soon the lighter sticks in Tusker's house began to blow away. Then the wolf gave a few more puffs and blew the whole place to pieces.

By this time the little pigs had realized that the wolf was bound to win and had run off helter-skelter to their brother's home. Porker welcomed them inside and then set about bolting and barring the windows and doors.

He had just finished by the time the wolf reached the brick house and knocked on the door.

"Little pig, little pig, let me come in!" he called.

"Not by the hair of my chinny chin chin. You're the big, bad wolf!" cried Porker.

"Then I'll huff and I'll puff and I'll blow your house in!" howled the wolf, taking an enormous breath. He huffed and he puffed and he puffed and he huffed, and when that didn't work he dashed himself against the brick walls and tried to knock them down.

"Go away!" cried Porker.

"Not till I've eaten you three little pigs for my dinner!" growled the wolf.

But the house was so well built that at last the wolf had to give up and go home.

He slunk away with his head between his shoulders, the way wolves do. He could hear a lot of high-pitched giggling coming from Porker's brick house. "Ti, hi, hi!" Curly went, and "Ha, ha, ha!" Tusker chimed in. Only Porker was thoughtful.

"We haven't seen the last of that wolf yet!" he warned his two brothers.

The following day there was a knock at the door.

"Who is there?" cried Porker through the keyhole.

"It's just the old man from the woods," croaked the wolf, trying to disguise his voice. "There's a field of turnips over there, going to waste. Come with me and we'll dig them up for tomorrow's dinner!"

"I'll meet you there in the morning when I've put my milk out to cool," Porker replied.

But instead, he told his brothers to milk the cow that morning, while he himself set off early to the field. By the time the milk had been put out in the bowls to cool, Porker was safely back in the house, with a sack full of turnips.

"Little pig, are you ready?" called the wolf.

"I've been and come back this half morning!" Porker replied. The wolf went away angrily.

Soon there was another knock at the door.

"Who's there?" asked Porker.

"It's old Nelly, my dear," the wolf cried, "There's a tree full of ripe apples on the hill over there. Come help me pick them!"

"I'll come tomorrow morning when my bread's in the oven," replied Porker.

He got up extra early the next day, and prepared the dough. But he did not wait for it to rise, and told his brothers to put it in the oven for him.

He set off briskly just as day was breaking, to get the apples, for he hoped to be back home again before the wolf. But just as he had climbed on to the highest branch of the tree he caught sight of the wolf below.

"That looks juicy!" said the wolf. Porker wasn't sure whether the wolf was referring to the apples or to himself.

"Yes, I'll throw you one!" he said, and he threw the apple up the hill so far that, while the wolf was loping off to fetch it, he'd jumped down the tree and run home. The wolf returned to his den exhausted. He realized he would need a lot of cunning to catch the three little pigs now. For days he prowled around the house, waiting for Porker to come out.

Sure enough, on market day, which was always a Tuesday, Porker appeared carrying a basket on his arm and trotted off briskly to do his shopping. The wolf settled down to wait for his return.

A few hours later Porker came back from the town with a basket full of shopping and a butter churn under his arm. As he reached the top of the hill above his house he saw the wolf, grew frightened, and crawled inside the churn to hide. But as soon as Porker had got into the churn, it began to roll down the hill, bumping from rock to rock with the little pig squealing and squalling inside it. The wolf, however, thought that this was a strange beast that meant to eat him and he was so terrified that he ran all the way home.

That evening he crept back to the pigs' house, which was shut fast again. The only opening was the chimney for the smoke to escape. Stealthily, the wolf scrambled up on the roof, intending to climb down the chimney. But the little pigs, knowing he wouldn't be satisfied until he had gobbled them all up, had laid their plans.

They had briskly set about making a rich stew with all the vegetables Porker had brought from market. Then they stoked up the fire and set the pot of stew to boil.

Up on the roof the wolf's nose twitched at the delicious aroma and at the prospect of making short work of that extra treat along with those juicy piglets. But as he came sliding down the chimney, Porker took the lid off the pot and the wolf fell straight into the boiling stew, and that was the end of

him. He had ruined the pigs' own supper, but it was well worth it.

After that Tusker and Curly both built themselves new homes of brick next door to their brother's house. They were made of brick all right, but Curly insisted on lining his with mud and Tusker had cabbage leaves for his bedding.

Beauty & the Beast

ONCE upon a time there was a rich merchant who had three daughters. They were all beautiful, but the youngest was the loveliest of the three. She was always known as Beauty, which made her sisters jealous. The merchant gave his daughters everything they could wish for, and his wealth seemed to grow with every day.

Then suddenly the merchant's luck changed. His ships were wrecked, his warehouses burned, and his goods stolen. Soon he had lost everything he owned and he and his family had to move from their grand house in the city to a little cottage in the country, which was all he had left.

As they were now too poor to have servants, the girls had to work hard growing crops and milking the cows to make a living. The two eldest complained long and loudly at their change of fortune. They hated the country and did as little work as they could. Only Beauty was cheerful; she sang while she worked and danced when the work was done. "Look at her," her sisters would say, "a peasant's life is all she is fit for."

For a year they continued to live like this. Beauty used to get up at four in the morning to bake the bread, then she would take a basketful of washing down to the stream and scrub the linen clean in the clear water. Her two sisters would rise at ten and spend all day sighing and grumbling at their life. Then one day their father heard that one of his ships which had been believed lost had come into port at last, laden with goods.

"We are rich again," he told his daughters, "And I must go to the port at once to meet

my ship. What presents would you like me to bring you?"

"I want," said his eldest daughter, who had kept in touch with what the fashionable people in town were wearing, "I want some new metal hoops to make my petticoat bigger, and a pair of shoes with up-turned toes and diamond buckles."

"And I want," said the second daughter, who was even better informed on the matter, "A pink umbrella made of taffeta and a fan of French lace and humming bird's feathers. I also want a set of gold boxes, one with tiny scissors in it, another with a nail-cleaner and an ear-cleaner, and a third with little ivory plates on which to make notes."

"Very well," their father replied, hoping to remember all these things. "And you, Beauty? What do you want?"

"Oh, father," his youngest daughter replied, "You know that I want nothing. But if you really wish to give me something, then let it be a rose. I love roses above all other things that grow, and should like to plant one here outside our cottage."

The merchant rode off to the city, only to find when he arrived there that other men had cheated him of his cargo and had taken it for themselves. Sadly, he set off on the long journey back to his house, as poor as when he had left it. He had to go through a forest on his way home, and as it grew darker, a

terrible storm came up and he lost his way in the driving snow. Night fell, and the snow was so dense that he feared he would die of cold or be eaten by the wolves he could hear howling all around him.

Suddenly the snow cleared and he found himself in an avenue of orange trees, at the end of which stood a great palace with candles burning in every window. Thankfully, he hurried towards it and entered the courtyard, which was lined with stables. Every manger was stocked with hay and oats, but there were neither horses nor stableboys to be seen. The merchant led his tired and hungry horse into one of the stalls to rest and feed while he himself went into the palace. He climbed the great staircase and walked through several splendidly furnished rooms and galleries until he reached one in which a fire was burning.

He waited here for someone to come. But nothing happened to break the silence, except for the crackling of the ash logs on the hearth. At last he heard the palace clock chime eleven. He had grown so hungry that he decided he would not be polite any longer. He poured himself a glass of wine from the jug on the table and drank it. Then he sat down and helped himself to the meal; it was the most luxurious food he had ever tasted. He ate green truffles and salmon, and delicious blancmanges and jellies moulded into the shapes of strange creatures. He began to feel very tired and, walking back to the great fireplace once more, he stretched himself out on the wooden settle in the chimneybreast. A great weight seemed to press his eyelids down, and he fell into a deep sleep.

He awoke feeling refreshed. Someone had placed new logs on the fire, and had laid the table for breakfast. The merchant gratefully drank the chocolate and cream, and ate the fresh white bread. Then he noticed that a set of magnificent clothes had been put out for him, to replace his shabby ones. He slipped into the velvet coat with its beautiful fine silk cuffs, and put on the satin shirt and silk stockings and shoes that went with them.

Feeling more and more curious about the place, the merchant began to search through the palace for a sign of his host or some servants. He found no-one. At last he came to a long room whose roof and walls were made of glass. It was an orangerie, with rare trees growing in wooden tubs along either side. The merchant walked on, into a garden. Here the air was soft and sweet, filled with the scent of lavender and rose-mary, and of roses in full bloom. He was surprised to see this, for outside it was still winter and the ground was extremely hard. Then suddenly he recalled his promise to Beauty. He reached out and picked a rose.

At that moment there was a loud roar behind him. He spun round in terror and saw a terrifying Beast who spoke to him in a voice filled with anger:

"You ungrateful man! I saved your life by giving you food and a bed for the night, and now you steal my roses, which I love more than anything in the world. For such a crime you must certainly die!"

"Forgive me, my lord!" begged the merchant, falling on his knees. "I did not mean to offend you. I could see no one here and so I picked a rose to take back to my daughter Beauty, who had asked me for one." And he told the Beast about his three daughters and his fruitless journey.

The Beast listened, then he said more gently, "Old man, I forgive you on one condition—that one of your daughters will take your place."

The merchant protested and begged for mercy, but the Beast insisted. "I give you a month to return here. See if one of your daughters is brave enough and loves you

enough to come and save your life. She must come willingly, though, or not at all." So the merchant gave his promise, but with a heavy heart. No sooner had he agreed than his horse appeared before him already groomed and harnessed, with a chest strapped behind its saddle that was filled with gold and jewels.

When he arrived back at his house the merchant was bent with sorrow. "Here is your rose," he said to Beauty, and then he told his daughters of the terrible price he had agreed to pay for it.

"You shall not die, father," Beauty said at once. "Since the Beast is willing to accept one of us, I will give myself. I would rather die in order to save you than die of grief at losing you."

When the month was up she divided her possessions between her sisters and said goodbye to everything she loved. Her sisters cried when she left, but they had rubbed onion juice into their eyes to bring the tears. They were jealous of Beauty for her good looks and hoped that now she was out of the way, they would find rich husbands for themselves.

On the way through the forest to the Beast's palace Beauty's father still tried to persuade her to go back, but she refused. While they were talking it grew dark. Then, to their surprise, coloured lights began to blaze in front of them and the cold damp air grew soft and warm. They followed the lights until they reached the avenue of orange trees. Ahead of them was the palace, brilliantly lit, with sweet music coming from its rooms.

The merchant led Beauty through the splendid doorway and into a great hall. Here they found a table laid with every kind of food fit for princesses: larks' eggs and oysters, sucking rabbits and turtle soup, pink, yellow and green blancmanges. In the centre of the table was a large gold bowl filled with sugared violets, rose petals, honeysuckle and peach blossom. Relieved that her surroundings were so attractive,

Beauty ate what she could, though fear stopped her father from swallowing even a mouthful. But she had hardly finished her meal when the noise of the Beast's footsteps could be heard, and in a moment he appeared in the room. The sight of him struck terror into Beauty's heart, but she tried to hide her fear and greeted him politely.

"Good evening, Beauty," he said in a voice that was as terrifying as his looks. "Have you come to me willingly, and will you be content to stay here when your father leaves?"

Beauty answered bravely that she had. Then the Beast told her to accompany her father to the courtyard, where his horse was waiting for him. It had again been laden with chests of rich treasures for the merchant to take home. After they had embraced, Beauty, in tears herself, waved goodbye to her weeping father and wandered sadly back to her room, where she cried herself to sleep.

She dreamed that she was walking by a stream bordered with myrtle trees and roses when a young prince, handsomer than anyone she had ever seen, came up to her.

"You must not be unhappy, Beauty," he said in a voice so gentle that it touched her

heart. "You will be rewarded for your goodness. Do not trust to your eyes alone, and do not desert me whatever you do."

Beauty longed for the dream to continue, but presently a clock woke her by calling her name softly twelve times. When she rose her dressing table was equipped with everything she could wish for and beautiful clothes had been set out for her to wear. When she had dressed, and eaten the meal she found waiting for her in the next room, she noticed a door with the words *Beauty's Room* written on it. She opened the door quickly and was dazzled by the room she saw: its walls were lined with white silk hangings and among the graceful furniture was a large bookcase filled with books. Under the window stood a harpsichord and a lute with many sheets of music beside them. Beauty took down a book from the bookcase. On its cover was written in gold letters:

Welcome Beauty, banish Fear,
You are Queen and Mistress here;
Speak your wishes, and by me
They will swiftly answered be.

"All I wish for," thought Beauty, "is to see my father again and know what he is doing at this moment." No sooner had she thought this than she happened to look into a mirror that hung on the wall and in it she saw her father riding up to their house and being met by her sisters. He looked very sad, but her sisters could hardly hide their pleasure.

In an instant the picture had gone and Beauty saw only her own face in the mirror. But she could not help thinking that the Beast must be a kind one and that she had no reason to fear him.

Her thoughts returned to the prince in her dream. "Maybe he is somewhere in this palace," she said to herself, and opened the door that led from her room. She found herself in another room, where mirrors hung from every wall. A great crystal chandelier hung down from the centre of the ceiling, and the sunbeams dancing on it made the crystal flash blue and red, yellow and green. Beauty saw a diamond bracelet hanging from the chandelier and lifted it down. On the bracelet was a portrait of a man: the prince in her dream. She slipped the bracelet onto her wrist and walked into the next room.

This one was a picture gallery, filled with paintings by many different artists. But each portrait showed the same face: the face of the prince in her dream. And each picture,

as it looked out of its frame, seemed to smile.

Beauty opened the door to the next room. Here she found every kind of musical instrument of that time. A lute and a dulcimer, a viol and a psaltry were there, while a little-known instrument called an angelica stood propped up against a large organ. Beauty picked up a cittern and began playing softly to herself, singing these words:

"I thought as I lay sleeping
A dream enchanted me;
I heard sweet music playing
That set my heart strings free.

A stream flows through my garden
With water sweet and clear
That feeds the rose in winter;
Oh, that my love were near!

I pick the gillyflowers
The rosemary and rue;
Red roses fill my bower;
I lack, sweet love, but you."

She got up and went into the next room. Here Beauty found a copy of every book that had ever been printed. By this time it had grown dark and she could no longer read the beautiful manuscripts. Suddenly some candles flickered alight, and then more and more candles lit up wherever she turned.

Her supper was served just at the time she liked to have it, to the accompaniment of delightful music, but still she could see no sign of another person anywhere. Then, just as she was beginning to feel lonely, she heard the noise of the Beast approaching and tried not to shiver.

"Good evening, Beauty," the Beast said. "May I watch you eat?"

"You are the master here," Beauty replied, trembling.

"No," the Beast answered, "you are the mistress here and you have only to tell me to go if you want me to. You find me ugly, don't you?"

"I must tell the truth—I do," Beauty replied. "But I believe you are good and

kind, and when I think about your kind heart I cannot find your looks so *very* ugly."

The Beast talked to her for a while longer, then, as he rose to go, he asked:

"Will you marry me, Beauty?"

"Oh no, Beast!" cried Beauty, though she was sorry to hurt him.

"Goodnight, then, Beauty," the Beast groaned most pitifully, and then he left the room, looking back several times as he went.

"He is really so kind," Beauty said to herself when he was gone. "It is a shame he is so ugly."

That night she again dreamed of the prince walking with her by the stream and among the roses, but he seemed saddened by his thoughts.

In the morning she found a new room in the palace, full of every kind of cloth and silk for her to sew. The prettiest small singing birds flew around the room, and perched on the tapestry frames and sang to her as she embroidered.

"How I wish these pretty creatures were nearer my room that I might hear them sing!" she thought. When she opened the door she found that it led into her bedroom, though she had thought it lay on the other side of the palace.

Every evening the Beast would visit her and talk to her while she ate her supper, and she grew to enjoy their conversations. The Beast was better company, she found, than many of the men she had met in her father's house. Indeed, she would often look at her watch to see if it was nine o'clock yet, for that was the time when the Beast regularly appeared.

Just one thing distressed her. Each evening, before he said goodnight, the Beast would ask her to marry him, and when she refused, he looked so sad and wistful that she genuinely grieved for his distress. But she could not *marry* the Beast although she felt most friendly towards him.

The days passed quickly. After a while Beauty grew tired of being alone, and then another strange thing happened. There was

one room that she had not bothered to explore before; it was empty and dull-looking, except that under each window stood a comfortable chair. The windows all seemed to have black curtains behind them, for nothing could be seen through them. One day Beauty walked through the room, feeling sad and alone. She sat down in one of the chairs. Immediately the window lit up and harlequins and columbines danced before her eyes. She tried every chair in turn, and each time a new window lit up on another group of dancers or musicians or actors.

From time to time her mirror would show her how things were going at home, and that was how, one day, she found out that her father was very ill. That evening she begged the Beast to allow her to visit him.

"If you go, you will never come back," the Beast said, looking at her sadly. "And I will die of grief."

"Indeed, I *will* come back!" cried Beauty. "I promise I will only stay a week and then I will return."

So the Beast agreed. "You will be there tomorrow morning," he said to Beauty. "But remember your promise. When the week is over, just turn this ring round on your finger and say, 'I wish to return to my Beast and my palace.'"

Next morning Beauty woke up in her father's house once more. The moment the merchant saw her he began to look better, and Beauty nursed him with such love and care that he was soon well again. Her sisters were both married, but they were already dissatisfied with their husbands. So envious were they of Beauty's fine clothes and happy looks that they determined to bring about her downfall. By pretending to be dreadfully distressed whenever Beauty said that it was time for her to return, they persuaded the kind-hearted girl to stay several days longer than the week she had promised the Beast.

Then one night Beauty dreamed she was wandering in the gardens of the Beast's palace when she heard groans. Running to see what was the matter, she found the Beast stretched out on the bank of a stream, apparently dying. Beauty was so frightened that she woke up at once. "How could I hurt the Beast when he has been so kind to me?" she said to herself, in tears at the thought of her ingratitude. She said goodbye to her father immediately, then went to her room, turned the ring round on her finger, and said:

"I wish to return to my Beast and my palace."

She fell asleep instantly and woke to hear the palace clock chiming "Beauty, Beauty," twelve times. Everything seemed unchanged in the palace and Beauty cheerfully dressed herself as becomingly as she could, and waited impatiently for the evening to come.

The clock struck nine, but no Beast appeared. Then Beauty remembered her dream and began to fear that something had happened to him. She ran down into the gardens to look for him. Down the avenues and up the paths she ran, calling him. At last she came to a stream that she recognized as the spot she had seen in her dream. And on the bank lay the Beast. He was unconscious and seemed to her to be close to death.

Beauty dropped to her knees beside him and stroked his furry head. Then she scooped up some water from the stream and sprinkled it over his face. At that he seemed to revive, and in her joy Beauty bent down and kissed him. Then the Beast opened his eyes and said:

"Ah, Beauty, you have come just in time. I was dying because it seemed that you had forgotten me."

Then he added softly, "Beauty, will you marry me?" and she replied, "Yes, dear Beast," for now she knew she loved him.

As she spoke there was a sudden blaze of light all around them, and across the avenue of orange trees was written:

Long live the prince and his bride!

in letters made out of fireflies.

Turning to ask the Beast what this could mean, Beauty found that he had disappeared and that in his place stood the prince of her dream.

"Beauty," he said, smiling at her, "you have had the courage to love me for the goodness of my heart alone. Your love has ended the spell that a wicked fairy put upon me, and restored me to my true form once more."

Hand in hand, they returned to the palace,

which was once again filled with servants, and Beauty was delighted to find her father there, waiting to welcome her. Preparations for the marriage began at once: musicians played constantly, while the gardeners decorated every room with fruits and flowers.

When Beauty's sisters heard of their sister's good fortune they determined to profit by it too. They came to the wedding without being invited, and with hatred and malice in their hearts instead of joy and generosity. They came flouncing up the avenue of orange trees in their gaudy finery, but they had no sooner set eyes on the prince than their envy and greed froze them into statues depicting those vices. Rooted to the spot, they suffered the cruel punishment of having to watch Beauty's happiness every day without being able to share in it, or even complain about it.

Meanwhile, the marriage feast was celebrated with the greatest splendour. The dancing and feasting went on for a year and a day, but the happiness of Beauty and her prince lasted for the rest of their lives.

The Golden Goose

THERE was once a woodcutter who had three sons. He and his wife were very proud of the two elder boys, whom they thought were sure to do well in life and make their way in the world. But they had less than no patience with the youngest boy whom they called Blockhead because they judged him to be so stupid that they sneered and jeered at whatever he said and did.

One day the eldest son went to the forest nearby to cut down a tree at his father's bidding, and his mother packed his lunch bag with a rich fruit cake and a bottle of her best wine.

When Blockhead saw his brother about to set off, he asked his parents if he might go with him. "No," was the answer he got. "All you'll do is waste your own and your brother's time. You know you can't put your hand to anything useful."

The woodcutter's eldest son soon found the tree in the forest that his father had marked to be cut down. It was a large oak and after inspecting it he decided it would be a good idea to eat his lunch first. But he had scarcely dug his teeth into the fruit cake when a little grey man appeared seemingly out of nowhere right there beside him.

"Good morning," he said. "I see you have a fine lunch there. Please give me some of it; I am so hungry and thirsty."

"Certainly not," the clever son replied. "I don't know you and I don't need you. I want all this cake and wine for myself." The little old man looked at him for a moment with the merest hint of a glint in his eyes. Then he turned away and without another word disappeared again into the forest.

When the eldest son had finished his meal he set to work. But he had not made more than one or two small dents in the bark before the axe slipped and gashed his arm to the bone. He managed to stagger home, but the wound was so severe that he was away from his work for many weeks.

Then the father asked the second son to go to the forest to cut down the tree. His mother packed him a fresh gooseberry pie and another bottle of her good wine for his lunch. While his brother was sharpening his axe, Blockhead begged his parents to be allowed to go too this time. But they fobbed him off again, with the same mocking reasons as before.

When he reached the marked tree, the second son also decided to have his lunch before getting down to work. So he unwrapped the pie his mother had baked, took the bottle of wine out of his hamper and started in on his meal.

Just as he was taking his first bite out of the juicy pie, the little grey man, whom he had not even seen approaching, stood there in front of him, saying, "Please would you share your lunch with me. I'm hungry and thirsty and have no food or drink."

"Indeed I won't!" retorted the second son. "If I give you any of my food there'll be less for me. Be off with you."

The little man looked him up and down with a rather queer expression on his wrinkled face, then with no further word disappeared as elusively as he had come into the forest.

Soon afterwards the second son set to work on the tree. He chipped off a little more than his brother had done. Then his axe slipped and cut so deeply into his leg that when he dragged himself home his parents feared he might lose the use of that leg for ever.

The next day Blockhead said, "Father,

156

there. Please let me share your food and drink with you. I have nothing of my own."

Blockhead felt sorry for the poor little man and without a second's thought told him, "It isn't very much, but you're more than welcome to half of it." Imagine his surprise when he opened the satchel in which he had stowed the bread and beer his mother had given him and found instead a delicious nut cake and a bottle of the choicest wine.

Just as much as the unexpected feast itself, however, Blockhead enjoyed the good company. For once they were both propped comfortably against the tree and got down to eating, the skimpy old man with the knobbly bones, scrawny neck and wisp of a beard became the merriest little fellow, full of fun.

When they had eaten their fill in great good spirits, he got to his feet and said to Blockhead with a twinkle, "Because you have a kind heart and will help people, I shall help you too. Cut down that tree and among its roots you will find something valuable." Then all at once he was gone again.

Blockhead swung his axe many times into

let *me* go out and cut down that tree!" But his father answered, "If your two brothers couldn't do it, *you* certainly won't. But maybe a day in the forest will knock some of that nonsense out of your head." So his mother gave him a grudging crust of bread and a flask of stale beer, and Blockhead set off.

No sooner had he arrived at the tree than the little grey man materialized before him as well and said, "I see you have a lunch bag

158

the tree until at last it gave way and came crashing down. Its roots were pulled out of the earth, and among them he suddenly saw a shining golden goose. Carefully, he lifted the bird and, as he stroked its feathers, he realized that they were made of pure gold. Blockhead realized that this was indeed something valuable—too valuable to take home to his unkind family. So he tucked the bird under his arm and carried it to a nearby inn, where he took a room for the night.

Now the landlord of the inn had three daughters, and as soon as they saw the goose each one of them longed to have one of its golden feathers. That night, once Blockhead was asleep, the girls crept into his room. Swiftly the first one grabbed at the goose's tail. But instead of pulling out a feather, her fingers stuck fast to the goose, and she found she could not take her hand away.

The second daughter tried to show her sister how to do it. But the minute she touched the goose she too was stuck fast to it. Then the third daughter came up and tried to push her sisters out of the way so that she could get at the goose. But no sooner did her hands touch their shoulders than they stuck fast there. So all three sisters had to spend a

very uncomfortable night with the goose.

Next morning Blockhead woke up, tucked the goose under his arm, and left the inn, apparently unaware of the three girls who were still stuck to it. They had to run to keep up with him, as Blockhead, who knew perfectly well that they were there, set off through the fields. To tell you the truth, he liked seeing them twisting and turning behind him. In one field they met the

minister on his way to the church. Shocked at the sight of them, he cried out: "Shame on you, you bold hussies! What do you mean by running after a young man like this?" And he grabbed the youngest girl by the hand to try to draw her away. But as soon as he touched her he was stuck fast too, and had to run along with the rest.

Soon afterwards the parish clerk came along the road. His mouth fell open in astonishment at the sight. "Why, where are you going, sir?" he cried. "Don't forget the mayor's baby is being christened today!" He ran after them and pulled the minister by his gown, and so was caught himself.

As the five of them jogged on behind the goose, two farmhands came along the road on their way home from work. "Get me loose!" cried the minister, as soon as he saw them. But no sooner had they touched the

clerk than they stuck fast too. Now there were seven of them running along shouting behind Blockhead and his goose.

After a time they came to the castle where the king of that country lived. He had one daughter, whose mind was so full of sad thoughts that she never laughed. The king had decreed that whoever managed to make her laugh should marry her if he wanted to.

When Blockhead was told this he took his goose and its followers into the castle yard and marched them up and down in front of the princess's window. Sadly, the princess glanced outside, then all at once she began to laugh out loud. Blockhead waved up at her cheerfully and she liked him and waved back.

So then Blockhead went to the king and claimed the princess as his bride. But the king was reluctant to make such an odd fellow his son-in-law.

He set Blockhead three seemingly impossible tasks before he could win the princess: the first was to find a man who could drink up a whole cellarful of wine, the second was to find a man who could eat a mountain of bread, and the third was to bring him a ship that could sail over land as well as sea.

At that the little grey man appeared once more. "Don't worry," he said to Blockhead. "I will drink up the cellarful of wine and eat up the mountain of bread, and I will find you a ship which can sail on land as easily as on water."

The little man was as good as his word. First he emptied a cellarful of wine so vast that he needed to shinny up and down a ladder the while in order to reach all the bottles lining the shelves from floor to ceiling. And yet he did it in no time at all, and with not the slightest sign of tipsiness or any other ill effects.

Next he set himself down at the foot of a pyramid tall as any mountain, composed entirely of crusty, freshly baked loaves. Maybe it was a little tougher for his stumpy old teeth to chew their way through the

bread than it had been for his hardy old throat to swallow the wine, but in less time than it would take most people to eat one loaf, he cheerfully munched away that whole bread mountain until no crumb was left.

Lastly, on a morning shortly afterwards, and to the wonder of all those watching from the windows, his wizened little frame could be seen almost tripping up the road towards the palace gates, a grin proudly splitting his face from ear to ear as he effortlessly steered by the slenderest towline as splendidly rigged a ship as ever sailed the high seas, and that yet had wheels that could propel it on land.

The king, who was really quite glad to exchange his daughter for such a marvellous ship, ordered the wedding celebrations to begin. The chief guest, naturally, was the little grey man, and at Blockhead's request all the people who had been stuck to the goose were set free and made welcome at the feast. Blockhead became the king's heir, and when he and the princess finally inherited the kingdom, they ruled it with as much wisdom as any and more than most.

Aladdin & His Lamp

IN Arabia people tell this story about a boy called Aladdin, who lived with his widowed mother in a city in China, many, many years ago.

Aladdin's mother used to spin cotton on her wheel. By working from sunrise to sunset she could earn just enough money to buy bread and goat's milk to keep herself and Aladdin alive. The boy played in the streets all day, for nobody cared enough about him to teach him a trade, nor even how to spell his name. He was always hungry and dirty and his only friends were beggars and thieves. His dreams, however, were like those of other people: he dreamed that one day a magician would come along and make him the richest and most handsome man in the land.

When Aladdin was fifteen years old, he was coming out of his house one day when a stranger who was walking by stopped and looked at him. He was an evil magician from Africa, who had been watching Aladdin secretly for quite a while. He needed a boy to help him with a plan he had made—a boy whom nobody would miss if he never returned.

"Aren't you Mustapha's son?" he asked.

"Yes, sir, I am," answered Aladdin. "But my father has been dead for many years. He was a poor tailor, and since he died we have become poorer still."

"My child," said the magician at once, "I am your uncle. I have been travelling abroad for many years, but now I have come back to look after you and your mother. You need never go hungry again."

He pressed some gold pieces into the boy's hand and told him to buy wine and food so that they could celebrate his homecoming.

The magician promised Aladdin's mother that he would set her son up in a shop of his own. He bought Aladdin fine new clothes and invited him to come and see the sights of the city with him. They visited the shops of the richest merchants and admired the Sultan's great palace. Finally, when the sun had climbed high in the sky and they were hot and tired from their sightseeing, the magician led Aladdin into a cool, shady garden, full of flowers.

After they had rested a while, he led Aladdin through a small door in the wall to another garden even lovelier than the first. They rested here too, until the magician said he wanted to show Aladdin another garden—and yet another.

Soon they had left the outskirts of the city far behind, but the gardens were so cunningly arranged that Aladdin did not realize how far he had travelled. Beyond the last garden they found themselves in a deep valley, with mountains on either side. The ground was bare, save for a few sticks and one large stone, and there was not a living thing to be seen.

The magician led Aladdin up to the big stone and told him to collect enough sticks to make a fire. Then he set the sticks alight and threw a few drops of oil on the flames. A thick, dense smoke immediately curled up like a snake around them. The magician chanted strange words, and suddenly a bronze ring appeared in the stone.

"Aladdin," the magician said, "you are the only person in the world who can collect the treasure that lies beneath this stone. Raise it, and go down the steps you will see into a cave. This will lead you to a garden, which is filled with treasures beyond human imagination. Collect what you like there; all I want you to bring me is the lamp you will find burning on the garden terrace.

"Take this ring," the magician went on.

"Put it on your finger and it will keep you from harm."

Aladdin lifted the stone by the bronze ring and climbed down into the cave.

The underground garden in which he found himself was unlike any he had ever known or could have believed possible. Each blade of grass was spun of the palest jade, the paths glowed with amber. Exotic flowers bloomed in abundance, their foliage fashioned of malachite, their petals shimmering in a blaze of diamonds and sapphires, amethysts, garnets and opals. An exquisite bird of paradise hovered close beside a slender tree trunk, its plumage brilliant with a myriad flashing gems.

The boy's gaze rested on the trees laden with pearls, emeralds, and rubies more perfect than any in the world. He had never seen jewels before and thought they were just coloured glass. But they were beautiful, so he picked as many of them as he could. Then he found the lamp and put it carefully in his shirt before hurrying back to the cave

entrance where the magician was waiting impatiently.

"Give me the lamp first," he shouted to the boy, "then I'll help you out."

But Aladdin called back, "I will give it to you when I come out—help me up first." They argued like this for a long time until the magician flew into a fury, slammed the stone down over the entrance, and disappeared.

Aladdin had been so excited that he had forgotten to be afraid. Now, locked underground in the darkness, he was terrified and clasped his hands together in prayer. In doing this he accidentally rubbed the ring the magician had given him. Immediately a

huge genie appeared before him. It was so big that it seemed to fill the entire cave.

"I am the slave of the ring. What can I do for you, master?" it asked.

"I want to go home," cried Aladdin, and immediately found himself standing in front of his mother. They hugged each other, weeping for joy, while Aladdin told her his adventures. Then, realizing how hungry he was, he asked for some food. His mother began to weep again, because she had none in the house and no money to buy any.

"We can sell the lamp I found in the cave," suggested Aladdin, and his mother fetched some water and sand to rub it clean. No sooner had she begun rubbing it than another genie appeared, even larger and fiercer than the slave of the ring.

"What do you command?" it thundered, and Aladdin at once replied, "Some food, please." The genie reappeared an instant later carrying silver dishes laden with meat and fruit and silver cups filled with wine. Then it disappeared, while Aladdin took care of his mother, who had fainted at the first moment she caught sight of the genie.

The food and wine lasted them for two days. Then Aladdin took the dishes to the market and sold them for so much money that they had plenty to eat for the rest of that year.

For several years they went on living like this, spending their money carefully and using the genie of the lamp only when they really needed help. Aladdin had grown into a handsome young man, and he spent his time wisely, learning from the merchants of the city. One day he happened to see the Sultan's daughter being carried through the streets on a litter borne by slaves. She was so beautiful that he instantly fell in love with her and wanted her for his wife.

He brought out the jewels he had gathered from the trees in the magic garden—whose true value he now knew—and asked his mother to carry them to the Sultan and ask for his daughter's hand in marriage. When the Sultan saw the superb jewels, his interest in the unknown suitor was great.

"Tell your son to bring me forty times the gold and jewels he has given me here," he said to Aladdin's mother, "and I will give him my daughter's hand in marriage."

Overjoyed, the woman hurried home to

tell her son the good news from the palace.

Aladdin commanded the genie to bring him the presents and in an instant there appeared forty black slaves and forty white slaves, each one carrying a basin of gold filled with pearls, diamonds, rubies, and emeralds. For Aladdin there was a robe that was more splendid than any king's clothes had ever been, and a magnificent horse with a harness studded with jewels. As he rode through the streets to the palace his slaves threw pieces of gold to the people, who cheered this handsome and generous young prince until their voices grew hoarse.

The Sultan was so impressed by Aladdin's splendour that he summoned the grand judge of the city and commanded him to draw up the marriage contract at once. Then Aladdin went home and rubbed his lamp once more.

When the genie appeared, Aladdin said, "I command you to build me a palace tonight, opposite that of the Sultan. It must be worthy to receive my bride—its walls must be of lapis lazuli and jasper, its floors of marble, its stairs of porphyry, and its window frames inlaid with diamonds, rubies, and emeralds. I want stables that are as beautiful as other men's palaces, filled with the finest horses. Go now, and only return when everything is completed as I have commanded."

The next morning the Sultan was amazed

to see a new palace opposite his own, richer and more beautiful than anything that had ever been seen before. The wedding was celebrated at once and a hundred female slaves danced and sang while the court sat down to a banquet that surpassed all other feasts in excellence.

The years passed, and Aladdin and his princess lived together most happily. Then one day, while Aladdin was out hunting with his men, the African magician returned. He had heard of Aladdin's wealth, and knew it could only have come through the magic of the lamp. Determined to get the lamp for himself, he disguised himself as a pedlar and walked up and down the street beneath the princess's window, carrying a tray of brightly polished brass lamps.

"New lamps for old, new lamps for old!" he cried, and to each of the servants from the palace who brought him a tarnished old lamp he gave a shiny new one.

At length the princess heard him and remembered the old lamp Aladdin kept in his room. She sent one of her slaves to exchange it for a new one, knowing nothing about its magic powers until it was too late and the magician had made the genie of the lamp transport the princess and her entire palace and all its inhabitants to his home in Africa.

On his return that evening Aladdin was dismayed to find that both the princess and

the palace had vanished. The Sultan immediately had him arrested and brought before the executioner. In despair, Aladdin pressed his hands together to say his last prayer. But he had forgotten that he still wore the magic ring, and when he now accidentally rubbed it, the genie reappeared.

"What do you wish?" it cried, and Aladdin replied, "Take me to where my princess is hidden." The words were hardly out of his mouth when he found himself in Africa, face to face with his beloved again. The princess told Aladdin everything that had happened and how the magician was trying to win her love. Aladdin gave her a deadly poison, which he told her to pour into the magician's cup when he came to visit her. Then he hid himself close by.

As the moon rose that evening the magician made his way to the princess's chamber. But instead of greeting him with tears as before, the princess welcomed him

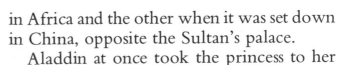

in Africa and the other when it was set down in China, opposite the Sultan's palace.

Aladdin at once took the princess to her father, and the three embraced with tears of delight. The Sultan made Aladdin and the princess his heirs, and in due course they succeeded him and reigned over the country with wisdom and prosperity.

inside. She beckoned to him to sit beside her, and then she offered him the cup of wine. The magician accepted it eagerly, drained it to the last drop, and fell lifeless to the ground.

Aladdin hurried from his hiding place and removed the lamp from his body. The moment he rubbed it the genie of the lamp appeared, and with its help the palace and everyone in it was transported home again. Only two slight shocks were felt; one when the palace was lifted up from where it stood

The Sprig of Rosemary

THERE is a story told in Spain about a girl who used to go into the forest to collect firewood. By chance one day she pulled out of the earth a sprig of rosemary, and as she did so, a handsome prince appeared before her enraptured gaze. He in turn was so captivated by the girl's vivid beauty that, unwilling to let her out of his sight, he took her by the hand and led her unresisting to his palace, which lay in a valley below the forest. There, within its noble-pillared walls, he scarcely needed to woo his new-found love before winning her heart forever as his chosen bride.

Now the prince was, unbeknownst to the girl, under the malicious spell of a wicked witch, and he earnestly cautioned his young wife that she could go anywhere she wished in the palace and open all the doors except one. The girl accepted this without question at the start. Radiantly happy as she was, she would have consented to anything her prince asked of her. And thus for a while they lived happily together.

At length, however, the girl found herself increasingly tantalized each time she passed

that one room closed to her. Eventually she became so consumed with curiosity that one morning when her husband was out hawking, nothing could stop her having a peep at what lay behind the forbidden door.

No sooner had she turned the key in the lock than there was a shaking and a roaring around her, and the entire palace became earth and disappeared.

The girl stood alone in the forest again, and shed bitter tears at the loss of her husband. She decided to travel the world over to find him.

She went up to the sun, whose light shines on every place, to ask him if he had seen the prince, but the sun had not. She climbed up to the moon, who sees the secrets of the world while people are asleep, and asked her if she had seen the prince, but the moon had not.

Finally she went to the wind, who flies everywhere and sees everything, and the wind replied as he whistled softly about her, "Yes, I have seen him. He is the prisoner of a cruel king and is to marry his ugly daughter this very day. The prince is under a spell, and all memory of his love for you has vanished."

Then the wind wrapped the girl in his cloak and carried her to the country where her lover lay imprisoned. She stood in the courtyard of the king's palace and saw all around her preparations being made for the wedding. In her despair she picked another sprig of rosemary from the king's herb garden and held it against her heart. Just then the prince came by on his way to meet his new bride. She touched him with the rosemary and he remembered her, and the spell was broken. The prince kissed her and declared that she, and none other, was his true wife. Together they left the king's castle, and lived happily together all the days of their lives.

171

The Ugly Duckling

IT was summertime and a mother duck was sitting on her eggs. She had hidden her nest at the far end of a pond, among the waterweeds that grew there. She was longing for her little ducklings to hatch out for she was lonely. Hardly anyone bothered to visit her; the other ducks preferred to swim about in the pond rather than sit under a dock leaf quacking with her.

At last the eggs cracked open one after the other. "Peep! Peep!" the little ducklings said, sticking their heads out of the shells.

"Quack! Quack!" said the mother duck, and then the little ones scuttled out as quickly as they could, and began peering under leaves and twigs.

"Oh, how big the world is!" said the ducklings. And it certainly was much bigger than the eggs that they had been lying in.

"Do you imagine that this is the whole world?" the mother duck said. "Why, it goes a long way past the other side of the garden, right to the edge of the field, but I've never been as far as that." She got up from her nest, thinking that all the eggs had been hatched. But then she noticed that there was still one egg left, the largest one of all. She sat down again.

At last the big egg cracked. There was a gentle "Peep! Peep!" from the young one as he fell out, looking so large and ugly. The mother duck looked at him and said, "My! What a big duckling he is! None of the others looked a bit like that."

Then she plopped down into the water. "Quack! Quack!" she called to the ducklings, and one after the other they all jumped in. The water closed over their heads, but in a moment they had popped up again and were floating along beautifully.

"Look how well they use their legs," the mother duck said proudly, nodding at the ugly grey one among them, who was swimming along as strongly as the rest. "Now let me show you the world and introduce you to the barnyard. But keep close to me so that nobody steps on you; and watch out for the cat."

There was a lot of noise going on in the farmyard, for two families were fighting for an eel's head, and in the end it was the cat that got it. The other ducks in the yard stared at the new arrivals and said loudly, "What do we want more ducks for? Ugh! What a sight that duckling is! We can't possibly put up with him!" And one duck immediately waddled up to the duckling and bit him in the neck.

"He's so awkward and peculiar," they all said. "We'll just have to squash him."

"Not on your life!" said the duckling's mother. "He's not handsome but he's good-tempered and he can swim just as well as the others. The trouble with him was that he lay too long in the egg—that's why he's that peculiar shape. Anyhow, he's a drake, so it doesn't matter if he isn't handsome. He looks as if he'll be strong one day, though."

"Your ducklings are charming, my dear," said an old, important-looking duck, and so they were allowed to make themselves at home in the farmyard. But the poor duckling who was so ugly was pecked and jostled and teased by every fowl in the barnyard. The duckling didn't know where to turn and was terribly unhappy.

Things grew worse and worse as the days went on; even his brothers and sisters began saying, "If only the cat would get you, you clumsy great goof!" until the mother duck herself wished he were far away.

One day, when the girl who fed the

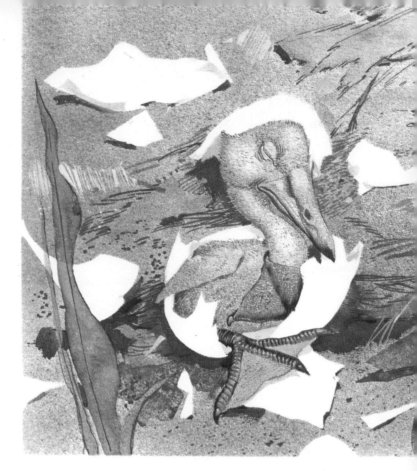

poultry kicked at the duckling with her foot, he ran away. He fluttered over the hedge, and the little birds clustered there grew frightened and flew into the air. "That's because I am so ugly," thought the duckling, and ran away even farther. At night he came to the great marsh where the wild ducks lived and lay there, tired and dejected.

In the morning the wild ducks flew up to look at him. "Who are you?" they asked. "What a scarecrow you are! But that doesn't matter as long as you don't marry into our family." Poor thing! He wasn't dreaming of getting married; all he wanted was to stay quietly among the rushes. But even this he was not allowed to do, for some men came with guns and shot the wild ducks dead, and big dogs broke through the rushes and picked them up in their mouths. One dog pushed its muzzle right down to the duckling, crouching in the rushes. Then it bared its teeth and went off without touching him.

"I'm so ugly that even the dog won't bite me," he thought, and hurried away from the marsh as fast as he could.

It was a cold, bleak day, and he had never been so far before nor felt so lost and lonely.

Towards evening he came to a poor little

cottage, so rickety that it hardly knew which way to fall and therefore stayed upright. He slipped into the house through a crack in the door, to shelter from the wind.

An old woman lived there with her cat and her hen. The cat could purr very loudly and the hen was a good layer, and the woman loved them like her own children. When she saw the duckling she was glad, for she hoped it too might lay eggs for her.

The hen, who was very proud of herself, said, "Can you lay eggs?" and the duckling replied, "No."

The cat asked, "Can you purr?" and again the duckling had to say, "No."

"Well, then, you're no use here," they both said, and he was made to sit in the corner. Suddenly he remembered the fresh

air and the sunshine, and he felt a great longing to swim in the water.

"It would be so lovely to duck my head down under the water and dive to the bottom," the duckling told the cat.

"You must be crazy," she replied.

"I think I'll go out into the wide world again," said the duckling.

"Yes, do," said the hen and the cat.

And so the duckling went off. He swam in the lake; he dived down to the bottom but still he could not make friends with any of the other creatures, because he was so ugly.

Then autumn came. The leaves in the wood turned yellow and brown, the wind carried them off the branches and danced them about, while the sky took on a frosty look. The clouds were heavy with rain and

sleet, and the raven who perched on the fence kept squawking, "Ow! Ow!" because he felt so cold.

One evening, when there was a lovely sunset, a flock of large, handsome birds appeared on the lake. The duckling had never seen such beautiful birds; they were shining white and had long, graceful necks. They gave a weird cry, spread out their great wings, and flew from this cold country to warmer lands and open lakes.

They rose high and the ugly little duckling felt strange as he watched them. He turned round and round in the water like a wheel, and craned his neck after them, letting out a cry so shrill that it quite frightened him. Ah! He could never forget those beautiful, fortunate birds; and directly they disappeared from his sight he dived under the water, for he was almost beside himself with excitement. He did not know what the birds were called, nor where they were flying to, and yet they were dearer to him than anything he had ever known. Yet he did not envy them in the least, for he never dreamed he could be part of such loveliness.

It was a very cold winter. The duckling had to keep swimming about in the water to stop it freezing under him. But every night the pool he was swimming in grew smaller and smaller; the ice froze so hard that it cracked and froze again. The duckling had to keep his feet moving all the time to stop the ice from closing in. At last he grew faint with exhaustion, and lay still. Finally, he froze fast in the ice.

Early next morning a farmer came by and saw him. He broke the ice around him with a stick, and carried him home to his wife. And there she revived the duckling.

The children wanted to play with him, but he was afraid of them and flew in panic right into the milk bowl, so that the milk splashed all over the counter. The woman screamed and clapped her hands in the air, and then he flew into the butter tub and from there into the flour bin and out again.

What a sight he looked! The woman screamed again and hit at him with the poker, while the children ran around trying to catch him, laughing and shouting. It was a good thing that the door was open; the duckling darted out into the bushes and sank down exhausted into the soft snow.

It would be too sad a story to describe all the misery the poor duckling went through during that hard, cold winter. He was sheltering among the reeds in the marsh when the sun at last began to get warmer and the days lighter. Spring had arrived.

Suddenly he felt he had to try his wings; they were stronger than before, and they carried him higher. Almost before he realized it, he found himself in a garden with apple trees in blossom and sweet-smelling lilac

dangling over the stream. Everything here was lovely and soft and fresh. Then three beautiful white swans came in sight, floating lightly on the water. The duckling recognized them and was overcome with a feeling of sadness.

"I will fly across to those royal birds," he thought. "They will peck me to death because I am so ugly. But it's better to be killed by them than be pecked and nipped by the other creatures and go through another terrible winter." As he swam over to them, the birds came hurrying towards him, "Kill me!" cried the duckling, and bowed his head to the water, awaiting death. But what did he see there in the clear stream? It was a reflection of himself, but he was no longer a clumsy, grey, ugly bird—no, he was

himself a graceful long-necked swan!

You see, it doesn't matter being born in a duck's nest as long as you are hatched from a swan's egg.

The three great swans swam round and round, stroking him with their beaks. Some little children came into the garden and threw bread into the water. "There's a new swan!" they cried. "It's the prettiest of them all—so young and handsome!" And the older swans bowed to him. He ruffled his feathers, raised his lovely neck, and was touched to his heart by all that had happened to him. "I never dreamed of so much happiness, when I was the ugly duckling," he thought to himself.

The Legend of Sleepy Hollow

SOME distance north of New York City, the great Hudson River broadens into the Tappan Zee, a name given it by the old Dutch navigators who first sailed up the river centuries ago. On the eastern shore of this inland sea lies a small port called Greensburgh, or, more often, Tarrytown. This name was given it by the housewives of the surrounding district because of their husbands' habit of lingering around the taverns on market days.

About two miles from Tarrytown there lies a valley between high hills, which must be the quietest place in all the world. The only sound to be heard is the occasional whistle of a quail and a brook makes just enough murmur to send you to sleep. This drowsy atmosphere, and the nature of the valley's inhabitants, who are descended from those early Dutch settlers, have given the place the name of Sleepy Hollow.

One story is that an Indian chief used to hold pow-wows there before Hendrik Hudson ever discovered the river named after him. Another says that a German doctor bewitched the valley long ago. Certainly a spell hangs over the place, which causes the people to walk dreamily and believe in all kinds of strange things. More visions, hauntings, ghosts, dismembered voices and music in the air are heard and seen in Sleepy Hollow than anywhere else I can think of. But the chief of all these ghosts is the figure of a horseman without a head. He is said to be the ghost of a trooper whose head was knocked off by a cannon ball during the American War of Independence. The ghost has been seen riding out at night to seek its head, not only in the valley but around a church nearby, where the trooper's body is thought to be buried. This spectre is so well

known that it has been given the name of the Headless Horseman of Sleepy Hollow.

In this quiet spot there lived some hundred and fifty years ago a man called Ichabod Crane, who used to say he "tarried" there in order to teach the children. He came from Connecticut, a state famous for frontier woodsmen and schoolmasters.

His name was appropriate to his appearance, for he was very tall and thin, with long arms and legs which ended in huge hands and spadelike feet, all of which hung loose and hardly seemed to be joined to each other.

His head, into which were set large green eyes, enormous ears and a thin beak of a nose, stood up on a long spindly neck like a weathercock. To see him striding along a ridge on a windy day, with his ill-fitting clothes flapping about him, you would think that a scarecrow was taking a walk.

The schoolhouse in Sleepy Hollow was a large building, crudely made of logs, whose one room had windows made partly of glass and partly patched with sheets from old copybooks. When the schoolhouse stood empty, the place was kept shut by means of

a tough, flexible willow twig, twisted around the handle of the door. Wooden stakes were set against the window shutters, so that, though a thief might easily break in, he would have great difficulty in getting out again.

The house stood in a lonely place beneath a wooded hill with a brook running by and a big birch tree standing at one end of it. On a drowsy day the murmur of his pupils' voices could be heard like the hum of bees, as they read their lessons aloud, interrupted from time to time by his authoritative tones of command, or, occasionally, by the awful switch of the birch rod. For Ichabod, though he was not a cruel master, followed the rule, "Spare the rod and spoil the child," and did not spoil them.

When school was over, however, he would often become the companion of the older boys, and be sure to take safely home the smaller ones who had pretty sisters or mothers who cooked well. For he needed to be on good terms with his pupils. His earnings from the school would never have fed him because he ate so much. So, following an old custom, he used to lodge for a week at a time with the families of his pupils, carrying his belongings about with him in a large handkerchief.

In order that the farmers in whose houses he stayed would not complain too much about the expense of having to keep him, he tried to make himself useful to them in various little ways.

He did earn a little extra by serving as choir master in the local church. He had a curious style of singing and a loud, noticeable voice. On a calm Sunday, one can still hear from a distance of half a mile away, strange sounds coming from that church, which are the remains of Ichabod's teaching. So the

schoolmaster managed to make his living, although there were those who thought he had a pretty easy life.

To the country people of those days the schoolmaster was a man of some importance, especially to the ladies. If he came to tea, his hostess would set out an extra dish of cakes or her best silver teapot. The girls would favour him with smiles, and on Sundays between services he could be seen picking grapes for them from the wild vines, or escorting a group of them beside the mill pond, to the envy of the shyer village boys.

He was always ready to listen to—and to believe—almost any strange story. No tale was too much for him, and he would spend many a long hour after the children had gone home, reading and studying Mather's *History of New England Witchcraft*.

He was in fact an odd mixture of simple understanding and superstition. He always hungered for marvellous things, and loved to imagine that they were happening all around him.

He liked to take himself off, in the late afternoons, to the little stream by the schoolhouse. Here he would lie in the clover and pour over books of dreadful tales, until the sun had set and the falling night blurred the print before his eyes. Then, as he made his way past swamp and stream and mysterious woodland to whichever farmhouse he was lodging in, he would be startled out of his wits by every sound of the countryside. He would jump at the moan of the whippoorwill and at the cry of the tree-toad as it warned of storms to come. His heart would leap at the hooting of the screech-owl and at the sudden rustling in the thicket of birds frightened from their nests. The fireflies too, which sparkled vividly in the darkest places, filled him with unease. If by some ill luck a huge beetle actually crashed into him the poor man nearly died of fright, believing himself to be the target of some evil spirit. His only weapon against this unseen and malevolent army was to sing psalms and hymns as bravely as his wavering heart let him. And so it was that the good people of Sleepy Hollow were in turn frightened out of their wits to hear his strange nasal voice borne through the night air as he wound his way homeward.

Another of his pleasures was to pass long winter evenings with the old Dutch wives as they sat spinning by the fire, with a row of apples roasting and spluttering along the hearth, and listen to their marvellous tales of ghosts and goblins, haunted fields and haunted brooks, haunted bridges and haunted houses, and particularly of the Headless Horseman of the Hollow. The schoolmaster in turn would terrify them with his stories of witchcraft and of the dreadful signs and symbols around them. He would frighten them with descriptions of comets and shooting stars, and with the alarming fact that the world did most certainly turn round, and that they were half the time topsy-turvy!

But however much he enjoyed all this, sitting snugly of an evening in a chimney corner warmed by the woodfire, he always had to suffer dearly for that pleasure on the long walk home afterwards. What fearful shapes and shadows barred his path, how like a ghost each shrub looked as it crouched half-hidden under the snow! He did not dare look back, for fear he should see some frightful being following him. When a sudden gust of wind blasted its way through the tree tops, he was thrown into a terror as he imagined the Headless Horseman himself on his nightly ride.

However, all these spectres of the night passed with the break of day, allowing Ichabod Crane's life to continue its uneventful, happy flow. He would undoubtedly have passed the rest of his life in Sleepy Hollow had not his path been crossed by someone more disturbing to man than any devil or hobgoblin—a woman.

Among the singing class, which met once a week, was a lovely girl of eighteen, Katrina Van Tassel. She was the only daughter of the wealthiest of the Dutch farmers, and was famed not only for her plump, healthy beauty, but for the fact that she would inherit her father's money in due course. This had made her a little coquettish, and she used to dress in a daring mixture of old and new fashions, decorated with the beautiful gold ornaments her great-great-grandmother had brought from Holland, and with a provokingly short petticoat which displayed her attractive feet and ankles.

Ichabod had a soft and foolish heart, and it is not surprising that he soon took notice of this girl, especially once he had visited her at her family mansion. Old Baltus Van Tassel, Katrina's father, looked the perfect picture of a well-off, contented, friendly farmer. He seldom let his thoughts go beyond the boundaries of his own farm, but everything enclosed therein was snug, happy and well cared for. His farm lay on the banks of the Hudson river, in one of those green, sheltered fertile spots in which the Dutch farmers are so fond of settling. A great elm tree spread its broad branches over it, at the foot of which bubbled up a spring of the softest and sweetest water, in a little well, made of a barrel, and then stole sparkling away among alders and dwarf willows. Near the farmhouse was a vast barn that might have been used for a church. Through every window and door of the barn could be seen the rich produce of the farm, while numberless swallows, martins and pigeons fluttered in and out among the eaves. Sleek, fat porkers were grunting contentedly in their pens surrounded by a troop of sucking pigs. Some stately geese were swimming in a nearby

pond, while ducks, turkeys and guinea fowl pecked and scratched and gobbled their way around the farmyard.

As Ichabod's large green eyes surveyed all this abundance, his imagination, stirred by his appetite, saw every roasting pig running about with its belly full of stuffing and an apple in its mouth, the pigeons laid to rest in a bed of piecrust, and the geese swimming in their own gravy. As for the turkeys, he saw them already trussed and cooked with necklaces of sausages.

But his heart was quite won over when he entered the house. It was one of those spacious farmhouses with high-ridged, but lowly sloping roofs, built in the style handed down from the first Dutch settlers. The low, jutting eaves formed a piazza along the front, which would be closed up in bad weather. Under this were hung flails, harness, various farm tools, and nets for fishing in the nearby river. Benches were built along the sides for summer use; and a great spinning wheel at one end, and a butter churn at the other, showed the various uses to which this important porch might be put.

From the piazza the schoolmaster entered the hall, which formed the centre of the house and the place where the farmer and his family usually lived. Here, rows of fine pewter, ranged on a long dresser, dazzled his eyes. In one corner stood a huge bag of wool ready to be spun, in another a pile of linsey-woolset just from the loom; ears of Indian corn, and a string of dried apples and peaches hung in gay festoons along the walls, intermingled with the red peppers. An open door gave him a peep into the best parlour, where the claw-footed chairs and dark mahogany tables shone like mirrors, and irons, with their matching shovel and

tongs, glistened from among the asparagus tops; while mock-oranges and couchgrass decorated the mantelpiece. Strings of various coloured birds' eggs hung above it; a great ostrich egg hung from the centre of the room, and a corner cupboard, left open on purpose, showed an imposing display of old silver and well-mended china.

Having seen all this, Ichabod could not rest until he had won the heart of Van Tassel's daughter. But unlike the knight errants of history who had only to contend with giants and dragons, Ichabod had to contend with the whims of a country co-quette and the opposition of her rustic admirers.

Chief among these was Brom Van Brunt, whose fame and feats of strength had earned him the nickname Brom Bones. Known for his extraordinary skill at horsemanship, he was always at the front in a race or test of strength, sure to be found in the midst of any fight or prank. Many a night he could be heard on his horse, accompanied by his four companions, clattering past a farmhouse with whoops and yells. Then the old women would shake their heads and say, "There goes Brom Bones and his gang."

For some time Brom Bones had paid court to Katrina, but although he was as gentle at the art of lovemaking as a bear, it was said she did not discourage him. When his horse was tied to Van Tassel's gate on a Sunday night his rivals would ride by, not wanting to cross Brom Bones when he was out courting.

This was Ichabod's rival, and he would have deterred a stronger or wiser man, but Ichabod was persevering and pliable. He would bend under the lightest pressure, but when it was off he would return to where he was before.

He could not take the field openly against his rival, for he did not want to lose. He made his advances quietly, under cover of his position as Katrina's singing master. While Katrina's mother bustled about the house or sat on the porch spinning, and her father sat at the other end of the porch smoking his pipe, Ichabod would pay court to Katrina beneath the great elm in the gathering twilight.

How women's hearts are wooed and won has always been a matter of mystery to me, and only a remarkable man can keep a firm hold on the heart of a coquette. This Brom Bones could not do. From the moment Ichabod began to pay his attentions, Brom Bones's horse was no longer seen outside the Van Tassel farmhouse on Sunday nights. A deadly feud rose between the two men.

Brom would have liked to settle their rival claims in a fight, but Ichabod was far too well aware of his rival's strength to allow him an opportunity. He had overheard Brom boast that he would fold the master in two and lay him on a shelf in his own schoolhouse. This peaceful resistance only provoked Brom more, but all he could do was annoy the schoolmaster by playing all the

turned into a whirlwind of activity. The lessons were hurried through, the benches thrown aside, and the whole school was let loose an hour before time, whooping and yelling, like imps let loose into the yard. Ichabod spent a full hour arranging his hair and brushing his best and only rusty black suit. Then he borrowed a horse from Hans Van Ripper, the old Dutch farmer he was currently staying with and, mounted like a knight of old, he set out on his adventure.

The animal he rode was a broken-down old ploughhorse called Gunpowder who had once been Van Ripper's best horse but had outlived everything but his viciousness. He was a gaunt shaggy beast with a head like a hammer. One eye stared blindly but the other gleamed with sheer devilment.

His rider was no less strange a sight, with his knees drawn up, his elbows stuck out and a big wool hat resting on his nose. Shambling out of Van Ripper's gate with his coat tails flapping way out behind and his whip held up like a sceptre, Ichabod was as strange an apparition as had ever been seen around there.

It was one of those fine autumn afternoons when the sky is clear and serene and the countryside bathed in rich golden hues. The forests had turned a deep brown and yellow, with a few trees already dyed orange, purple and scarlet by the early frosts. Streaming files of wild ducks winged their way across the deep blue sky; the sound of the squirrel could be heard from among the beech trees and the hickory nuts, and the thoughtful whistle of the quail rose occasionally from the neighbouring stubble-field.

Small birds fluttered, chirped and frolicked from bush to bush and tree to tree, lost in the chase after ripe berries which flashed before their eyes so abundantly that harvest. There was the scarlet robin, the favourite game of little boys, with its persistent song; and the twittering blackbirds flying through the air like small black clouds; the golden-winged woodpecker with his crimson crest, his broad black neckband and splendid wings

tricks he knew. He smoked out his singing class by blocking the chimney, and he broke into the schoolhouse and turned everything over. Worse, he taught a dog to whine and gave it to Katrina to be a rival to her singing master.

Things went on like this for some time, without any change in the rivals' positions, until one fine autumn afternoon, as Ichabod sat in his schoolhouse, a servant came clattering into the yard to invite Ichabod to a ''quilting frolic'' at the Van Tassels' that evening.

At once the subdued schoolhouse was

and yellow-tipped tail, and his little cap of feathers; and finally the blue jay, that noisy fellow in his gay light-blue coat and white underclothes, screaming and chattering, nodding and bobbing and bowing, and pretending to be on good terms with every-one.

Ichabod jogged slowly on his way, noting with pleasure the ripe apples on the trees and in the baskets and barrels by the road-

side, ready to be taken to market or crushed in the clean-scrubbed cider presses.

He rode through great fields of Indian corn, and in his mind's eye he already saw the cakes and hasty-puddings that would be baked with the corn.

His eyes travelled happily over the yellow pumpkins lying on the earth, their fair round bellies lying turned sunward. He passed by the fragrant buckwheat fields, breathing in the fine smell of beehives, and in his imagination he now saw the dainty flap-jacks, well buttered and covered with honey or treacle, offered to him by the delicate little dimpled hand of Katrina Van Tassel.

The sun gradually wheeled his broad disc down into the west. The wide surface of the Tappan Zee lay motionless and glossy, except for a gentle wave here and there. In the distance floated the blue shadow of the mountain. A few amber clouds hung in the sky, without a breath of air to move them. The horizon was of a fine gold tint, changing gradually into a pure apple-green and from that into the deep blue of midheaven. A slanting ray lingered on the woody crests of the cliffs, giving greater depth to the dark grey and purple of their rocky sides. A boat was drifting in the distance, dropping slowly down with the tide, her sail hanging uselessly against the mast. As the reflection of the sky gleamed along the still water, it seemed as if the boat was suspended in the air.

Towards evening, he arrived to find the great house thronged with people. There were farmers in their best homespun breeches, blue stockings and huge, pewter-buckled shoes. The older women had on close-crimped caps and long-waisted gowns. Their daughters were dressed just as quaintly, except for perhaps a daring straw hat, and their sons wore square-skirted coats with rows of large brass buttons.

The hero of the scene was Brom Bones, who had arrived on his favourite horse, Daredevil, as mischievous a creature as his master. Bones could not abide quiet horses, thinking them unworthy of his spirit.

Of all the glorious sights that met Ichabod's eyes as he came into the mansion, it was not the bevy of pretty girls who held his gaze, but an old Dutch tea table loaded with the fruits of autumn. There were doughnuts and pastries, sweet cakes and short cakes, ginger cakes and honey cakes. There were peach pies, pumpkin pies and apple pies, preserved plums, peaches and quinces, broiled fish, slices of ham and smoked beef, as well as roasted chickens, with bowls of milk and cream, all surrounding higgledy-piggledy a great motherly teapot sending up puffs of steam. He did justice to every dish.

Ichabod was the kind of man whose spirits rose in proportion to the amount that he ate. As he did so his great green eyes rolled round, and he thought that one day, quite soon perhaps, all this splendour might be his. He would leave the schoolhouse behind for ever, along with his niggardly patrons like Van Ripper.

The sound of the fiddle summoned them all to the hall to dance. Here a grey-haired Negro was scraping the strings of a violin as old as himself. Ichabod thought himself as much a dancer as a singer, and his loose-jointed body clattered around the room like

St Vitus himself. He could not be otherwise than happy, for Katrina was his partner and was smiling at him, while Brom Bones sulked in a corner. When the dance was over, Ichabod went over to join a group of old men who sat at one end of the porch around old Van Tassel, smoking and telling stories about the war for independence.

This was a neighbourhood full of famous exploits, for the British and American lines had been quite near and the district had seen robbers, cowboys and all sorts. Enough time had gone by, however, to allow each story to turn out to the advantage of the teller, and make everyone present a hero.

But these tales were nothing to the ghost stories that followed. If there were more tales of the supernatural than usual, it was because of the closeness of Sleepy Hollow, which infected the whole region with its atmosphere of dream and fancy. Strange wailings had been heard around the tree where the unfortunate Major André had been taken prisoner by the Americans and later hanged as a British spy. But most of all they talked about the Headless Horseman. He had been seen quite often in recent weeks, they said, near the church in the Hollow.

At one side of the church is a woody dell with a stream rushing through it. Near the church a wooden bridge crosses this stream, and both the bridge and the road that leads

to it are so overshadowed by tall trees that it is a dark place even in daytime. It is here that the horseman is most often seen. This is the spot, they said, where Brom Bones challenged the goblin horseman to a race for a bowl of rum punch; and Bones was winning until, as they came up to the bridge, the ghost vanished in a flash of fire.

Ichabod drank in all these tales, told in an undertone in a darkness lit only by the glow of pipes, and told in return stories about his own experiences in the Hollow and in his native Connecticut.

The party gradually broke up with the farmers and their families rattling away over the hills in their wagons while the girls rode pillion behind their lovers.

Only Ichabod stayed to talk alone with Katrina, confidently expecting to be accepted. But something went wrong, and he came away in a little while looking very downcast. Could the girl have been leading him on, just to make sure that his rival would propose? No one knows, but Ichabod came away like someone who had been caught stealing eggs from a henhouse. Without a glance at the scene he had so often gloated over, he went to the stable, roused his horse with great kicks, and set off home in the blackest of moods.

The blank expanse of the Tappan Zee lay below him, and an indistinct bark of a dog on the opposite shore only made the great space more immense. There was no sign of life save for a bullfrog's croak as it moved in its muddy bed. All the evening's stories turned in Ichabod's mind as he drew closer to Sleepy Hollow. He passed safely by the old tree where Major André had been taken, but more dangers lay ahead.

A short way from the tree a stream crossed the road and ran into a dense, marshy wood of oaks and chestnuts. It was in this wood that Major André's captors had hidden. The bridge over this stream was well known to be haunted, and as Ichabod approached it he gave the horse half a dozen kicks to try to dash across the bridge. To his dismay the animal ran up against the fence instead. Fearful at this delay, Ichabod kicked it again, only to drive it against the opposite fence. As he whipped and kicked the perverse animal, it suddenly dashed forward—only to stop dead at the bridge. It was then that Ichabod heard something moving.

His hair stood on end. In the darkness he could see a great, towering, misshapen figure. "Who are you?" he stammered out, but there was no reply. He could not go back, so, beating Gunpowder as hard as he could with his whip, he began to sing a hymn to keep his spirits up. The figure moved out on to the road, where Ichabod could see that it was an enormously tall man on horseback.

Without attempting to do Ichabod any harm, however, it simply trotted along on the blind side of Gunpowder, who had by now completely recovered from his fright.

Remembering Brom Bones's adventure with the goblin horseman, Ichabod quickened his pace to try to leave the figure behind, but the figure kept up with him. Ichabod was so frightened by the manner of this horseman that he could not even sing; his tongue seemed stuck to the roof of his mouth. Then as he reached the top of a hill and could see his companion clearly against the sky, he was horror-struck. This gigantic horseman had no head! Instead, he appeared to be carrying it at the pommel of his saddle.

In terror Ichabod rained blows on poor old Gunpowder, who started off down the road, with sparks flying from his hooves. But the spectre started off too, and followed them at a gallop. Ichabod's thin, fluttering form stretched out over the horse's neck as if he hoped to reach home before his horse.

When they reached the place where the road turned off to Sleepy Hollow, Gunpowder, apparently possessed by the devil, turned sharply to the left and plunged down the lane that led through the dark, woody dell and over the haunted bridge to the church on the hill.

Up to now Gunpowder's panic had given Ichabod an advantage in the chase, but they were only halfway through the wood when the girths of his saddle gave way. He tried to hold the saddle by its pommel, but it slipped from his grasp and he was just able to grab the horse's neck before the saddle fell to the ground, to be trampled by the horse behind. He thought for a moment how angry Van Ripper would be, for it was his best saddle. But then all he could think of was how to keep his seat as he bounced along on Gunpowder's sharp backbone, with the spectre close on his heels.

Through an opening in the trees he saw the bridge ahead, and remembered thankfully that it was here that the ghost was said to disappear. He could hear the pursuer's horse panting behind him and, kicking Gunpowder in the ribs, he sprang over the bridge. But when he looked back he saw that the ghost was throwing its head at him!

He tried to dodge, but it was too late. The head crashed into him, and he tumbled to the ground as Gunpowder and the ghost thundered past and away up the hill . . .

The next morning Gunpowder was found grazing at his master's gate, without his saddle. Ichabod did not appear at breakfast or at lunch. The school children played along the stream. Hans Van Ripper began to be worried about Ichabod and his saddle, but a search discovered the saddle on the path to the church, which had been trampled by horses at furious speed. Near the bridge where the stream runs deep and black, Ichabod's woollen cap was found, together with a shattered pumpkin. The stream itself was searched, but nothing more was found. Hans Van Ripper, acting as Ichabod's executor, disposed of his belongings, which were very few. Among them was a book of dreams and fortune-telling in which were some loose sheets of paper with poems written on them to Katrina Van Tassel. These Van Ripper burned, promising never to send his children to school any more since no good ever came of reading and writing.

The mystery of Ichabod's disappearance caused great speculation in the Hollow. But as he was single and not in debt, no one troubled very much about it. An old farmer who visited New York some years later brought back the news that he was alive, and had become a politician and journalist there.

However, the old wives still maintained that he was spirited away by the Headless Horseman, and the deserted schoolhouse was said to be haunted by his ghost, singing thinly. But Brom Bones, who married Katrina soon afterwards, used to burst into hearty laughter whenever anyone mentioned the pumpkin that was found by the bridge. And this made some people suspect that he knew more about the matter than he chose to tell.

Jack the Giant-Killer

IN the days of King Arthur, when there were as many giants in the world as there were fairies, a young boy called Jack lived in the English county of Cornwall. Now Jack was very brave and always ready for an adventure. He had heard many stories about the giants who terrorized England at that time. One giant in particular, named Cormoran, lived quite close by and was feared by everyone.

Cormoran was eighteen feet high and nine feet round, and he lived in a cave on the top of a mountain that was half buried in the sea. Whenever he was hungry he would take three large strides over the water and land right in the middle of Cornwall, where he would devour a whole flock of sheep for his breakfast.

Jack, who was a farmer's son, resolved to put an end to the giant's marauding. He took a horn, a shovel, a pickaxe, and a lantern, borrowed a boat from a friend, and rowed himself over to the mountain where the giant lived. At nightfall he set to work outside the giant's cave and dug a pit twenty-two feet deep and twenty feet broad. He covered the top over to make it look like solid ground. Then he blew so loudly on his horn that the giant woke up and stamped out of the cave brandishing his club. In his haste he did not notice the pit, so he fell headlong into it and Jack was able to strike him such a blow on the head with his axe that it killed him.

When the news of the giant's death reached the people of Cornwall, they were so grateful to Jack for freeing them from Cormoran that they gave him a belt with *Jack the Giant-Killer* embroidered on it.

A few months later Jack's father sent him to Wales to buy some sheep. On his way Jack had to pass through a large and lonely forest and, feeling weary from his long journey, he lay down under an oak tree and went to sleep.

Now the forest was owned by another giant named Blunderbore, who happened to come by while Jack was asleep. He stopped to take a look at him and read the boy's name on his belt.

"Ho, ho," he chuckled, "a giant-killer! We'll see about that!" and he lifted Jack up by his little finger and tucked him into his pocket. When he reached his castle, he locked Jack up in a tower and went off to ask his brother, who lived nearby, to join him in eating Jack for supper.

Jack was wide awake and waiting as the two giants came into the castle yard, which was strewn with human bones. He had found two long pieces of rope in a corner of the room and had made a noose in each one. As the giants were unlocking the door to his tower he threw the noose over their heads and knotted the ropes together behind the window bars. The more they struggled, the tighter the ropes drew around their necks, until at last they both choked to death.

Jack slid down the rope, took the keys off Blunderbore's belt, and freed the many other prisoners who were shut up in the castle. Then he went on his way to collect his father's sheep. But it had been an exhausting day and by nightfall Jack was growing tired again.

He came across a large farmhouse and knocked on the door to ask for a bed for the night. To his surprise it was opened by another giant, who had two heads, each with a long white beard, and was dressed entirely in bearskins.

"Come in, come in!" the giant called out in a friendly way. "Please do make yourself at home in my spare feather bed."

With that he showed Jack into a room with a large bed in one corner. The giant then went off to the kitchen, while the tired Jack got straight into the bed. Just as he was falling asleep, however, he heard the giant next door humming these words to himself:

"Another human, oh what fun!
I'll eat him up e'er day is done."

"Is that so?" thought Jack to himself. "So that's how you treat your guests!"

Getting out of bed, he groped around the room until he found a log of wood. He laid this in his place in the bed and pulled the covers over it. Then he hid himself in a corner of the room.

At midnight the giant came in with a heavy club and struck the bed with it several times, thinking he was breaking every bone in Jack's body. Then he went out again.

The next morning Jack heard the giant moving about in the kitchen. "Good morning!" he called out, coming through the door just as his host was about to sit down to breakfast. The giant leaped with fright to see him still alive. Then, recovering himself, he asked if Jack had spent a comfort-night.

"Yes, thank you," Jack replied, "save for a rat that came and slapped me with its tail a couple of times."

The giant was amazed at Jack's strength and, to gain time, he offered him some oatmeal porridge in a huge wooden bowl. It was much more than Jack could eat, so he tipped most of it into a leather sack he had hidden inside his coat. The giant, who had not noticed this, wondered at Jack's enormous appetite.

"That was good porridge," said Jack, "and now I will show you a fine trick. I can cut off my own head and put it on again! I can even do this—" and with that he slit open the bag under his coat and the porridge poured out fast all over the floor.

"Oddsboddikins!" spluttered the giant. "If you can do it, so can I!" And with that he slit open his stomach with a carving knife and fell dead to the ground.

When Merlin the wizard, who lived in those parts, heard about Jack's feats he decided to help him by giving him a horse, a cap of knowledge, a sword of sharpness, and an invisible cloak. Jack thanked him for his gifts, mounted the horse, and rode on in search of more giants.

He did not have far to go, for soon he heard the cries of a boy and a girl who were being dragged into captivity by a giant. Jack put on his invisible cloak and began attacking the giant with his sword of sharpness. Because the giant was so tall, Jack could only reach to his knees and the giant thought a bee was stinging him. He let go of the children to swat at Jack, who kept on dodging, until at length the giant stumbled and fell to the ground. Then Jack managed to stab him through the heart, and that was

the way in which Jack disposed of him.

Jack took the children home and then went on his way, travelling over hill and dale until he reached the foot of a very high mountain. Here there stood a house in which an old man lived alone. He invited Jack to supper and listened with interest while he recounted his many adventures with giants.

"You are most welcome here," the old man told Jack, "for on the top of this mountain there is an enchanted castle kept by the giant Galligantus and an evil magician. They have just seized a princess and transformed her into a deer."

Jack immediately set off to rescue the princess and free the land from the giant. At the entrance to the castle he saw two fiery dragons keeping guard, but he wrapped his invisible cloak around himself and passed by them unseen. All around him he could hear the cries of the giant's prisoners, whom the magician had turned into birds and beasts.

He found the giant and the magician seated opposite each other at supper, the giant gnawing on a great bone and sharing a joke with the bewhiskered magician who was mopping up a bowlful of pea soup. Neither of them was paying any heed to a slender dappled deer standing forlorn beside the table. From its grace and the pleading look in its gentle blue eyes, Jack was sure that this was the captive princess. He at once leaped upon the giant and the magician and, because he was still wearing the invisible cloak, he was able to kill them both unawares with two strokes of his sword. With that the spell was broken and the princess and all the giant's other prisoners returned to their natural forms and were set free.

By now Jack's fame had spread far and wide, and King Arthur wanted to reward him for having freed England from the last of the giants. Jack, who had fallen in love with the princess whom he had rescued from being a deer, asked for her hand in marriage. The king gladly agreed and gave them a large castle and fine lands in Cornwall, where Jack and his lady lived in happiness for many years.

Cinderella

ONCE there was a rich man whose first wife died, leaving him with a small daughter. After some years the man married again, but his second wife was as proud as she was mean and loved no one except her own two ugly daughters. These girls, in turn, were jealous of the man's first child and soon made themselves the centre of the household, forcing the girl to become their servant. She had to scrub the floors and wash the dishes, shake out the heavy feather beds and, worst of all, get up before dawn each day to clean out the cinders in the hearth.

The poor girl slept in an attic under the roof on a sack full of straw. In wintertime, when the snow blew through the tiles and covered the sack like an eiderdown, she would lay herself down near the ashes and cinders in the kitchen hearth in order to keep warm. For this reason, and because her clothes were always dusty with the ashes from the fire, the two sisters used to call her Cinderella. In fact, they were jealous of her, for no matter how hard Cinderella worked nor how ragged her clothes were, she still looked far prettier than they.

One day the king's son gave a ball and invited all the fashionable people to it. Cinderella's stepmother and her daughters were invited along with the rest, and the ugly sisters set to work at once ordering elaborate gowns, petticoats and wigs for themselves. They made Cinderella starch the lace and pleat the frills, steam the velvet and iron the silk.

"I'm going to wear a red velvet gown with French trimmings," said the elder.

"I *think*," said the younger, "that I shall wear a gold-flowered blue bodice with my diamond stomacher, which is far from being the most ordinary one in the world."

They sent for the best hairdresser they could get to make up their wigs, and the most fashionable dressmaker to sew their new robes, and they bought beauty patches from the smartest shop in the city to stick on their faces.

While Cinderella helped them arrange their hair they teased her about the ball. "Wouldn't you like to go too?" they asked. "Oh, but of course you can't. Everyone there would laugh at the cinder dust on your dress."

Anyone other than Cinderella would have done their hair badly and ruined it, but she was a good, kind person and made them look as beautiful as she possibly could.

On the day of the ball the ugly sisters spent hours admiring themselves in the oval mirrors in their rooms. These could tip up or right down, and only the finest households had them. At last the hour of the ball drew near and they stepped into their coach and drove off to the palace in a cloud of red and blue flounces and frothy lace.

Cinderella watched them until they were out of sight. Then she went back to her seat by the fire and cried her heart out from loneliness and sorrow. Suddenly there was a tapping at the window, and a strange lady entered the kitchen. She had green eyes and a long cloak and she carried a small wand in her hand. She asked Cinderella what was the matter.

"I wish I could—I wish I could—" Cinderella was crying so hard that she could not finish her sentence.

"My dear, you wish you could go to the ball. Well, so you shall. A long time ago, when your mother was still alive, I became your fairy godmother. Now be a good girl and run into the garden and bring me a large, golden pumpkin."

Cinderella hurried into the garden and with the help of a lantern chose the finest pumpkin there and brought it to her godmother. That lady took a little silver knife out of her pocket and scooped out the centre of the pumpkin, leaving nothing but the rind. Then she struck it with her wand and it instantly turned into a fine coach. The girl had seen carriages with their grand ladies driving through the street when she was scrubbing the front steps, and she had wistfully seen her sisters riding haughtily off to the ball in their stylish coach, but she had never seen a coach like this, all covered in gold the colour of a pumpkin.

Next, her godmother asked her to look in the mousetrap in the pantry, where she found six mice, all alive. The fairy told Cinderella to lift up the little trap door, and as each mouse scuttled out, she gave it a tap with her wand and turned it into a fine horse with a long, flowing mane. In no time they were harnessed to the coach, and made a handsome team of six horses with beautiful, mouse-coloured grey coats.

"We still need a coachman," she said to Cinderella, who at once had an idea. "There's a rat trap in the shed," she cried. "I'll go and see if there's a rat in it that we could make into a coachman."

So she brought in the trap and inside it they found a stout rat with splendid whiskers, whom the fairy turned into a fat, jolly coachman with the smartest moustache you ever saw. After that she said to Cinderella, "Go into the garden again and you will find six lizards behind the watering can. Bring them to me."

Cinderella had no sooner done so than the godmother turned them into six footmen in livery who skipped up behind the coach and hung onto its straps as tightly as if they had done nothing else all their lives. Then the fairy turned to Cinderella and asked her if she was pleased.

"Oh, yes!" cried Cinderella. "But how can I go to the ball dressed in rags like this?"

Her godmother touched her once with the wand and her clothes were turned into a gown of Indian muslin edged with swansdown and pearls, silver and white like a summer's night. On her head lay a crown of starry flowers and on her hand she wore a ring of gold and precious stones. Finally the fairy changed the wooden clogs on her feet into slippers of spun glass lined with swansdown.

As Cinderella was just about to drive off in her coach and six, her godmother called out, "Remember to come back before midnight. If you stay a moment longer, the coach will be a pumpkin again, the horses mice,

the coachman a rat, the footmen lizards, and your clothes as ragged as before."

Cinderella promised to leave the ball before twelve, and then away she drove, trembling with joy.

When they saw her step out of the coach the prince and all the court were struck dumb with admiration. The lords and ladies left off dancing and the violinists stopped playing, the better to admire Cinderella's beauty. Then, as the prince asked her to be his partner, the violinists took up their bows again and the music sounded more sweetly than ever before.

The king, the queen, and everyone present praised Cinderella's beauty and her graceful dancing, and wondered who she could be. But as the evening wore on and the prince danced with no one else, tongues began to wag behind fluttering fans,

matronly dowagers with marriageable daughters could not help looking askance beneath their heavily painted eyelids at this usurping stranger, while the slighted young misses themselves pouted increasingly at their less favoured partners—who were doing their own share of ogling the fair unknown. Cinderella and the prince, however, were oblivious of all this as they danced the evening away at what might have been their own private ball.

It is hard to say which of the two was the more transported—the girl, who seemed made of starlight, or the prince who held her luminous in his arms. Certain it is that the prince was so entranced by her that he did not even notice when supper was served and ate not a morsel of the rich banquet that had been prepared. Cinderella sat down by her sisters, politely offering them some of the

sugared oranges and lemons that the prince had given her. This flattered the two vain girls, who never recognized the lovely stranger as the girl they had left in the ashes at home.

Then the clock struck a quarter to midnight and Cinderella rose to go. She curtsied to the company and hurried away before anyone could even ask her name.

When she reached home, she told her fairy godmother what a wonderful time she had had and that the prince had begged her to attend the ball the following evening too. She was still thanking her godmother when she heard the sound of a coach pulling up, and ran to open the door for her sisters.

While Cinderella helped them undress and get ready for bed, they boasted to her about the lovely princess who had been so charming to them at the ball. Cinderella had

to turn away so that they would not see her smiling.

Next evening the two sisters went to the ball again, and so did Cinderella, but this time she was dressed even more bewitchingly than before. The prince never left her side and the two of them danced and talked until they felt they had known each other all their lives. So lost were they in each other that Cinderella quite lost track of the time. As the clock began striking midnight, she started up and fled through the palace like a deer. The prince hurried after her, but he could not catch her. As she ran down the great staircase one of her glass slippers came off, and the prince picked it up and put it in his pocket.

The guards at the palace gate were asked if they had not seen a princess go out. They had seen nobody, they said, save for a young girl in rags, who looked like a kitchenmaid.

When the ugly sisters returned from the ball they told Cinderella that the prince had quite lost his heart to the mysterious princess who had vanished so suddenly, and that he had done nothing but gaze at her little glass slipper for the remainder of the evening.

The prince ordered that the slipper should be laid on a silk cushion and carried in state through the city, while his heralds read a proclamation that he would marry the girl whose foot the slipper fitted. It was to be tried on every unmarried lady, beginning at the top with the princesses and the duchesses.

The turn came for the ugly sisters to open their door to the royal messenger. The slipper was brought to the elder sister to try on, but push as she might, her foot was too big. So greedy was she to become a princess that she actually snipped off her big toe with a pair of scissors and managed to squeeze her foot into the slipper. But the royal messenger saw the blood through the glass and disqualified her.

Then the second sister tried on the slipper, but this time it was her heel that was too big. So she pared it down with a kitchen knife until the shoe fitted. However, she limped so badly that the messenger discovered her trick and disqualified her too.

Then Cinderella laughed and said, "Let *me* try on the slipper."

Despite her sisters' protests, the messenger kneeled down and slipped it on her foot. It fitted her as if it had been made of wax. Then Cinderella pulled out the other slipper from her pocket and put it on her other foot. The fairy godmother appeared at that moment and changed Cinderella's clothes into robes that were more magnificent than any she had worn before.

Then her two sisters recognized her as the beautiful lady at the ball, and they threw themselves at her feet and begged her pardon for their ill treatment of her. Cinderella kissed them and said she would forgive them gladly if they behaved to her like a sister, which they both promised they would from now on.

She was brought to the prince, who thought her more charming than ever, and a few days later they were married. Cinderella, who was as good as she was beautiful, found husbands for her sisters too, who were wealthy and kinder than they had any right to expect.

The Fisherman & his Wife

THERE was once a fisherman who lived with his wife by the sea. They were so poor that their only shelter was a pigsty. One day as the man cast his line into the sea it was dragged deep down under the water by a great fish that was caught on its hook. As he pulled it in to the shore, the fish cried out to him:

"Spare me, spare me! I am not a fish; I am an enchanted prince. Throw me back into the water!"

So the fisherman, who had a kind heart, set the fish free and went back to his wife to tell her the strange story.

"What?" she exclaimed. "You mean to say you let it escape without first asking it for something?"

"What should I ask for?" he said.

"Oh, for somewhere decent to live, away from this pigsty, of course. Go back, and tell the fish we want a little cottage by the sea."

So the fisherman reluctantly set off down to the sea again, which now had turned yellow and green. He called to the fish until it appeared again.

"What do you want?" it asked the man.

"My wife says I should ask you for a little cottage for us to live in, as a reward for setting you free."

"Go home then," replied the fish. "She is in it already." So the man went back home and found in place of the pigsty a pretty cottage with a garden and fruit trees and chickens and a cow, and his wife sitting in the middle of it all.

"Ah! How happy we shall be now!" the man exclaimed, but his wife said nothing. They lived like this for a month or two, until one day his wife said:

"Husband, there's not enough room in this cottage. Go back to the sea and ask the fish to give us a castle instead."

The fisherman was dismayed at her words, but he did as she asked. This time the sea had a blue-black heaviness lying over it. The air was still as the man called to the fish.

"Well, what do you want now?" it asked when it reappeared.

"Please, my wife says the cottage is too small for us; we need a castle."

"Go home then," said the fish. "You have it already." So away went the man and found his wife standing at the gate of a grand castle, with the keys to every door in it hanging around her waist. There were servants in every room, waiting to do their bidding.

"Oh, how happy we shall be here!" the fisherman exclaimed, but his wife said nothing. A few weeks went by and then she said to her husband, "Go back to the sea;

211

the fish must make me queen over the whole of the land."

Sorrowfully the man returned to the sea, which had turned dark grey. He called to the fish, and told it what his wife demanded. "Go back then, and you will find that she is queen already," said the fish.

It had spoken the truth, and for a while the woman was happy to be queen over all the land. But the day soon came when she said:

"Husband, I see that I am meant for greater things. Go back to the fish and say that I must be empress of many lands. And hurry back!"

The husband was filled with fear at her words and returned to the sea with a heavy heart.

"Well, what does she want now?" the fish asked. The water had turned quite black around him.

"She wants to be empress over many lands!"

"Go back then, and you will see that she already is."

So he went home again and found his wife sitting on a throne of gold. On her head was a crown of diamonds and rubies, and in her hand an orb and sceptre that flashed like fire.

212

"Now you are the most powerful woman in the world," he said. "Now surely you must be happy."

"No, I want to be more powerful than any man or woman in the world," she replied. "Go back to the fish and tell him that he must make me Pope."

The fisherman was stricken with terror at her words, but he did not dare to refuse her and so he ran back to the sea with her message. The water had turned black and white, as if a terrible storm was brewing.

"What does she want now?" the fish asked. "She says she must be Pope," stammered the man, and the fish replied, "Go back. She is Pope already." The man returned, and found his wife on the throne of Saint Peter.

"Husband," she cried as soon as she saw him. "I see that I cannot rest until the sun and the moon and the stars are at my command!"

The man, who knew that disaster was near for both of them, returned to the sea for the last time. A terrible storm had arisen, and there were waves as large as mountains.

"Oh fish, she says she must have the sun, the moon and the stars at her command!" he cried, and his voice was carried away by the wind.

"Go home!" thundered a voice from the deep, "and see—your wife has been thrown back into the pigsty again."

The Swan Maiden

THERE lived in the north in a land of great forests and tall trees a young nobleman whose favourite sport was hunting. He liked nothing better than to take his bow and arrows, mount his white horse, and set off at sunrise to shoot the wild creatures of the forest.

One day he was stalking three swans that had landed on a nearby lake. He drew his bow and aimed his arrow at the most graceful of the three as it came gliding towards him through the water. But in the moment he was about to release the arrow he stayed his hand as his incredulous eyes saw that each of the swans had slipped off its mantle of white feathers and transformed itself into a beautiful young girl. The one at which he had aimed his arrow was the loveliest of the three. Her hair was pale gold as the new-risen sun, her skin delicate as gossamer wafted on a summer breeze, and when the young man saw her emerge from the water, clad in dazzling white, he knew that he would love her to the end of his days.

He may only have imagined that her limpid eyes rested on him for a fleeting moment before she transformed herself again into a swan and flew away, high up over the treetops, with her two sisters.

The young man was so bewitched by her beauty that he lingered beside the lake the whole of that day and the whole of the next, aching for her to return. And at sunset that second evening he again heard the beating of their wings and again saw the three swans descend onto the water.

This time he watched where they slipped off their feather mantles, and as soon as the three shimmering girls had swum into the lake he hid his beloved's feather mantle.

Soon afterwards he heard two swans fly away, but the third maiden remained behind, turning her head here and there about her with the bewildered look of a lost child on her fragile face. At last she came slowly towards him and sank to her knees, im-

ploring him to return her mantle to her.

"No, do not ask that of me," the young man replied as he raised her gently to her feet. "I cannot live without you." And he carried her tenderly in his arms, set her down close to him on his horse, and rode away with her to his castle, where shortly thereafter she became his bride.

For many years their lives were blessed with the greatest love and happiness, their home enriched by the fairest of children.

One day, however, the swan maiden was drawn, as though by an invisible cord, up to the topmost tower of the castle where, in a hitherto unknown wooden chest, she came upon a mantle of swan feathers. In wonderment she slid it over herself and on the instant was transformed once more into a swan. Spreading her wings, she flew out of the window, soared ever higher away over and beyond the tall castle towers and was never seen again.

The Adventures of Pinocchio

ONCE upon a time there was . . .
"A king!" you will say at once. But that is where you are wrong.

Once upon a time there was a piece of wood. It was not a special piece of wood, only an ordinary log like one you would burn in your fire.

One day this piece of wood found its way into the shop of an old carpenter named Master Antonio. Everybody, however,

called him Master Cherry because the tip of his nose was red and shining as a ripe cherry.

No sooner had Master Cherry seen the piece of wood than he rubbed his hands together in delight and said:

"This is just what I'm looking for. It will make a fine table leg." He took hold of his axe and was about to chop it into shape when he suddenly heard a little voice saying:

"Don't hit me too hard!"

Master Cherry nearly jumped out of his skin with fright. There was no one in the room, and he thought his ears were playing tricks on him. He decided not to take any notice, and gave the piece of wood a great blow with his axe.

"Oh, oh! You've hurt me!" cried the same little voice.

Master Cherry dropped his axe. He was trembling all over. "Where on earth can that voice come from? It couldn't come from that piece of wood, could it? Why, it's just a log. If it were thrown on the fire it would hardly burn enough to heat a pot of beans. All the same, I don't trust it—I'll get rid of it as quickly as I can."

Just then there was a knock at the door and in came a lively old man called Geppetto, who lived nearby.

"Good morning, neighbour Geppetto," said the carpenter. "What can I do for you?"

"Well, as a matter of fact, I need a piece of wood. I'm going to make myself a puppet, a wonderful puppet that will dance and turn somersaults. I want to travel round the world with it, so that I can earn a crust of bread and a glass of wine."

Master Cherry was delighted. He picked

up the troublesome piece of wood from his work bench and handed it to the old man.

"Here is a present from me," he said.

Geppetto thanked him warmly and set off with the piece of wood under his arm. As soon as he reached home he brought his tools out and began to saw and chisel and drill and carve the wood into the shape of a puppet. He took a great liking for the little thing, and said to himself:

"What name shall I give him? I think I shall call him Pinocchio. I once knew a family who had that name and all of them were very lucky. The richest one was a beggar."

Then he began to carve the puppet into the shape of a little boy. First he made the hair, then the forehead. When he had finished the eyes, he noticed to his amazement that they blinked up at him. No sooner had he made the nose than it began to grow. It tilted up cheekily and wagged at him. Poor Geppetto tried to cut it down to size again, but the impertinent thing took no notice of him and just grew to the length it wanted to be, which was quite long.

After that Geppetto made the mouth. It was hardly finished before it began to laugh at him and to tease him.

"Stop laughing!" cried Geppetto indignantly. "Stop it, I say!" The mouth stopped laughing, but it stuck out its tongue at him instead. Geppetto pretended not to see, and went on to carve the chin, the neck, the shoulders, the stomach, and the hands.

The hands were hardly finished when the old man felt his wig snatched from his head. He turned round— and what did he see? His yellow wig was in the puppet's hands!

"Pinocchio! Give me back my wig this minute!" he cried. But Pinocchio, instead of giving the wig back to Geppetto, put it on his own head. "You rascal, you! You're not even finished yet and already you're showing no respect for your father. That's bad, my boy." And the old man wiped away a tear.

He still had to carve out the legs and the feet, but no sooner had he done so than they flew up and kicked him on the nose.

"I deserve that," said the old man. "I should have thought of it sooner. But now it's too late to tie him down."

Then he lifted the puppet, who was still very stiff in the joints, onto the floor and showed him how to walk. When Pinocchio understood what he was supposed to do with his legs, he began to scamper and skip all around the room. Then he skipped out of the house and ran off down the street. Poor Geppetto rushed after him shouting, "Stop him! Stop him!" But the people in the street had never seen a puppet running like the wind, and they just stood by and laughed.

At last a policeman appeared and stood himself firmly in Pinocchio's path. When the puppet tried to dart between his legs, he snapped them together and trapped Pinocchio between them. He handed him back to Geppetto, who took the puppet by the scruff of the neck, shouting angrily:

"Just wait till we get home— I'll settle up with you there."

But Pinocchio refused to go a step further with the angry old man. The crowd of busybodies who had gathered around them started to cry out, "That poor puppet! No wonder he won't go home with that old man. Geppetto has a filthy temper, and he'd beat the life out of him at home!"

They made such a fuss that in the end the policeman set Pinocchio free and arrested Geppetto instead. He locked the poor old man up in prison, while the puppet ran off home as fast as his legs would carry him.

The next day Pinocchio was wakened by a loud knocking at the door.

"Who is it?" he cried.

"It's me," answered Geppetto's voice. "They let me out of prison because I had done nothing wrong."

Pinocchio ran to unbolt the door and let the old man in. "Oh, Papa!" he cried, "I will be a good boy in future and go to school and do everything you tell me to. But first, please will you make me some clothes?"

"Good boy," replied Geppetto, smiling with pleasure. Then, because he had no money to buy Pinocchio any clothes, he made him a suit out of wallpaper, shoes from the bark of a tree, and a cap of breadcrumbs.

"I look very smart now," said Pinocchio proudly after he had admired himself in the mirror. "But I still need something for school—the most important thing of all."

"What is that?" asked Geppetto.

"A spelling book."

"Of course," said the old man sadly. "I shall have to buy you one." And he put on his old coat and went out into the snow. When he came back he had a spelling book in his hand, but no coat on his back.

"Where's your coat, Papa?" asked Pinocchio.

"I sold it because I was too hot," the old man replied, shivering as he did so. Then Pinocchio understood that his poor father had

sold the coat to buy him the book, and he kissed him gratefully.

He set off for school the next morning, but long before he reached it he heard the sound of fairground music. Imagine his delight when he heard a drummer boy call out, "Roll up! Roll up for the puppet theatre! Grand gala performance! Roll up! Roll up!" Pinocchio was so excited that he decided to miss school and go and see the puppets instead. But he needed money to buy a ticket. After much bargaining he sold

his new spelling book to a street pedlar for two pennies.

By the time he entered the puppet theatre the play had already begun. There were two puppets on the stage, who immediately recognized him and began shouting at him to come up and join them. There was so much commotion and noise, with the other puppets rushing onto the stage too and the audience demanding that the play go on, that the puppet master was furious with Pinocchio for interrupting the performance.

He had just dragged him away and was about to throw him into the fire when Pinocchio called out, "Papa! Papa—save me!" This softened the puppet master's heart so much that he set Pinocchio free and gave him five gold pieces to take home.

Pinocchio thanked the man and set off quickly to take the money to his father. But on his way home he met a sly old fox and a rascally cat, who set about getting his money by trickery. The fox pretended to be lame and the cat pretended to be blind, and between them they persuaded the silly puppet that all they wanted was to help him.

"Wouldn't you like your five little gold pieces to grow into a hundred even a thousand gold pieces?" asked the fox. Then, as Pinocchio nodded, he went on, "You must come along with us to the land of owls. There is a field in that land called the Field of Miracles. You dig a little hole and put your money in it. Then you water the earth, sprinkle two pinches of salt on it, and go away. By the following morning the coins will have grown into a tree laden with gold pieces."

Pinocchio went with the fox and the cat, and it all happened exactly as the fox had said—except that, when Pinocchio went back to the field the next day there was no tree full of gold pieces—there were not even the gold pieces he had buried the night before. The fox and the cat had stolen them in the night, and that was the last the puppet saw of *them*.

In fact, it was even worse than that. For the wicked old fox and cat disguised themselves as robbers, ambushed Pinocchio, tied him up, and hanged him from an oak tree.

And there he would surely have died if a little girl, who happened also to be a fairy, had not noticed him.

"But that isn't how the story ends!" she exclaimed when she saw him hanging half dead from the tree. She clapped her hands together three times. At once a large falcon flew down and landed at her feet.

"Do you see that puppet over there?" she asked the bird.

"Yes, the wind is blowing him round and round like a dead leaf," the falcon replied sympathetically.

"Well, fly across and free him for me," the fairy commanded.

No sooner said than done. The bird pecked the rope in two with his sharp beak and Pinocchio found himself falling through the air. Then he lay quite still on the grass, keeping his eyes tight shut.

The fairy clapped her hands twice more. At this a magnificent poodle appeared, walking upright on his hind legs. He was dressed in a very grand manner, more like a footman than a poodle. On his head he wore a three-cornered hat, braided with gold, and his legs were tucked into crimson velvet breeches. Hanging down behind him was a kind of umbrella case, into which he slipped his tail when it rained.

"My dear Medoro!" exclaimed the fairy when she saw him, "Be quick and fetch me my best carriage! Rescue that poor puppet lying insensible over there!"

The poodle drove the carriage over to Pinocchio and laid him in it. But although the cushions were made of canary down feathers and the walls were lined with cream and egg custard, the puppet was too ill to enjoy it.

"Poor, poor boy!" the fairy sighed when she saw him. "Call the best doctors at once!"

The doctors, who were a crow, an owl and a cricket, came at once.

"Please tell me, gentlemen," the fairy

implored, "If this puppet is alive or dead!"

The crow hopped forward first. He felt Pinocchio's pulse, then he felt his nose, and finally the little toe of his foot. Having carefully done this, he croaked:

"In my opinion the puppet is quite dead; but if by some misfortune he were *not* dead, then it would certainly mean that he is still alive!"

"I am sorry," hooted the owl, "I am sorry to have to contradict my honoured friend and colleague, but I believe that the puppet is still alive. If by some misfortune he were *not* alive, then he would most certainly be dead!"

"And you—have you nothing to say?" the fairy asked the cricket.

"In my opinion, if a doctor doesn't know the answer," the cricket chirped, "He had better be silent. As it happens, I do know something. I know that this young puppet here is a no-good rumscullion who has run away from his old father!"

The cricket's sharp words made Pinocchio cry. "Oh, oh, oh!" he wailed loudly. The three doctors nodded happily and turned to go. Pinocchio was left alone with the fairy.

"I'm hot and I feel ill!" he cried.

"Then I will give you some medicine to make you better," said the fairy. She half filled a glass with water and stirred some white powder into it.

"Is it sweet or bitter?" Pinocchio asked suspiciously.

"It is bitter, but it will do you good."

"I don't want it."

"Listen to me: drink it."

"I won't have it."

"Drink it, and when it's all gone I will give you a lump of sugar to take away the bad taste."

"Where is the lump of sugar?"

"Here it is," said the fairy, taking a piece from a gold sugar basin.

"Give me first the lump of sugar, and then I will drink your medicine."

"Do you promise me?"

"Yes."

The fairy gave him the sugar, and Pinocchio crunched it up very quickly.

"Now drink your medicine." The puppet took the glass and held it up to his mouth.

"Ugh! It smells horrible!"

"It will make you better!" The fairy was very firm, and at last Pinocchio swallowed his medicine. It cured him immediately. He threw back the bedclothes and jumped up. The fairy took Pinocchio by the hand.

"Now tell me how it came about that those two rogues strung you up on a tree to die," she said.

So Pinocchio told her the whole story. "Well, there I was," he said, "On my way home to my father. I was walking along the road one night; it was so dark that I could not see my own nose. Suddenly two assassins beat me up and took all I had. They even tried to rob me of my four gold pieces," he said. "But they couldn't get at them because I had carefully hidden them under my tongue."

"And where are they now?" the fairy asked.

"I have lost them," Pinocchio said quickly. But he was telling a lie, for he had them in his pocket.

His nose began to grow bigger.

"And where did you lose them?"

"Er . . . in the wood near here."

At this second lie his nose grew bigger still.

"If you lost them in the wood, then we will find them again. That is a magic wood, and everything in it is always found."

"Ah, well . . . now I remember," replied the puppet, getting quite confused. "I didn't lose them there. I . . . um . . . swallowed them with the medicine."

At the third lie his nose grew to such an extraordinary length that poor Pinocchio could not move it in any direction. If he turned to the right, he struck his nose against the bed or the window; if he turned to the left, he struck it against the cupboard or the door; and if he raised it up a little he ran the risk of prodding the fairy with it.

The fairy began to laugh.

"Why are you laughing at me?" cried Pinocchio.

"Because of the lies you tell," she replied. "I can always tell when a boy tells lies. Some lies have short legs and others have long noses. Yours have a long nose."

She clapped her hands together and a thousand birds flew in through the window. They perched on the puppet's nose and began to peck at it.

"Help! They're very fierce!" cried Pinocchio. "Ouch! They're tickling me!" But the birds took no notice of him. They knocked and pecked and tapped away at the long piece of wood until at last his nose was the right size again.

Pinocchio was very happy with the fairy.

Sometimes he imagined that she was really his sister, sometimes his mother. They lived together in a little white house at the edge of the wood where the fairy had lived for more than a thousand years.

"I'm sick of being a puppet!" Pinocchio said one day to the fairy. "I wish I would be a boy!"

"That's quite easy to arrange," the fairy replied.

"Oh, please tell me what I must do!"

"You must learn to work a little and to help other people. You must learn to read and write, and to do that, you must go to school."

"I will do all these things," Pinocchio promised, and he began going to school the very next day.

At school the boys laughed at him because he had wooden arms and legs. But when the biggest bully in the class came near him to trip him up, Pinocchio gave him such a kick that the boy went flying across the field.

"Oh, what hard feet!" he yelled, rubbing the bruise that the puppet had given him.

"And what sharp elbows! They hurt even more than his feet!" cried another, who'd been punched in the tummy because

he'd tried very hard to push the puppet over.

After that the boys all made friends with him and liked him very much.

Pinocchio soon learnt to read and write, and the teacher was very pleased with him. But as time went on he mixed more and more with the naughtier boys at school. Then, despite his teacher's warning, he chose as his best friend a boy nicknamed Candlewick. Candlewick was the laziest and naughtiest boy in the school, but Pinocchio preferred him to all the others.

One day the puppet decided to give a party and went around inviting all his friends. He wanted to ask Candlewick, but the boy was nowhere to be found. At last Pinocchio discovered him hiding in a cottage doorway.

"What are you doing?" he asked Candlewick, who told him, "I'm waiting for midnight, and then I shall leave here."

"Where are you going to?"

"I'm going to live in Toyland, where there are no schools and no books—only play—and where the holidays last from the first of January to the last day of December. Come with me, Pinocchio!"

The puppet was very willing to follow his friend to Toyland, and together they climbed onto the coach that arrived at midnight. It was drawn by twelve pairs of donkeys, every one of which wore boys' boots made of leather. The coach was crammed with other boys, and the coachman was laughing and joking with them. It was a very jolly journey to Toyland.

When at last the coach arrived there, the boys all jumped out and hurried to join in the games. They played ball, rode bicycles, dressed up as soldiers, and did whatever they liked. This happy state went on for several months until one morning, without any warning, Pinocchio woke up to find that he had grown a pair of donkey's ears! He ran to Candlewick's room.

"Wake up, Candlewick!" he cried, "Look! You've got them too!"

"Got what too?" his friend asked sleepily.

"Why, donkey's ears!" Pinocchio shouted. He tried to pull his off, but they were stuck firmly to his head.

Before either of them knew what was happening, their hands had turned into hooves, their faces lengthened into muzzles, and their backs were covered with light grey hair. They had been changed into donkeys —and so had all the other boys who had so foolishly decided to leave school and go to live in Toyland instead.

The coachman wanted to sell them all as quickly as possible, and Candlewick was bought by a farmer and Pinocchio by a circus ringmaster. He was trained to dance and to jump and learned how to leap through hoops and walk on his hind legs. He led such a hard life that one day he hurt his leg badly while jumping and went quite lame.

"What can I do with a lame donkey?" thundered the ringmaster. "He's no use to me now!"

So Pinocchio was sold to a man who wanted to use the donkey's skin to stretch across his drum. He tied a rope to the animal's leg and threw it into the sea, so that it would drown. But instead of a dead donkey, he pulled out a live puppet, for a mass of little fishes had eaten the donkey's skin and flesh away and freed the wooden limbs of Pinocchio again.

The puppet laughed at the man's astonishment and jumped back into the water. He had not swum far, however, when a

monstrous shark reared up in front of him. It was too late to escape—the shark had seen him, and it opened its huge mouth and swallowed him whole.

When Pinocchio came to himself again he could not imagine where he was. Then he realized he was trapped in the shark's stomach. It was quite dark all around him, but in the distance he could see a faint light.

Slowly he groped his way towards it until at last he found his father, Geppetto, sitting at a table with a candle burning on it! The shark had swallowed him too, and he had managed to stay alive by eating the stores in his boat.

With the help of the good fairy the two managed to escape safely from the shark's stomach, and this time Pinocchio made up his mind to stay with his father and help him.

226

He learned to weave rush baskets to make a living, and he made an elegant wheelchair so that he could take his father out on fine days. He learned to read and write, and he did everything so well that he was rewarded in the best possible way.

One morning he woke up and was astonished to find that he was no longer a wooden puppet, but had become a real boy with brown hair and blue eyes. He looked at the old puppet propped up against a chair, with its wooden head on one side and its arms dangling lifelessly by its sides.

"How funny I looked when I was a puppet," he said to his father, Geppetto, "and how glad I am to have become a little boy!"

The Little Matchgirl

IT was New Year's Eve and terribly cold. In the twilight a little flaxen-haired girl walked barefoot in the street. Her feet and legs were blue and numb with cold. So were her hands, holding onto her bag containing boxes of matches that she was selling. She looked sad and downcast, for she had sold no matches all day and she dared not go home, for her father would beat her. The snow began to fall and settled on her flaxen hair, and the rich smell of roast goose floated into the streets from the lighted windows.

She stood by the railing at the corner of the street. It grew colder, and as she looked at her matches the little girl thought, "Dare I strike one?" Then she did, and the spluttering light thrilled and warmed her.

She fancied she was sitting by a warm stove, but as she stretched out her toes towards it the light went out. She struck another match. The cold wall beside her seemed to turn to gauze and she saw a plump goose stuffed with apples and prunes lying on a table elaborately laid for dinner, and the moment it caught her eye it jumped off its large platter and ran straight towards her. But then that light too went out. She struck another.

This time she beheld a great Christmas tree, its lights and bulbs hanging over her head. Presents wrapped in pretty paper and tied with gold and silver ribbons dangled from its branches, and at the very top a spangled fairy twinkled her wand. But as the little matchgirl reached out her hand to the nearest branch, the tree too quickly vanished.

A shooting star fell in the sky. "That's

someone dying," she thought. Her Granny had told her that. Then she struck another match and there, standing in the snow, was her Granny, who had always been kind to her and had died. "Take me with you, Granny!" she cried. She didn't want her Granny to disappear, like the stove and the goose and the tree, so she struck all her remaining matches, one after the other. They flared up, as bright as day.

Her Granny grew tall and beautiful and picked the little girl up in her arms and carried her into heaven, where there was no cold, nor hunger, nor fear.

In the first light of the New Year the little matchgirl was found, frozen to death and smiling, in the corner of the street. "Look how she was trying to keep herself warm," people said, but they didn't know how happily she had gone into the New Year with her Granny.

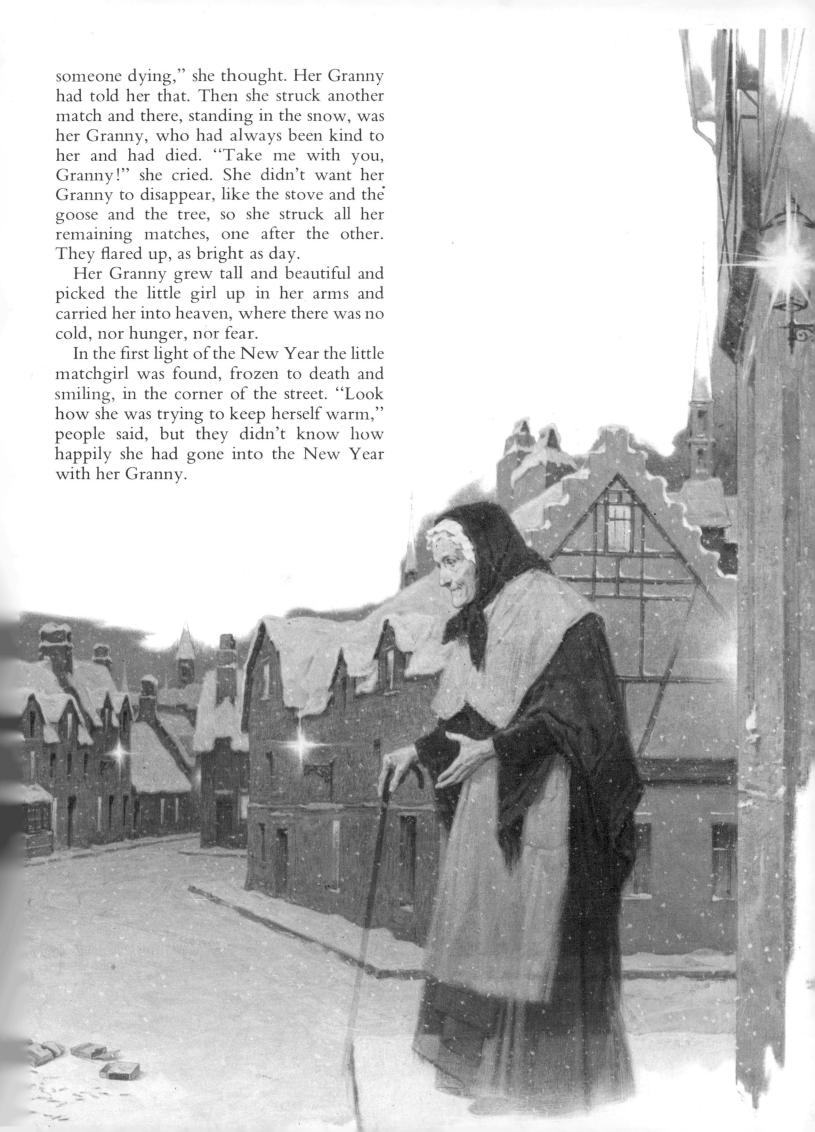

How Tom Sawyer Had His Aunt's Fence Painted

THIS story comes from a book by an American writer who called himself Mark Twain. He wrote about a boy growing up in the southern part of the United States well over a century ago, and the adventures of Tom Sawyer have become as well known to American children as any folk tale.

When my grandfather was still just a lad, a boy called Tom Sawyer lived with his aunt in a village in Missouri. The aunt was a kind lady and looked after Tom well, but she didn't think it right that he should like playing with other boys and getting into mischief better than going to school or helping her work.

In fact Tom hated work more than anything else, and he could think up more tricks for getting out of it than there were stones in the street. One day, after he had been in a fight with another boy and had come home late with his clothes all torn, his Aunt Polly decided to teach him a lesson.

"Drat that boy!" she said. "I'll make him work on Saturday, when all the boys are having a holiday. I've got to do my duty by

him, or I'll be the ruination of the child."

So she sent him off to paint her fence, and gave him a bucket of whitewash and a long-handled brush to do it with. It was a bright sunny day and everybody else in the village was carefree and happy because it was a holiday.

Tom looked at the fence gloomily. It was thirty yards long and nine feet high. He sighed and dipped his brush in the white-wash bucket. He passed the brush along the topmost plank slowly and stepped back to see what it looked like. He felt so depressed at how little he had done that he sat down on a stone, feeling discouraged.

Just then he saw Jim, the little Negro boy who lived down the road, come skipping along with a tin pail in his hand. He was singing.

Tom knew that Jim was on the way to get water from the town pump. It was a hateful job, Tom always thought, but this morning it struck him differently. There was usually plenty of company around the pump, boys and girls joking, larking about. You could spend a good hour dawdling there waiting to get your bucket filled.

"Say, Jim, I'll fetch the water from the pump if you'll whitewash some of this fence," Tom called out to him. But Jim shook his head and said that Tom's aunt had told him on no account to do the white-washing for Tom, and that she'd lick him if he did.

"*She!*" Tom said scornfully. "She'd never lick anybody—she just whacks 'em over the head with her thimble—and who cares for that, I'd like to know. She talks awful, but talk don't hurt. If you do it, I'll give you a marble, Jim—I'll give you a white alley! And—and—I'll show you my sore toe!"

Jim was only human—the temptation was too much for him. He put down his pail, took the marble, and watched while Tom took the bandage off his toe. But in another moment Aunt Polly had come up behind him and sent him flying down the street.

Tom went on with the painting, but all the while he was thinking of the fun he had planned for the day, and how the other boys would laugh at him for having to work on a Saturday.

Then he hit upon a brilliant idea. He took up his brush and went on working. Presently Ben Rogers came in sight—the very boy who would make the most fun of poor Tom's labours. Ben was coming along the street with a light-hearted hop, skip, and a jump. In between taking bites out of the apple in his hand, he was letting out long whoops, a ringing "Ling-a-ling-ling!" or orders like "Stop him, sir!" or "Lively, now! What're you about there?" for he was pretending to be a steamboat, acting the part of the captain and the engine bells at one and the same time.

Tom paid him no attention, just went on with his whitewashing. Ben stopped and stared over at him for a moment, and then said, "Hi-*yi*! *You're* up a stump!"

No answer. Tom surveyed his last touch with the eye of an artist, then he gave his brush another gentle sweep and surveyed the result, as before.

Ben steered up alongside him and said, "Hello, old chap, you got to work?"

Tom wheeled around suddenly. "Why, it's you, Ben," he said. "I wasn't noticing."

"Say, *I'm* going swimming. Don't you wish you could too? But of course you'd rather *work*, wouldn't you?"

Tom looked at the boy a bit, eyed that enticing apple, but then said carelessly, "What do you call work?"

"Why, isn't *that* work? You don't mean to tell me that you *like* it?"

Tom's brush continued to move. "Like it? Well, I don't see why I shouldn't like it. Does a boy get a chance to whitewash a fence every day?"

That put the thing in a new light. Ben began to watch Tom closely as he painted, and grew more and more interested.

"Say, Tom, let *me* whitewash a little," he begged at last.

"No, Ben, no, it wouldn't do. Aunt Polly wouldn't like it. She wouldn't let Jim do it, or one of the other boys who wanted to. She's awful particular about this fence. I reckon there isn't one boy in a thousand, maybe two thousand, that can do this fence the way it's got to be done."

"Oh, shucks, I'll be careful. I'll give you what's left of my apple if you let me."

Tom gave up the brush with reluctance in his face but eagerness in his heart. And while Ben Rogers worked and sweated in the sun, Tom sat on a barrel in the shade close by, dangled his legs, munched the apple, and bided his time.

Before long, more and more of the boys came by to jeer, but stayed to whitewash. The first one traded his kite for a chance with the brush, and the next one offered him not only a dead rat, but a piece of string to swing it on. It went on like this until, by the middle of the afternoon, Tom was literally rolling in wealth. Leaving aside what he had already bartered, he had acquired twelve marbles, part of a Jew's harp, a useless key, a toy cannon, a one-eyed kitten, and a couple of tadpoles. And that still didn't count, among the rest of the treasure, a brass doorknob, a bottle top, a tin soldier, a shaving of chalk, a dog collar, and some bits of orange peel. He had the while done not a lick of work, had plenty of company—and the fence had three coats of whitewash on it!

For Tom had discovered a truth about human nature, without realizing it—namely, that in order to make a man or a boy want something, it is only necessary to make it difficult to have. For in people's eyes work consists of whatever a person is *made* to do, and play consists of whatever a person is not *made* to do.

Bluebeard

ALONG time ago there was a proud and foolish widow who had two sons and two daughters, Anne and Fatima. Anne was not pretty, but she was quick-witted and brave. Fatima was beautiful, but her head was filled with dreams of fairy princes and magnificent castles, and she longed more than anything else to find a splendid husband who would carry her off to his domain. Her mother was just as anxious to have Fatima marry well, and kept a constant look out for a likely suitor for her daughter.

One evening, as Fatima was sitting by the window of their house doing her embroidery, she heard silver bells jingling outside. She looked up, and to her delight saw a fine gold-and-glass coach, drawn by four milk-white horses, driving up to the house. The coach halted outside their door, and a footman in white and gold livery called out to them to ask the way. At the sight of so much finery the foolish widow immediately invited the travellers in.

At this a dark and handsome man stepped from the coach, bowed low to the widow, and explained that the darkness of night would soon overtake them. The widow, who was charmed by his smooth voice and distinguished bearing, grew even more flustered at his words.

"But of course you must not dream of travelling further now that darkness is falling," she said. "Allow me to invite you to my little home. It is humble but warm, and my daughters will help you while away your time with us." To herself she thought,

"What a stroke of good fortune! At last an eligible husband for Fatima arrives on our very doorstep!" The stranger graciously accepted the invitation to stay the night, and the widow introduced him at once to her two daughters.

He instantly made a good impression on Fatima, for there was an air of mystery about

him that made her think of her longed-for fairy prince. Anne, too, felt the mystery, but to her it seemed to carry evil. She noticed above all his beard, which was so black that it was almost blue, and which he kept stroking with his fingers into the shape of a short, sharp scimitar.

At dinner that night the widow placed Fatima on their visitor's right, and the girl sipped her wine and ate her food so daintily that Bluebeard—for so he was called by his neighbours— declared himself bewitched by her beauty and grace. The very next morning he asked the widow for Fatima's hand in

marriage, and she replied that he had made her the proudest mother in the land.

The wedding was held without delay and at great expense, for Fatima insisted that there be fiddlers and trumpeters and silver dishes loaded with sugared almonds and sweetmeats. Throughout the feasting the bridegroom could be seen smiling at his bride and stroking his beard into the shape of a scimitar.

The next day the young couple and Anne, who had begged to accompany them, departed in the gold-and-glass coach for Bluebeard's castle. Great was Fatima's delight when she first set eyes on it, for it stood on the highest peak in the land and the setting sun had turned its walls and turrets blood red. And when Bluebeard led her into the castle itself, her eyes widened with rapture at its palatial splendour.

Some days later Bluebeard announced that unexpected business would take him away from home for a week or more.

"But in order that you may feel free to wander wherever you will while I am gone," he told his wife, "I shall leave with you the keys to every room in the castle." And with that he produced an iron ring hung heavy with keys of every shape and size.

"Take them, my dear," he said, "and explore each room at your leisure. You may use every key except this one." He detached a small dark key from the ring and held it up for her closer inspection. "*This* little key is for the room in the tower. You must *never* go there," he warned as he replaced the key on the ring he now handed to her.

For several days Fatima was content with discovering the riches in each new room she unlocked. But one night she could not sleep, consumed with curiosity to know what was hidden in the tower room. At last she slipped silently out of bed and lit a candle. Then she tiptoed down the long stone corridors and up the winding stairs to the forbidden door at the top of the tower.

She unlocked it—and a cold draught from the room nearly blew out the flame of her candle. Then she screamed, for the room contained the bloodied heads of all Bluebeard's former wives. At that instant she felt her husband's cold hand grasp her own head by the hair. He had returned home unbeknownst to her and she shrank as she saw the gleam of the curved sword in his raised hand.

"Mercy, mercy!" she begged in terror. "Give me time at least to say my prayers."

"You may have until dawn," said the cruel Bluebeard, "but by sunrise your head shall lie with the others."

As the sky began to grow light Fatima called out to her sister who was watching from a balcony below, "Sister Anne, Sister Anne, do you see help for me?" But Anne could see nothing but a flock of birds wheeling ahead. Once more Fatima cried, "Sister Anne, Sister Anne, do you see help for me?" Then Anne replied joyfully, "Yes; our two brothers are galloping towards the castle! They come, they come!"

At the moment that Bluebeard burst into the room with his scimitar raised to cut off Fatima's head, the brothers leaped at him and stabbed him to death. Then they buried the bodies of his poor wives, and took Anne and Fatima back with them to live quietly in their humbler home.

The Elves & the Shoemaker

THERE was once a shoemaker who worked very hard and made very good shoes, but still he could not earn enough to make his living. At last all his money ran out and he had only enough leather left to make one more pair of shoes. That evening he cut out the leather, ready to be stitched up the following morning, and then followed his wife upstairs to bed, feeling very sad.

He rose again at sunrise, said his prayers, and was about to settle down to work when to his amazement he saw the shoes all stitched up and ready on the table. The good man could not understand how it had happened; he examined the shoes carefully and found that they were quite beautifully stitched and finished off.

The same day a customer came into the shop and bought the shoes, and because they were of such excellent quality, he was willing to pay double the usual price for them.

With this money the cobbler bought enough leather for two more pairs of shoes. Again he cut them out, and again he left the leather on his bench overnight, thinking he would stitch them together the following morning. But when he awoke he found that the work had already been done for him. The two pairs of shoes were as beautifully made as the first and soon found willing buyers, and the shoemaker received enough money for them to buy leather for four more pairs.

So it went on for weeks and months. Each evening the shoemaker would carefully cut out the leather, say his prayers and retire to bed, and each morning he would find the shoes standing sewn and ready in neat rows on the bench. Eight pairs at first, then twelve, then twenty, then almost too many pairs to count. And he had so many customers that now he could afford to buy the finest skins and other costly materials besides. He cut out knee-high boots of the softest suede for the lords to wear when they rode off with their hounds to the hunt, and shoes of silk and brocade and velvet for the ladies to wear with their fashionable ball gowns.

And before many more months had passed, the shoemaker grew so rich that he

began to want to share his prosperity with his invisible helpers.

One night he and his wife hid behind a pile of leather hides to see who these helpers were. At midnight two naked little men appeared and hey presto! they stitched up all the shoemaker's shoes for him. Then they disappeared. The shoemaker's wife was very sorry for them because of their nakedness, and she at once set to work to sew them the loveliest little clothes while the shoemaker made them each a pair of pointed silk shoes. They laid the present out, and were on the watch again at midnight as the little men came in to do their work.

When the elves saw their clothes they were delighted. They put them on and laughed and danced all around the room, and then they skipped out into the street, never to be seen again.

But the shoemaker continued to be successful and prosperous in his work for the rest of his days.

The Thick, Fat Pancake

THERE was once a woman who lived in Norway, who had seven hungry children. The children loved nothing better than to eat pancakes, but because there were so many of them their mother decided that, instead of cooking seven ordinary-sized pancakes, she would cook them one enormous pancake that would do for the whole family. So she took flour, milk, butter, eggs, sugar and salt, and made the thickest, fattest pancake you ever saw.

The children jostled and pushed each other about the kitchen table, vying eagerly for a closer look as their mother whisked and stirred the creamy batter in her largest bowl. And they were so excited as they watched it sizzling and browning in the pan that they kept jumping up and saying, "Ooh! *What* a beautiful thick, fat pancake!" until the pancake said to itself:

"Well, I *must* be something really special; I am obviously far too good to be eaten!"

And with these words it jumped down from the pan and ran out the door, hoppity-

hop. On it ran, down the road, with the seven children chasing after it and calling on it to stop.

But the thick, fat pancake was too fast for the children, and too fast for the farm dog who joined in the chase, and too fast for the pet goat. It ran away from a rooster who wanted to peck it, and from a cow who wanted to lick it. It ran past the farmer's horses and out over the fields and rolling meadows, outstripping some gambolling lambs who tried to bite into it, and a flight of swooping hawks hoping to gobble it up. And it was just beginning to feel a bit out of breath itself when it came to a river.

Now the pancake couldn't swim, and was wondering how it could cross the water before all those noisy people and animals caught up with it, when a piglet that had been chasing the pancake from the start jumped into the river and came paddling up to it.

"Thick, fat pancake, would you like a lift across the river?" the piglet asked.

"Yes, please, I would," the pancake replied with a sigh of relief.

But no sooner had it landed on the piglet's snout than snap! he had bitten it in half, and swallowed the morsel then and there. But the other half leaped onto the bank and raced away, hoppity-hop. The piglet tried to catch it up, but he was too slow and the pancake was lost to sight over the hills and far away.

And that is why pigs sniff with their snouts on the ground: because they hope that some day they will find the other half of that thick, deliciously fat, round pancake.

The Emperor's New Clothes

Many years ago there lived an Emperor who loved fancy clothes so much that he spent all his money on elegant suits and cloaks. He took no interest in his army or the theatre or in driving through the country, unless it was to show off his new clothes. He had different clothes for every hour of the day and, just as you might say of an important person that he was in council, so it was always said of the Emperor, "He's in the wardrobe."

One day two swindlers arrived in the city. They told everyone that they were weavers and could weave the very finest materials imaginable. Not only were the colours and designs unusually attractive, but the clothes made from these materials were so fine that they were invisible to anyone who wasn't terrifically smart and fit for his job.

"Well!" thought the Emperor. "They must be wonderful clothes. If I wore them I could see which of my statesmen were unfit for their jobs and also be able to tell the clever ones from the stupid. Yes, I must get some of that stuff woven at once." And he paid a large sum of money to the swindlers to make them start work.

The swindlers then made a great fuss about setting up their workshop; they put up looms and pretended to be weaving, but there was no thread on the looms. They demanded the richest silks and finest gold thread, which they promptly hid in their own bags, and then they went on working far into the night at the empty looms.

"I wonder how they're getting on?" the Emperor thought, and then he became rather nervous. He was a bit worried at the idea that a man who was stupid or unfit for his job would not be able to see what was woven. Not that he thought he was no good—oh, no—but all the same, he'd feel happier if someone else had a look at the stuff first.

"I'll send my honest old prime minister to the weavers," he thought, "He's the best one to see the stuff first, for he has plenty of good sense and nobody does his job better than he."

So off went the honest old prime minister to the weavers' workshop, where they were sitting at their empty looms. "Good gracious me!" thought the old man in dismay, "Why, I can't see a thing!" But he was careful not to say so. "Good lord!" he thought, "Is it possible that I'm stupid? I never knew, and I mustn't let anyone else find out. Can it be that I'm unfit for my job? I must on no account admit that I can't see the material."

"Well, what do you think of our work?" asked one of the weavers.

"Oh, it's charming! Exquisite!" said the old minister, peering through his spectacles. "What a pattern and what colouring! I shall certainly praise it to the Emperor!"

The old minister listened carefully as the swindlers gave details of the colours and the design, and repeated it all to the Emperor.

The swindlers now demanded more money, more silk, and more gold thread, to continue the weaving. They stuffed it all into their own pockets and continued to pretend to weave on the empty frames.

By and by the Emperor sent another trusted official to see how the weaving was going on. The same thing happened to him as to the prime minister; he couldn't see

anything but the empty looms. "I know I'm not stupid," thought the man, "So it must be my fine job I'm not fit for. I musn't let anyone know!" And so he praised the material that he couldn't see, and told the Emperor of its charming shades and beautiful design and weave.

Then the Emperor himself said he must see it, and invited all his court to come with him. When they arrived at the workshop they found the cunning swindlers weaving for all they were worth at the empty looms.

"Look! Isn't it magnificent!" all the officials said, feeling sure that the others could see it.

"What's this?" thought the Emperor, "I can't see anything—this is dreadful! Am I stupid? Am I not fit to be Emperor? This is the most awful thing that could happen to me. . . . Oh, it's quite exquisite," he said aloud, "It has our gracious approval." He nodded at the empty loom, for he wasn't going to say that he couldn't see anything. Then all the courtiers nodded and smiled at the empty loom and said, "Yes, it's quite exquisite," and advised him to have some robes made of it, to wear at the grand procession the next week.

"Magnificent!" "Delightful!" "Superb!" were the words of praise that filled the air; everyone was enormously pleased with the cloth. The Emperor bestowed a knighthood on each of the swindlers, with a badge to wear on his lapel, and gave them the title of Imperial Weavers.

On the eve of the grand procession the swindlers sat up all night, with twenty candles burning in their workshop. People watched them from outside, busily finishing off the Emperor's new clothes. They pretended to take the material off the loom, they snipped away at the air importantly with scissors, they stitched away with their needles without thread, and at last they announced, "There! the Emperor's new clothes are finished!"

And when morning came, the Emperor ate his usual hearty breakfast, for he loved

food almost as much as he did clothes, and then, attended by his most noble gentlemen-in-waiting, went in person to the weavers' workshop to be arrayed in his new finery as befitted the great occasion.

"Ah, your imperial majesty!" The two weavers bowed and scraped low in unison as the Emperor made his entrance. "You do us honour!" And the one poised each thumb, each finger daintily aloft as if holding up a confection really too delicate for human handling. "Here, your majesty, are the breeches!" he said almost in awe, while the other went through the same gesturing motions with a fulsome, "And here is the robe! And now the mantle! You can feel they are as light as down; you can hardly tell you have anything on, your majesty—that's the beauty of them."

"Yes, indeed," chorused the gentlemen-in-waiting enthusiastically. But of course they were only fooling themselves and each other, for there was no more to be seen now than there had ever been.

"Will your imperial majesty now graciously take off your clothes?" said the swindlers. "Then we can fit you with the new ones, in front of that big looking glass."

So the gentlemen-in-waiting helped the Emperor out of the clothes he was wearing, upon which the swindlers set about their pretence of dressing him in the new raiment they were supposed to have made. They took their time about it, the Emperor twisting and turning this way and that the while, apparently admiring himself in the ample mirror, the swindlers consulting him and each other without cease as to the cut, set, appearance of each separate item.

"The breeches—not too tight, too loose about the waist? Ah no, I can tell, snug as kidskin," approved the one, with an appraising pat at the Emperor's paunchy stomach. And, "The ruffle, your majesty, a soupçon higher perhaps—so," suggested the other, tweaking at the air about the Emperor's throat. "Gentlemen," the first one at last challenged the bemused courtiers.

245

"Perfection, would you not say?"

"Goodness! How well they fit your majesty!" they all exclaimed. "What a cut! What colours! How sumptuous!"

The master of ceremonies came in to announce, "The canopy to be carried above your majesty's head is ready and the procession is waiting."

"Tell them I am ready," said the Emperor. Then he turned around once more in front of the glass, to make quite sure that everyone thought he was looking at his fine clothes.

The chamberlains who were to bear the train aloft groped on the floor as if they were picking it up; they walked solemnly and held out their hands, not daring to let it be thought that they couldn't see anything.

The Emperor marched off in the procession, under the grand canopy, and everyone in the streets and at their windows said, "Good gracious! Look at the Emperor's new clothes! They are the finest he's ever had. What a sumptuous train! What a perfect fit!" No one would admit to anyone else that he couldn't see anything, because that would have meant that he wasn't fit for his job or that he was stupid. The Emperor's new clothes were praised by everyone.

"But he hasn't got anything on!" exclaimed a little child. "Hush! what are you saying?" cried the father. The people around him had heard, however, and repeated the child's words in a whisper. Then someone said them a bit louder.

"He hasn't got anything on! There's a little child over there saying he hasn't got anything on!"

"That's right! HE HASN'T GOT ANY-THING ON!" the people all shouted at last. And the Emperor began to feel very uncomfortable and embarrassed, for it seemed to him that the people were right. But his royal upbringing prevented him from running away, and he thought to himself, "I must go through with it now, procession and all." And he drew himself up haughtily, while the chamberlains tripped after him, bearing the train that wasn't there.

The Wizard of Oz: Dorothy Kills the Witch

ONCE there was a little girl named Dorothy who lived on a farm in Kansas. One day the sky grew dark and a big wind began to blow across the flat prairies that stretched all around the farm. Dorothy ran into her house to take shelter but the tornado came closer and closer until—suddenly—it lifted Dorothy's house high up into the sky, with Dorothy and her little dog Toto still inside. The house came to rest at last in a magic country, as Dorothy realized the moment she opened the door and walked outside.

The first person she saw was an old lady. She looked just like any other old lady except that she was smaller and wore a high, pointed hat on her head with gold bells hanging from it, and a white gown. She was followed by three small men, all dressed in blue. They too wore high, pointed hats with bells hanging from them, and big boots that reached right over their knees.

"Who are you?" asked Dorothy.

"I am the Witch of the North, and I have come to thank you for killing the Wicked Witch of the East."

Dorothy looked surprised. "I've never killed anybody!" she replied.

"Well, your house did, when it landed here. It fell right on top of her and killed her—you can still see her silver shoes sticking out from under the wall there. Take them; they are yours now."

Dorothy looked down at her own shabby shoes. "Well, it's a long walk back to Kansas from here; I might as well get some good shoes for the journey," she said. "Can you tell me the way home, please?"

"Oh, no, my dear," the old lady replied. "Only the Great Wizard of Oz knows that. You will have to ask him."

"Where does he live?" asked Dorothy.

"A *long* way away, in the Emerald City. The road there is very dangerous."

"Will you come with me?" asked Dorothy.

"No, I can't do that, but I will give you my kiss, and no one will dare to hurt you if you've been kissed by the Witch of the North." She kissed Dorothy softly on the forehead. Where she had kissed her a round, shining mark appeared.

"Thank you," said Dorothy, but before the words were out of her mouth the witch and the three little men had disappeared.

Dorothy put on the silver shoes, tucked Toto under her arm, and set off to find the Wizard of Oz. The road was long, and many

things happened to her on the way there.

First she made friends with a Scarecrow and took him with her on her search. The Scarecrow was going to the Emerald City to ask the Wizard for some brains. The farmer who had made him had stuffed his head with straw, and nobody can think with a head made of straw.

Then she and the Scarecrow came across a Woodman who was made entirely of tin. He begged them to let him join their party, for he wanted the Wizard to give him a heart. A wicked witch had put a spell on his axe one day, and it had cut his body so badly that a smith had had to replace every part of it with tin. The only thing that the smith had not been able to replace had been his heart, and now he wanted more than anything in the world to get a new heart, so that he could feel sorrow and happiness as other people do.

Finally, as they were walking through a dark forest, they met a Lion who had a very fierce roar but who was in fact afraid of everything. Being so cowardly made him very unhappy, for he knew that as king of the beasts he ought to be braver than anyone else.

"Do you think Oz could give me courage?" the Cowardly Lion asked Dorothy.

"Just as easily as he could give me brains," said the Scarecrow.

"Or give me a heart," said the Tin Woodman.

"Or send me back to Kansas," said Dorothy.

"Then, if you don't mind, I'll go with you," said the Lion.

"You're very welcome," answered Dorothy, "for you will help keep away the other wild beasts on our journey."

So off they set, and after a great many adventures they arrived at the gates of the Emerald City.

There they asked to see the Wizard, and one by one they were admitted to his throne room to present their requests. But to each one he gave the same answer, "Your wish will not be granted until you have rid the country of the Wicked Witch of the West." To Dorothy he said, "When you can tell me that the Wicked Witch is dead, I will send you back to Kansas—but not before."

The little girl began to cry, for she thought she couldn't possibly kill the Witch and feared that this meant she would *never* get back to Kansas.

"What shall we do now?" she asked her friends sadly.

"We must go to the land of the West," said the Lion. "We must find this Witch and destroy her."

So they set off towards the Wicked Witch's castle.

It wasn't long before the Witch found out about Dorothy and her party. She was angry with them for coming without

asking her permission first and decided to punish them terribly. She took a tin whistle and blew on it three times.

The whistle was immediately answered by a great howl that seemed to come from all directions at once as a pack of great wolves bounded towards her.

"Go to these strangers," cried the Witch, "and tear them to pieces!"

"Very well," replied the wolves, and off they loped towards the little group.

Luckily the Tin Woodman heard the wolves coming from a long way off. "Let me deal with them," he said. "Get behind me; I'm going to kill them."

He took his axe in both hands and waited for the first wolf. When it was just an arm's length away, he swung the axe into the air and chopped the wolf's head off, and the beast fell dead to the ground. There were

forty wolves in all, and as each one jumped at the Woodman, he knocked it flying. When they all lay dead on the ground, he wiped his axe and put it away.

When the Wicked Witch saw what had happened, she was very angry indeed. She blew another three blasts on her whistle. Immediately a flock of fierce crows flew down and settled at her feet.

"Peck out the strangers' eyes and tear

them to pieces!" she commanded them.

The crows flew up and shot off towards Dorothy like so many arrows towards their prey.

The Scarecrow cried, "Let me fight them! Lie down beside me and I will protect you!"

He stretched up his arms and caught each bird as it flew down and broke its neck.

When the Wicked Witch saw all her crows lying dead on the ground, she grew even angrier than before. She blew three more times on her whistle. And at once she was surrounded by a swarm of black bees.

"Go to the strangers and sting them to death!" she cried, and the bees blew off towards Dorothy and her friends like so many bullets shot from a gun.

"Take out my straw stuffing and scatter it over yourselves!" the Scarecrow cried to Dorothy, Toto and the Lion, when he saw the swarm coming. "Then the bees won't be able to sting you!" They did as he said, and when the bees came down they found no one but the Tin Woodman to sting. They flew at him and broke their stings against his tin body and fell dead to the ground.

Then Dorothy and the Lion and Toto got up and stuffed the straw into the Scarecrow again, and they continued their journey.

The Wicked Witch turned purple with anger when she saw that her precious bees too had been killed by the strangers. She called her slaves, the Winkies, and told them to take their sharpest spears and kill the five of them at once.

So the slaves set off down the road, but they were frightened because they knew what had happened to the wolves and the crows and the bees.

When the Lion saw the Winkies coming, he gave a great roar and sprang towards them. "Help!" they cried, and scuttled off back to the castle as fast as they could run.

Then the Wicked Witch sat down and began to think hard. She could not understand how she had failed to destroy the little group, and she was more determined than ever to kill them.

She had in her safe a golden cap with a circle of diamonds and rubies curling around it. This was a magic cap, for whoever owned it could call on the winged monkeys and make them carry out any order they were given. But no one could call on the monkeys more than three times. Twice already the Wicked Witch had made them do her bidding. She could use the cap to call the monkeys only once more, and she did not want to do this until all her other magic had been used up. But she had tried everything she could against the strangers: her wolves and her crows and her bees were dead, and her slaves had been scared away. There was only the golden cap left.

The Witch took it out of her safe and put it on her head. Slowly she intoned in a chant.

"Ep-pe, pep-pe, kak-ke!"

Suddenly the sky went black, and a low

rumbling like the sea breaking over rocks could be heard. The air was filled with winged monkeys as they flocked into the castle. The biggest one among them flew up to her and said:

"For the third and last time we come at your call, Wicked Witch of the West. What do you want?"

"Go to the strangers and destroy them all except the Lion. Bring him to me. I want to harness him like a pony and make him drive me around."

"We go at your command," said the leader, as they flew off towards Dorothy and her friends. They swooped down and picked up the Tin Woodman and carried him through the air to a rocky place. There they dropped him so that he crashed down onto the rocks and was so battered and dented that he could not move.

Then they picked up the Scarecrow and

began tearing the stuffing out of his body. When they had scattered the straw, they tied up his clothes and threw them into a tree.

They threw coils of strong rope around the Lion and tied him up like a parcel. Then they lifted him up and flew away with him to the Witch's castle.

Dorothy was very frightened when she saw what the monkeys were doing to her friends. She stood with Toto in her arms watching them, knowing that it would be her turn next. The leader of the monkeys flew up to her and stretched out his long, hairy arms to snatch her away. Then he stopped suddenly. His face was quite close to hers, and he was looking at the round, shining mark that the kiss from the Good Witch of the North had left on Dorothy's smooth young forehead.

"Don't hurt her!" he cried. "She is protected by the power of good! It's much more powerful than the power of evil is!''

So they lifted Dorothy up gently and carried her through the air to the castle. Dorothy squeezed Toto tightly under her arm, and together they were set down in front of the Witch.

"We have obeyed you as far as we could," the monkey leader told her. "We dare not harm either the little girl or her dog. Now your power over us is ended, and you will never see us again." With that the monkeys flew off and disappeared into thin air.

The Wicked Witch was angry when she saw the shining circle that the Good Witch's kiss had left on Dorothy, for she knew now that she could not hurt her in any way. Then she noticed that

Dorothy was wearing magic shoes and that she did not seem to know they were magic. A cunning gleam came into the Witch's eye.

"Come here at once!" she shouted at Dorothy. "You must do exactly as I tell you. If you don't, I shall kill you as I have killed the Woodman and the Scarecrow!" She ordered Dorothy to set to work to clean up the whole castle and to stoke the fire in the kitchen. Then she went out into the yard to

see the Lion who had been shut up there.

"How grand I shall look," she thought, "when I'm driven through the streets by a lion." She opened the door cautiously. The Lion leapt up. "Arr-rr!" he roared, and the Witch's teeth rattled together in fear.

She jumped back to a safer distance and shouted at him, "If you don't do as I say, I shall starve you to death!" "Arr-rr!" the Lion replied and shook his mane.

When the Witch went to bed that night, Dorothy crept into the yard and brought him some food. She came to him every night and talked to him, trying to work out a means of escape for them both. But every gate and bridge around the castle was guarded by the Witch's slaves.

"I *must* get hold of Dorothy's magic shoes!" the Witch said to herself. "When I have them, I'll be so powerful that I'll have no more worries on earth." But Dorothy never took off her shoes except at night and when she went to have a bath. The Witch was too afraid of the dark to steal them in the night, and she was even more afraid of water. In fact she always made quite sure that she

kept right away from even the tiniest splash and carried an umbrella with her wherever she went.

Eventually the Witch tried to steal the shoes away by a trick. She put an iron bar in the middle of the kitchen and cast a spell on it to make it invisible. Dorothy did not see it and so she fell right over it. One of her shoes flew off and the Witch snatched it up at once.

"Ha-ha! It's mine now and you can't work the spell any more, even if you knew how to!" she said.

"I've got no idea what you're talking about," said Dorothy crossly. "Give me back my shoe at once!"

"I will not," hissed the Witch. "It's my shoe now!"

"You are wicked!" cried Dorothy. "That shoe belongs to me!"

"I shall keep it just the same, and some day I'll get the other one from you too!"

This made Dorothy so angry that she picked up the bucket of water she had just pumped up and threw it over the Witch, soaking her from head to foot.

"Aaah! Iiih!" screamed the Witch. She

began to shake and melt away at the edges. "See what you've done!" she cried. "I'm going to evaporate!"

"I'm sorry," stammered Dorothy, who was really frightened to see the Witch melting away before her eyes. "Was there anything wrong with that water?"

"No, there wasn't. But any sort of water is the death of me. Oh dear, oh dear, here I go!" And with these words the Witch melted right away into a little brown puddle.

Dorothy put her second silver shoe back on again. Then she picked up the Witch's bunch of keys and ran out into the yard to unlock the Lion's cage. "We're free! We're free! The Wicked Witch is dead!" she cried.

How Dorothy and her friends were reunited, how the Wizard of Oz granted them all their wishes, and how the little girl found her way back at last to her home in Kansas is a long story which you must find in another book.

The Wonderful Tar-Baby

MANY years ago there was a little boy who lived on a cotton plantation in the American South. His best friend was an old black man called Uncle Remus whom he was always begging for another story about Brer Rabbit, and Brer Fox who was always trying to catch him. But the rabbit was too smart and always got away.

"Didn't the fox *never* catch the rabbit, Uncle Remus?" the boy asked one evening.

"He come mighty near it one time, honey. One day Brer Fox got him some tar, an' he mixed it in with some turpentine an' fixed up a contraption that he called a Tar-Baby. An' he set this here Tar-Baby right smack in the big road an' then lay down in the bushes an' watched for to see what would happen.

"Pretty soon Brer Rabbit come prancin' along the road, lippity-clippity, sassy as a jaybird, till he spied the Tar-Baby sittin' there, an' then he fetched up on his hind legs lookin' mighty astonished. The Tar-Baby just sat there, doin' nothin', an' Brer Fox, he kept on layin' low.

" 'Mornin'!' says Brer Rabbit. 'Nice weather this mornin',' says he.

"Tar-Baby ain't sayin' nothin', an' Brer Fox, he lay low.

" 'How is the state of your health at present?' says Brer Rabbit to Tar-Baby. An' when there ain't no answer, 'Is you deaf?' he says, 'because if you is, I can holler louder.'

"Brer Fox wink slow, but Tar-Baby just sat.

" 'You're mighty stuck up, you is,' says Brer Rabbit. 'An' I'm goin' to cure you,' says he. 'I'm goin' to learn you how to talk to respectable people if it's the last thing I do,' he says. 'If you don't take off that old hat an' say howdy-do to me, I'm goin' to bust you wide open,' says Brer Rabbit.

"Brer Fox, he sorta chuckled, but Tar-Baby kept on sayin' nothin', till finally Brer Rabbit draw back his fist and *blip*— he hit Tar-Baby right smack on the side of the head. Right there's where Brer Rabbit made his big mistake. His fist stuck fast in the tar an' he couldn't pull loose. But Tar-Baby, he just sat. An' Brer Fox, he lay low.

" 'If you don't let me loose, I'll knock you again,' says Brer Rabbit, an' with that he fetched Tar-Baby a swipe with the other hand. An' *that* stuck. Tar-Baby she ain't sayin' nothin', an' Brer Fox, he lay low.

" 'Turn me loose,' hollers Brer Rabbit. 'Turn me loose before I kick the natural stuffin' out of you,' he says. But Tar-Baby ain't sayin' nothin'—just keeps on holdin' fast. Then Brer Rabbit he commenced to kick, an' the next thing he know his feet are stuck fast too. Brer Rabbit squall out that if Tar-Baby didn't turn him loose, he'd butt with his head. Brer Rabbit butted, an' then he got his head stuck too.

"Then Brer Fox, he sauntered out of the bushes, lookin' as innocent as a mockin' bird.

" 'Howdy, Brer Rabbit,' says Brer Fox, says he. 'You look sort of stuck up this mornin',' says he, an' then he rolled on the ground and he laughed and laughed till he couldn't laugh no more. 'I reckon you're goin' to have dinner with me this time, Brer Rabbit,' he says. 'I've laid in a heap o' nice vegetables an' things, an' I ain't goin' to take no excuse,' says Brer Fox."

Here Uncle Remus paused and raked a sweet potato out of the ashes on the hearth.

"Did the fox eat the rabbit, Uncle Remus?" asked the little boy.

"Well, now, that's as far as the tale goes," replied the old man. "Maybe he did—an' then again, maybe he didn't."

How Brer Rabbit Fooled Brer Fox

ONE evening, when the little boy had finished supper and hurried out to sit with his friend, he found the old man in great glee. Uncle Remus was talking and laughing to himself at such a rate that the little boy was afraid that he had company. The truth is, Uncle Remus had heard the child coming and, when the little chap put his head in at the door, was busy talking to himself and humming words that went something like this:

> *"Old Molly Har*
> *What you doing thar,*
> *Sitting in the corner*
> *Smoking your cigar?"*

Whatever this meant, it somehow reminded the little boy that the wicked Fox was still chasing the Rabbit, and he immediately said:

"Uncle Remus, did the Rabbit have to go right away from there, when he got loose from the Tar-Baby?"

"Bless you, honey, no he didn't. Who? Him? You don't know nothing at all about Brer Rabbit if that's the way you think he is. What should he go away for? He maybe stayed sorta close till the tar rubbed off his hair some. But it wasn't many days before he was loping up and down the neighbourhood the same as ever—and I don't know if he wasn't even more cheeky than before.

"Seems like the tale about how he got mixed up with the Tar-Baby got round among the neighbours. Leastways, the girls got wind of it, and the next time Brer Rabbit paid them a visit they tackled him about it. The girls giggled, but Brer Rabbit

he just sat there as cool as a cucumber, he did, and let them run on. Like a lamb, he sat there, and then by and by he crossed his legs and leant back and winked his eye slowly. Then he got up and said:

" 'Ladies, Brer Fox was my daddy's

riding horse for thirty years—maybe more, but thirty years that I know about,' said he. Then he paid the ladies his respects, and he tipped his hat, he did. And off he marched, just as stiff and stuck up as a stick.

"Next day Brer Fox came a calling on the ladies and when he began to laugh about Brer Rabbit the gals they got up and told him about what Brer Rabbit said. Well, Brer Fox he grit his teeth and he looked mighty grumpy. But when he got up to go he said, said he:

" 'Ladies, I ain't disputing what you say, but I tell you this: I'll make Brer Rabbit chew up his words and spit 'em out right here where you can see 'em,' said he. And with that, off went Brer Fox.

"As soon as he got to the road, Brer Fox shook the dew off his tail and made a straight shoot for Brer Rabbit's house. Brer Rabbit was expecting him, of course, and when he got there, the door was shut fast. Brer Fox knocked. Nobody answered. Brer Fox knocked again. Nobody answered. Brer Fox kept on knocking—then Brer Rabbit hollered out, but mighty weak:

" 'Is that you, Brer Fox? I want you to run and fetch the doctor. Something I ate this morning is killing me. Please Brer Fox, run quick, quick,' says Brer Rabbit, says he.

" 'I just come to get you, Brer Rabbit,' says Brer Fox. 'There's going to be a party up at the girls' house and I promised that I'd fetch you.'

"Brer Rabbit said he was too sick to go. Brer Fox said he wasn't—and then they had it up and down, disputing and contending. Brer Rabbit said he couldn't walk. Brer Fox said he'd carry him. Brer Rabbit said, How? and Brer Fox said, In his arms.

Brer Rabbit said he was afraid he'd drop him. Brer Fox promised he wouldn't.

"By and by Brer Rabbit said he'd go if Brer Fox let him ride on his back. Brer Fox said he'd do that. But Brer Rabbit said he couldn't ride without a saddle. Brer Fox said he would get a saddle. Brer Rabbit said he couldn't sit in the saddle unless he had a bridle to hold on to. Brer Fox said he'd get the bridle. But Brer Rabbit said he couldn't ride without blinkers on the bridle because Brer Fox might shy at stumps along the way and fling him off. Brer Fox said he'd get a bridle with blinkers.

"Then Brer Rabbit said he'd go. And Brer Fox said he'd ride Brer Rabbit most of the way up to the girls' house, but then he'd let him get down and walk the rest of the way. Then Brer Rabbit agreed.

"Of course, Brer Rabbit knew all along the sort of trick that Brer Fox was meaning to play on him, and he determined to outdo him. Well, by the time he'd combed his hair and smoothed it down, and twisted and twirled his moustache and spruced himself up, along came Brer Fox with the saddle and bridle strapped on, looking as pert as a circus pony. So Brer Rabbit hopped on him and they ambled off.

"Brer Fox couldn't see behind because of the blinkers he was wearing, but by and by he felt Brer Rabbit raise one of his feet.

" 'Well, what are you doing, Brer Rabbit?' said he.

" 'Shortening the left stirrup, Brer Fox,' said he.

"By and by Brer Rabbit raised up the other foot.

" 'What are you doing now, Brer Rabbit?' said he.

" 'Pulling down my pants, Brer Fox,' said he.

"All this time, gracious honey, Brer Rabbit was putting on his spurs. When they got close to the girls' house where Brer Rabbit was to get off, Brer Fox made a sign for him to stop. Then Brer Rabbit slapped the spurs into Brer Fox's flanks—

and Brer Fox streaked across that ground, fast as could be. When they got to the house, all the girls were sitting on the piazza. Instead of stopping at the gate, Brer Rabbit rode right on by, he did, and then came galloping back down the road and up to the horse-rack, and hitched Brer Fox to it. Then he sauntered into the house, he did, and shook hands with the girls, and sat there smoking his cigar same as any town man. By and by he drew in a long puff and let it out in a cloud. Then he squared his shoulders back and hollered out loud:

" 'Ladies, didn't I tell you Brer Fox was the riding horse for our family? He's sorta losing his gait now, but I reckon I can fetch him round in a month or so,' said he.

"Then Brer Rabbit sorta grinned, he did, and the girls giggled, and went tripping daintily round the pony, praising his whiskers and his tail. And Brer Fox was hitched fast to the rack, and couldn't help himself.

"Is that all, Uncle Remus?" asked the little boy, as the old man paused.

"Well, that ain't exactly all, honey—but it wouldn't do to give out too much cloth for to make one pair of pants," replied the old man sententiously.

267

The Straw, the Coal & the Bean

An old woman once hung a pot full of beans on a chain in her chimney and built a fire under it to heat it up for her supper. She lit the fire with a handful of straw, but as she did so, a piece of the straw slipped from her hand and dropped to the ground. While she was stirring the beans in the pot, one of them fell unnoticed to the floor where it rolled alongside the straw. By this time the fire was crackling away, and out jumped a red-hot coal and landed beside them.

"Dear friends," said the straw, "please tell me where you have come from."

The coal replied, "Oh, I made a quick jump out of that fire, for if I hadn't I'd have been burned to cinders."

"As for me," said the bean, "I too was lucky enough to escape with a whole skin, for if I hadn't jumped out of that pot I'd have been boiled to pulp along with the other beans."

"I should certainly have fared no better," said the straw, "for I should have gone up the chimney in smoke just like all the rest of my straw brothers."

"Well," said the coal, "since we've been chosen to stay alive, what shall we do with ourselves?"

The straw, the coal, and the bean then decided that since fate had thrown them together like this, they should without a doubt set off and see the world in each other's company.

For a while they had a fine, carefree time, tumbling merrily down hillsides, lolling lazily about under leafy trees. Poking their noses into farm kitchens, they congratulated themselves on their own cleverness at sight of other straw and coal burning away to ashes, beans simmering in steaming pots. The straw got almost more than he asked for when, tickling the ear of a rooster in a barnyard, he would have been chewed up for his pains had a sudden flurry of wind not whipped by and deposited him safely on the other side of the barnyard fence. And the bean was just about to be squashed under the hoof of a skittish foal in a meadow when the filly sprinted off in its mother's whinnying direction.

And so they wandered about the countryside until they came to a stream that ran between two fields. They looked up and down stream for a bridge, but they could not find one. So the straw laid himself across the stream and invited his friends to use him as a bridge instead.

The coal was the first to cross. But when he reached the middle he stopped for a moment—long enough, unfortunately, to burn through the straw so that they both fell hissing and burning into the water.

The bean, who was watching from the bank, literally split his sides with laughter. And that is how he would have remained had not a kind-hearted tailor come by, who pulled out his needle and thread and stitched the bean together again. The thread was very thick, however, and that is why every bean you see has a long thick seam down its side.

The Red Shoes

THERE was once a little girl who was very pretty but so poor that in summer she had to go barefoot and in winter wore only heavy wooden clogs which rubbed against her bare feet until her delicate skin was red.

A shoemaker's wife who lived in the same village felt so sorry for the girl that she made her a pair of red shoes out of strips of leather that she found in her husband's workshop. The shoes were soft and light, and the little girl loved to wear them.

One day her mother died, and because the little girl had only her red shoes, she wore these as she followed the humble wooden coffin to the churchyard.

Just then a large old-looking carriage drew up, with a large old-looking lady inside it. Feeling sorry for the little girl who was now all alone in the world, she invited Karen, for that was the little girl's name, to come and live with her. Karen felt she had only been asked because the old lady liked her red shoes, but she went to live in the old lady's house. However, as soon as she moved in the shoes were taken away from her and burned. The old lady had Karen taught to read and to sew, and gave her new clothes and a pair of black shoes.

One day Karen saw the queen passing through the town with her little daughter. The princess was wearing a beautiful white

dress. She had no train, nor did she wear a golden crown as in the fairy tales, but on her feet were a pair of lovely red leather shoes. Karen thought there was nothing in the world as beautiful as red shoes.

By now Karen was old enough to go to church with grown-up people. She was given a new white dress and taken to the shoemaker to have a new pair of shoes made. He led her into his own private room where there were glass cabinets full of elegant leather shoes and shining boots. Among the shoes was a red pair just like the ones the princess had been wearing. "Oh, can I have those ones?" asked Karen, and the old lady, whose sight had become so bad that she could not make out the colour, bought them for the eager young girl.

So Karen went to church in red shoes—which at that time seemed a very shocking thing to do. She could think of nothing but the shoes, even when the bishop laid his hand on her head to bless her. When the old lady heard from her neighbours that Karen had worn red shoes to church, she was shocked and told her that from now on she must only wear black ones.

Next Sunday when Karen was dressing to go to church, she looked at the black shoes, and then longingly at the red. . . . And in the end she slipped the red ones on. With the old lady she walked to the church through the dusty cornfields. Outside the door an old soldier was standing leaning on a crutch. He had a strange long beard that was more red than white—in fact, it was quite a brilliant red. He dusted off their shoes for them before they entered the church and when he came to Karen's he said, "My! What lovely dancing shoes! Stay on tight when you dance!" And he gave the shoes a tap with his hand.

Karen heard nothing of the service; she forgot to sing the hymns and she forgot to say the prayers. All she could think of was the red shoes.

Presently everyone came out of the church and Karen heard the old soldier call out again, "My! What lovely dancing shoes!"

Karen couldn't resist—she just had to dance a few steps. And she went on dancing right over the graves, as if the shoes had some power over her. At last someone caught her and carried her home and pulled her shoes off. Then her legs kept still.

By and by the old lady fell ill, and asked Karen to stay by her bedside to watch over her. A ball was being held in the town and Karen had been invited and badly wanted to go. She knew that the old lady could not live long and she ought not to leave her. But then she looked at her red shoes, and she just *had* to put them on and go to the ball.

It was a splendid ball. All the important people were there, the mayor and mayoress, all the town councillors and their ladies, and all the most notable people from many miles around. It was Karen's first ball and when she had all but floated up the wide staircase, she halted for one enchanted moment at the entrance to the ballroom as if on the threshold of some fairy queen's palace, alabaster-walled, illumined by chandeliers sparkling brilliant as diamonds. But once the musicians took up their instruments and embarked on their lively tunes, she was lost to everything in the room save her own dancing feet.

There were other pretty girls at the ball, gowned in satin and brocade, shod in gold slippers, silver slippers, pink, pale blue, lilac slippers. But it was Karen who caught at all eyes in her ballerina dress of white organza, a slim white ribbon banding her glossy dark

hair and, beyond all else, her distinctive scarlet shoes. And no girl there had more partners as the evening went by.

Not that she paid much heed, or could even have said who was partnering her at any particular moment. Which was not exactly flattering to all the young men, older gallants as well, competing with each other to dance with the lightest-footed girl in that or any room. All she knew, all that she cared about was that she was dancing . . . dancing . . . dancing . . . without pause, no matter with whom—short or tall, dark or

fair, tender or bold. Scarcely could she even have told *what* she danced—waltz, minuet, gavotte, polka, whatever the music played, she whirled, twirled, pirouetted with equally bewitched rapture in her fleet red shoes.

But when the ball was over, Karen found she could not stop dancing, for the shoes carried her down the stairs, through the streets, and out by the town gate, still dancing. She danced on and on, away into the dark forest, where she saw the old soldier up among the trees, laughing and nodding and saying, "My! What lovely dancing shoes! How beautifully you dance!"

This frightened her, but no matter how she tried, she could not kick off her shoes. She had to dance on, over field and furrow, in rain and sun, by night and by day. The shoes whirled her away, over thorns and stubble, stony brook and untamed meadow.

Some people say that she is out there dancing still somewhere. On a clear day, when the sun hangs high and there is not a cloud in the sky, you may yet see her dancing in her red shoes, on and on, for ever and ever, over the hills and far away.

Johnny Appleseed

IN the early years of the last century, when the settlers were moving west across America, a strange man roamed the forests of the Ohio Territory planting appleseeds wherever he went. His real name was John Chapman, but people always called him Johnny Appleseed because he was so fond of planting apple trees wherever he wandered.

He used to wear ragged remains of other people's clothes. Often all he had as a hat was a pot turned upside down, and winter or summer he never wore shoes. When someone once asked him why he went

barefoot, he replied, "This foot offended by stepping on one of God's creatures—a snake—and so I am punishing it. The other did the same—and crushed a worm—and so it is receiving the same punishment."

He loved all living things; he made friends in the forests with wild animals. One day he found a wolf caught by its leg in a trap. Most people would have been afraid to go near it, but Johnny freed it and treated the wound until it was healed. The wolf was so grateful that it followed him about like a dog for a long time afterwards.

Johnny once rescued a little girl from the Indians who had captured her. He came across her by chance one day as he was walking near the shores of Lake Michigan. She was barefooted and dressed in a deer-skin shirt and an Indian wrap-around leather skirt. Johnny noticed that her skin was fair and her hair light brown. She was minding an Indian baby as it slept on a wooden cradle board, wrapped tightly in a cloth to stop it falling out.

"What is your name?" he asked.

"My name is Sophie," she replied. Then the little girl picked up the baby and ran off into the woods. Johnny followed her until he came to an Indian village. Here he saw some women kneeling on the ground, grinding meal by rubbing it between two stones. The houses in the village were made of elm bark, and strange wooden masks and war clubs hung from their doorframes.

The Indians knew all about Johnny Appleseed. They liked him because he had never tried to hurt them or take their land, and because he too could make strange and beautiful things out of wood.

In his wanderings Johnny had come across the little girl's parents, and had heard the story of how she had got separated from them. They had been travelling on a wagon trail going west from Pennsylvania to Ohio when Sophie had wandered off into the woods on her own. They had searched for her for days without finding her, and in the end the wagons had had to move on, believing that the child had been killed by a bear or a rattlesnake. But a tribe of Indians had found her and adopted her as one of their own.

Now Johnny looked at the Indians and then at the little white girl in their midst. He tried to think of something to give them in exchange for the child. Slowly he untied his belt. It was a wampum belt, made of purple clam shell beads, and it had been given him by some Indians in exchange for a horse. The Indians did not use money, and they prized these wampum belts as highly as white men do gold coins. Johnny handed the chief his belt and the wooden carving knife that he always carried on him. The Indian nodded his head in the direction of the child and Johnny led her away.

And so it was that Sophie rejoined her father and mother and her sister Sarah. She

lived for many years in a small wooden cabin on Lake Erie, and when she had grown quite old she used to gather her grandchildren around her to show them a little doll made of corn husks. It was an Indian doll, and it reminded her of the days when she too had been a bare-footed little Indian girl in the forest.

Johnny had never had a wife nor had he had any children of his own. He did not even have a house. On nights when the weather was so bitter that he couldn't be outdoors he would knock on a cabin door and, although he would always be offered a bed for the night, he would just stretch out on the floor and rest his tired feet against the rough logs of the wall and go to sleep just as comfortably as if he were in a real bed.

His outdoor life made him strong and hardy. Once he had set out across a frozen lake with another man when night caught them unawares. It grew so cold that the other man froze to death, but Johnny managed to keep warm by rolling on the ice like a dog, and in the morning he crossed the lake safely. In his wanderings he often met

bears, but he never carried a gun and they must have sensed that he would not hurt them, for they never harmed him.

One snowy evening he lit a fire at one end of a hollow log, meaning to crawl into the other end and shelter there for the night. But a growl came from inside, and Johnny saw that a bear with some cubs was already sheltering there. So he put out the fire and slept in the snow.

He gave apple trees to everyone who could not afford to buy them, and he carried a Bible in his shirt and read from it to the settlers in their cabins. One day when someone asked him if he wasn't afraid of rattlesnakes biting his bare feet, he pulled out his Bible and said that this was his protection. In fact a rattlesnake did bite him one day, and the Indian who was with him killed it. Johnny was quite angry, saying that the snake hadn't meant to hurt him. Someone who knew Johnny said that his skin was so tough from his outdoor life that it would kill a rattlesnake to try to bite through it. Everyone laughed at Johnny, but he had a good wit himself. Some lawyers were teasing him one day about heaven, and asking him if they too would practise law in heaven. "No," said Johnny, "in hell."

"Then would we do there what we do now?" asked the lawyers.

"Exactly the same," said Johnny. "You would stand up to your knees in filth and spend your days throwing it in each other's faces." Everyone laughed, except the lawyers.

Someone else asked him if all people would keep their earthly jobs when they were in heaven.

"Yes," said Johnny. And would we die there?

"No," said Johnny.

"Then I would be out of a job," said the man, "for I am a gravedigger."

He had a generous heart. He was known to have given away as much as fifty dollars at one time to a needy family. He was always giving away his apple trees. In fact the men

who worked for him at the orchard he planted had standing orders to give trees to anyone in need, and when a family of six children lost both mother and father he gave the oldest boy sixty trees, which became the foundation of a fine orchard of six hundred trees.

If Johnny ever had any money he never put it in a bank but hid it under the roots of a tree—and often just gave it away. Once a settler saw Johnny walking through the snow in torn shoes and gave him a good pair—only to find him the next day walking barefoot again.

"Where are your good shoes?" the man asked.

"Oh, I gave them to a poor family moving west," said Johnny. "They needed them more than I do."

Johnny could bear physical pain and

he couldn't understand why he had escaped and not the horses; in the end he reasoned that it must have been because the Indians needed the horses more than he did.

He sometimes showed people how he could bear pain by sticking pins into his flesh without flinching. If he cut himself he would first sear the place with a fiery iron, then treat it as a burn.

Yet he could not bear seeing other creatures in pain, nor could he bring himself to kill them. He once built a fire, and clouds of mosquitoes flew towards the light and were consumed by the flames. Johnny took off his tin hat, filled it with water, and put out the fire, saying, "God forbid that I should make a fire for my own comfort that would be the cause of another's death."

Another time an old hunter chanced on Johnny playing in the woods with three bear cubs, while the mother bear looked on.

He took his turn working on the public roads, and one day, in Green Township, someone disturbed a wasps' nest. One of them flew up the leg of Johnny's trousers, but instead of killing it he gently worked the wasp back down the leg, though it stung him time after time, until it escaped. When someone asked why he hadn't killed it, he said that the creature was only obeying its

danger as well as any Indian brave. The Indians were said to respect him as a man who could work strong medicine. He walked in the forests without a gun, where other white men would certainly have been killed. One day the Indians did carry him off and his horses; but it was only the horses they wanted.

He had come by the horses because of his kind nature. In those days all the old, useless plough horses and others like them were turned loose into the wilderness to perish. Johnny would collect these old horses and feed them and care for them, sometimes nursing them back into good shape again. Then he would lend them or give them away to people who were in need.

One day, when he was riding through the woods with ten horses he had collected, the Indians took him prisoner. But they soon released him, keeping only the horses. To Johnny, such things were all God's will, but

nature and that it didn't *intend* to hurt him.

However, he once had to kill a forest animal. He was walking in the wilderness when a bear suddenly rose out of the bushes and reared to attack him. Johnny grabbed a long branch to protect himself, but the branch broke at every blow he struck until it was only about three feet long. Yet he managed to club the bear to death and when he had built a fire and feasted on the meat, he carried its hide and a quarter of the animal into the nearest settlement, where the hungry pioneers were glad indeed to receive it.

Johnny had originally wanted to be a preacher, and he would always read from his Bible to anyone willing to listen. But he spent most of his time in what Christ called *witnessing*; planting his appleseeds and doing simple acts of goodness to both men and animals around him. And although he was often laughed at for his strange ways, he was respected and admired by all who met him for his overwhelming kindness.

Far into his old age Johnny Appleseed still roamed the states of Ohio, Indiana, and Illinois that had been established in the land he used to know as the Ohio Territory. He would visit the nurseries and orchards that had sprung from his appleseeds, and help cultivate them. He still slept outside, often in a hammock slung from the tops of two springy young trees. If you came upon him in one of his orchards, lying down to rest from the hot sun under a thorn bush, he would probably be hoeing with one hand the weeds within his reach.

He was in a way a kind of saint, spending his life doing little acts of kindness wherever he went. He had traded the comforts of a home and family to lead his strange wandering life, and he made the best of it so that he could help the poor, struggling families who were trying to gain a foothold on the land of the midwestern settlement.

At seventy Johnny continued to travel, walking miles through the forest to visit his apple trees and see that they were cared for. He was still dressed in his strange tin-pot hat,

torn, cast-off shirt and trousers, and a coat of his own invention. This was a single length of stuff stretching to his ankles, with a hole cut in it for the head and straight sleeves cut into holes at the side. And he still walked barefoot. He had spent his life planting apple trees and caring for everything living around him. As he said of himself, "It's a comfort to think I have done good in this world, though I haven't done much."

But he had done more than he thought. Even before his death, he had become a legend. Books and poems were written about him and songs sung of him. People who met him were warmed by his kindness, but so were those who only heard about his strange and good life. His example bore

fruit for generations, just as his apple trees did. The way he lived still inspires people, and whenever they see apple trees blossom they think of Johnny Appleseed and do a little better.

Eventually his roaming days came to an end. He was staying with friends when he heard that some cattle were trampling trees in one of his nurseries, and without a thought he walked twenty miles to the place, drove the cattle off and mended the fence. He returned exhausted, and lay down in the garden to rest. That night he was dead.

The world is a poorer place without him. Few men are born as kind as he was, and even fewer use their kindness as well as he did. The many friends he had helped missed him sadly, and the forest birds and animals looked for him in vain along the leafy paths that his bare brown feet had trod for so long. The children missed their presents, and the apple trees their care.

But they say that certain people—children whose thoughts have not yet turned away from simple things and older folk with goodness in their hearts—passing the old cemetery at Duck Creek in Washington County, Ohio, can sometimes see him still. Some of Johnny's family are buried there, and the tale goes that he himself sometimes sits in the gnarled branches of an old apple tree, munching an apple and swinging his berry-brown feet in the air, singing, or reading from his Bible, or just smiling.

Rumpelstiltzkin

THERE was once a miller who was poorer than most, but he had a beautiful daughter. The girl was the apple of his eye, and her father boasted that she was lovely enough to be a queen.

One day the king rode by. He noticed the girl by the mill stream, washing linen.

"How beautiful she is!" the king thought to himself. Aloud he said, "What is your name?"

Before the girl could answer, her father replied, "If you please, Sire, that is my daughter. A finer girl you will never see!"

The king looked down at them both with interest from his beautiful dappled grey horse.

"Indeed! She has a lovely face!" he replied. The miller's heart swelled with pride.

"To be sure, to be sure! But there's more to her than her face!" he said.

"What do you mean, miller?" the king asked curiously.

"She can . . . she can . . ." the miller tried desperately to think of something that would impress a king. His eyes met the king's, and he looked down at his feet. He watched the chickens scratch around in

the yellow straw, looking for grain.

"She can spin this straw into gold!" he exclaimed with a look of immense triumph.

"But father . . ." his daughter broke in, dismayed at his untrue words.

"A rare girl indeed!" the king said, and smiled. "If your fingers can really turn straw into gold, then your place is in my castle. Come with me, and I will see if it is true."

The girl had no choice but to obey her king, and together they rode to his castle. When they arrived there, he led her to a high, dark room that was filled with straw. A spinning wheel stood in the centre. The king said:

"You have until sunrise to spin this dry straw into gold. But if you do not, and if your father has lied to me, then you must surely die!"

The girl heard the bolts being drawn

across the door, and she was so terrified that she started to cry. Then she noticed a little man standing in front of her.

"What is the matter?" he asked. "I'm so unhappy," wept the girl. "The king has commanded me to spin all this straw into gold by the morning, and I haven't a notion how to do it!"

"What will you give me if I do it for you?" the little man asked.

"The locket around my neck," she replied. The little man took the locket, sat himself down at the wheel, and in no time at all the bales of straw were spun into a pile of bobbins full of rich gold thread.

As soon as the sun rose the king came, unbolted the door, and was delighted to see so much new gold around him. But his privy purse was still not nearly full, and he needed a lot more gold to pay the soldiers who guarded his land from greedy neighbours. He took the miller's daughter into a much larger room, and told her to spin all the straw into gold by the next morning.

That night the girl began to cry again, for she knew her task was hopeless. But again the little man appeared, and again he said, "What will you give me if I spin the straw into gold for you?"

"The belt around my waist," she said. The little man took the belt, and whirr! round went the spinning wheel again, and bobbin after bobbin was filled with the fine gold thread, until there was no straw left.

The king was pleased beyond measure at the sight. He knew that with just a little more gold in his treasury, he could really get the country going again. So he filled his largest room with straw and led the girl into it.

"If you can spin all this away during the night," he said, "I will take you as my wife, and then you need never spin straw again."

When the girl was alone the little man appeared for the third time, and said, "What will you give me if I spin the straw for you again?"

"I have nothing left to give you," she replied. "Then promise me that you will give me your first-born child when you are queen," said the little man.

The girl thought that a lot of things could happen before that, so she promised him what he demanded. When the king came in the morning he found great heaps of gold where the straw had been.

"Oh, miller's daughter," he said, "You have spun more gold for me in three nights than I could hope to find in three score years. Your skill is only matched by your great beauty. Will you be my queen?"

So the girl, who already loved him dearly, became his wife, and in time she gave birth to their son. She had quite

forgotten her promise to the little man, until one day he stepped into the room and said, "Now give me what you promised." The queen was dismayed, and begged him to take all her jewels and riches instead. He refused but then he said, "Since you cry so bitterly at the loss of your baby, I will give you one chance to save him. You may have three days in which to guess my name, and if you do, then you may keep him."

The queen stayed awake all night, trying to remember all the names she had ever heard. When the little man arrived the following day she began with Nicholas, Timothy, Hereward, and all the other names she knew, but after each one he called out, "That is not my name." The next day she read all the books in the royal library and memorized all the uncommon names in them. She asked, "Is your name Nimrod or Noah or Marmaduke?" but he always replied calmly, "That is not my name."

The third day she sent messengers all over the country to learn what names people were calling their children. At length one messenger came back and said:

"I have not been able to find any new names, but on a high hill where the foxes and hares bid each other goodnight I saw a little man dancing around a fire, singing:

'Oh, little thinks my royal dame,
That Rumpelstiltzkin is my name!'"

Imagine the Queen's delight when she heard that name, but when the little man arrived that night, she asked first:

"Is your name Roger?" "No."

"Is your name Robert?" "No."

"Is it, perhaps, Rumpelstiltzkin?"

"The devil it is, the devil it is!" he screamed, and stamped his foot into the ground with such fury that he split in two.

Thumbelina

THERE was once a woman who lived all alone. What she wanted most of all in the world was to have a little child, but she had not the faintest idea where to find or even look for one. So eventually she went to a witch who had recently settled in the neighbourhood and said to her, "I would so dearly like to have a little child. I beg you, do please tell me where I can possibly go to find one."

"Oh," said the witch, "I only wish everyone wanted something so easy of me. You don't even have to go far for it." And while the cat curled up beside her gave a knowing wink and the wide-eyed owl nodded its wise agreement from its perch behind her, the witch fumbled in her pocket for a moment, then said, "Here, take this barleycorn. It's a very special one, of course. But all you have to do is plant it in a flower

pot, and you'll soon see what happens."

"Thank you more than I can say," breathed the grateful woman, giving the witch a penny. And she went home and planted the barleycorn.

In no time at all the grain began to put out the palest green shoots and as the woman watered, tended and watched it as no one had ever watered, tended or watched a plant before, the shoots grew into long, furled leaves protecting an invisible stem, until one morning the woman awoke to find that the stem had tapered overnight into a lovely, slender flower. It looked like a tulip, but the petals were shut tight as though it were still in bud.

"What a pretty flower!" the woman exclaimed, and leaned over impulsively to give the petals a kiss. Directly her lips touched them, the tulip burst wide open, and there, sitting in the middle of the flower, was a tiny, perfectly formed little girl. Her skin was tenderly pink as almond blossom, her hair burnished gold as a harvest moon, and marvel of all, she was no taller than your thumb, so the woman immediately gave her the name Thumbelina.

A well-varnished walnut shell served as her cradle, blue violet petals for her mattress, and a rose leaf for her blanket. In the daytime she was allowed to play about on the table, where the woman had put a plate with flowers. Their stalks stood in water, and a large tulip petal floated in the middle of the plate. Thumbelina liked to sit on this and row herself from one side of the plate to the other, using a couple of white horsehairs as oars. She used to sing while she rowed, in the sweetest voice you ever heard.

One night, as she lay in her walnut cradle, a hideous toad came hopping in through the window. It was big and ugly and slimy, and it jumped straight down onto the table where Thumbelina was lying asleep under her rose leaf.

"She'll make a good wife for my son!" thought the toad, and snatched up the cradle with Thumbelina still in it. Then she hopped

with it back through the wide-open window and out into the dark and gloomy night.

A stream ran through the garden; it had a muddy bank, and here the toad lived with her son. Ugh! what an ugly and horrible creature he was! "Coax, coax, brekke-ke-kex!" was all he could say when he saw the lovely little Thumbelina in the walnut shell.

"Sh! Not so loud, or you'll wake her," said the old toad. "She might run away from us, for she's as light as thistledown. Let's put her out in the stream on one of those large water-lily leaves. She's so small and light that the leaf will be like an island for her. She can't escape from there, and in the meantime we'll clear a hole out of the mud for you two to live in."

The old toad swam out and placed the walnut shell with Thumbelina still sleeping in it on the largest leaf she could find.

Early the next morning the little girl woke up and, when she saw where she was, she cried bitterly. The toads decorated the new room they had made with rushes and yellow water lilies, and then they swam out to Thumbelina. The mother toad made a low curtsey to the girl and said, "Here is my son. He'll make you a fine husband, and you will live happily together down in the mud."

"Coax, coax, brekke-ke-kex!" was all that the son could say. Then he and his mother took the walnut bed and swam away to put it into the bridal chamber.

Thumbelina sat on the green leaf and cried, for she didn't want to marry the toad. Some fishes, swimming around under the lilies, had overheard the toad's words, and they were sorry for her. So they swarmed together and nibbled at the water-lily stalk until the leaf came loose and floated downstream, far away from the two toads.

The sunshine gleamed on the water like fine gold, and the birds sang all around Thumbelina. A dainty little white butterfly fluttered round her, and at last it settled on her leaf. Thumbelina took the ribbon out of her hair and tied one end of it to the butterfly, while she made the other end fast

to the leaf. So the butterfly flew ahead, pulling the leaf with Thumbelina on it. Just then a large cockroach flew down and caught Thumbelina by the waist and carried her up into a tree. But the leaf went floating on, with the butterfly still tied to it.

What a fright it gave Thumbelina! But what upset her even more was the thought of the butterfly that she had tied to the leaf. It would starve to death unless it could free itself. The cockroach told her how pretty she was, which pleased Thumbelina but made all the women cockroaches in the tree spitefully jealous. "Why, she has only got two legs!" they scoffed, squatting there on their own six. "And she hasn't any feelers!" they sniffed, flaunting theirs as boastfully as young ladies might their ostrich-feather headdresses at a ball. "And did you ever see such clothes!" they taunted, disdainfully eyeing Thumbelina's primrose-leaf bodice and rose-petalled skirt. "Isn't she ugly!"

When the cockroach heard all the others criticizing Thumbelina, he took another look at her himself and decided she wasn't so pretty after all and he would waste no more time on her. Upon which, he promptly flew her down from the tree and left her sitting on a daisy, crying because she thought she was so ugly.

Thumbelina managed to live alone in the wood right through that summer. She took blades of grass and plaited them into a bed, and she hung this under a dock leaf to be out of the rain. She sipped the honey in the flowers for food, and drank the dew on the leaves in the mornings and at night.

And she did, somehow, have company from time to time. A sparrow hopped by one morning and scattered some crumbs for her from his bill. When she protested that she really couldn't deprive him of his own lunch like that, he chirruped "Nonsense!". "I can always get more where they came from. I can even bring you some more tomorrow." And he did too, staying each time to watch her nibble away at this

unexpected treat before he flew on again. A shame, he said, that he couldn't take her with him, but he didn't think his wife would exactly welcome sharing their nest with such a pretty young rival.

Her next visitor was an unusually agreeable caterpillar who, seeing her sitting lonely on a dandelion, offered her a ride on his back. Thumbelina, who had of course never been on a switchback, readily accepted, thinking it would be a nice change to see a bit more of the countryside than she could on her own tiny feet. But after she had humped and bumped along for no more than a yard or so on that bristly back, her head felt so dizzy and her fragile skin so sore that she had to ask to be let down. Being a well-mannered little girl who preferred not to give offence, she made the excuse that the sun had become rather hot. "Just my luck!" shrugged the caterpillar sadly, nearly toppling Thumbelina off head first. But although disappointed at losing such a desirable passenger so quickly, he crawled obligingly over to a clover leaf in whose shade he set her gently down, then went tactfully on his way, humping and bumping along as he had come. He too would very much have liked her for a wife, but he had modesty enough to know that so exquisite a little creature could never be happy with such an awkward fellow as himself.

"It hasn't really been such a bad summer" Thumbelina thought. A glowworm had given

her some companionable light one moonless evening on her way home from a rendezvous with a grasshopper. Sociable ants would sometimes pause for a chat when scurrying to build another industrious colony. Once a hedgehog hunched up crossly beside her and stayed for two whole days, letting her diminutive fingers soothe the prickle he had blunted on an even pricklier thorn. Thumbelina was a bit scared of him at first, but she got used to his grousing about thorns and their tricks, and he did thank her, in his own gruff way, when he moved on again.

But the summer was over now. And then the winter came—the long, cold winter. All the birds that had sung to her now flew away to warmer countries; the winds blew away the flower petals and the leaves from the trees, and the great dock leaf that she had been living under furled itself into a faded yellow stalk. She felt the cold terribly, for her clothes were torn and thin. It began to snow, and every snowflake that fell on her was like a shovelful of snow being thrown on one of us. She wrapped herself in a dead leaf and shivered with cold.

On the edge of the wood was a cornfield, but the corn had long been harvested and only the bare stubble still stood in the frozen earth. To Thumbelina it was like walking through a forest, but at length she came to a fieldmouse's door. It was just a little hole, but it led to a roomful of corn and a splendid kitchen and parlour. Poor Thumbelina stood just inside the door like a beggar girl, and asked for a barleycorn, for she had not eaten for days.

"You poor little thing!" the fieldmouse said. "Come in and have a bite with me in my warm parlour." She liked the look of the little girl, and added, "You're welcome to stay with me for the winter, as long as you'll keep my rooms tidy and tell me stories in the long dark evenings." So Thumbelina stayed with the fieldmouse, and was comfortable there.

"We shall have a visitor before long," said the fieldmouse one day. "My neighbour is coming to see us. He is much richer than I am, and he wears a lovely black velvet coat. Try and get him for a husband, and then you can live in comfort. But his sight's very bad: you'll have to tell him all the nicest stories you know."

Thumbelina had no intention of marrying the neighbour, for he was a mole. He came and called on them in his black velvet coat. He was very learned, but he couldn't bear sunshine or flowers; he said all sorts of nasty things about them, never having seen them. The fieldmouse made Thumbelina sing to him, and the mole fell in love with her, but he didn't say anything—he was much too cautious for that.

He invited Thumbelina to stroll through the passage between his house and hers and told her not to be afraid of the dead bird that was lying there. It was a swallow; its pretty wings were folded to its sides, and its head and legs were tucked in beneath its feathers. The poor bird must have died of cold, and Thumbelina felt sorry for it. But the mole just kicked it and said smugly, "What's a bird got to show for all its twittering and singing in the summer? In the winter it must starve and freeze. But I suppose that's considered a great thing these days."

Thumbelina didn't say a word, but when the mole had gone on she stooped down and kissed the swallow's closed eyes. Then she plaited a big fine blanket of hay and carried it down and spread it over the dead bird. She took some soft thistledown she had found and tucked it around the swallow so that it might lie warm in its last resting place. "Goodbye, little bird!" she said, and rested her head against its breast for a moment. She sprang up again in a great fright, for she had heard a kind of thumping inside. It was the bird's heart! The swallow wasn't dead; it had been unconscious with cold, and now, as it grew warmer, it was reviving.

Thumbelina tucked the thistledown still more closely around it and fetched a curled mint leaf that she had been using for her own counterpane and spread this over the bird. The following night she again stole down to the passageway and this time the swallow was conscious and could open its eyes.

"Thank you, my child," it said. "Thanks to you I shall get back my strength and be able to fly again."

Then Thumbelina brought the swallow some water in a gorse petal. The bird drank it and told her how it had torn its wing on a bramble and so had not been able to fly away with the other swallows.

Thumbelina continued to nurse the swallow, but neither the mouse nor the mole knew anything about it, or they would have forbidden her.

Spring arrived, and the sun began to warm the earth again. The swallow flew off into the woods and would have taken Thumbelina with it if the little girl had not feared to upset the fieldmouse by leaving her.

She felt so sad, for she was never allowed to go out in the sunshine. "You will have to start making your wedding trousseau soon," said the fieldmouse, "for you will need a lot of woollens and linens when you're married to the mole." The fieldmouse then engaged four spiders to spin and weave for Thumbelina and the mole. They were to be married at the end of the summer for the mole very much preferred the cold seasons to the warm.

Thumbelina wept bitterly

because she didn't want to marry the mole.

"Don't be so pig-headed, my girl," said the fieldmouse, "or I'll bite you with my teeth. He'll make you a splendid husband. The queen herself hasn't anything as fine as his black velvet coat. You ought to thank heaven he's yours."

The wedding day arrived. Thumbelina couldn't bear to say goodbye to the sun and live deep down under the earth for ever. She ran to the doorway and stretched out her arms. "Oh, my dear swallow! Where are you now?" she cried.

"Tweet-tweet!" called a voice over her head. She looked up, and there was the swallow, just passing. It was delighted to see Thumbelina again. She told it how she was being forced to marry the mole and live under the earth with him.

"The cold winter will soon be here," said the swallow, "and I'm flying far away to the south. Will you come with me? You can sit on my back and tie yourself on with your sash. Where I'm going it's always summer and there are lovely flowers all the year round. Dear Thumbelina, do come with me."

"Yes, I'll come," said Thumbelina, and climbed onto the bird's back. She settled her feet on its outstretched wings and tied her sash to its strongest feathers. Then the swallow flew high up in the air, over lakes and forests, and over the mountains. Thumbelina shivered in the cold air, but then she nestled closer under the bird's warm feathers and looked down at the snow-capped peaks beneath her.

At last they reached the south. The sun shone brightly there, and the sky was blue and seemed much farther away. There were vineyards on the hillsides and groves of olive trees and oranges. The air smelt sweetly of myrtle and curled mint, and lovely, dark-eyed children darted around after butterflies.

The swallow kept flying on and on, till at last they came to an ancient palace of white marble standing beside a blue lake. The tall pillars were covered in vines, and on the top of one of these was the swallow's nest.

A large white marble column was lying on the ground by the lake. It had fallen and broken into several pieces, and around these were growing the loveliest coloured flowers. The swallow flew down with Thumbelina and placed her gently on one of the petals. There, in the middle of a flower, sat a little man who wore a gold crown on his head and had folded wings on his shoulders. He was the guardian of the flowers, and in size he was no bigger than Thumbelina. He fell in love with her, and asked her to be his wife. She gladly agreed and, as a wedding present, he gave her a pair of beautiful wings, so that she too could fly from flower to flower.

The Goosegirl

ONCE upon a time there was an old queen who had a beautiful daughter. When she grew up the queen set about looking for a suitable husband for the girl, and finally arranged with a neighbouring king that she should marry his son.

The queen gave her daughter many costly jewels, pearls and rubies and emeralds, to

carry with her on her journey, and dressed her in the finest robes of gold and satin. She commanded the grooms to untie her magic horse named Falada, and harness him with a gold saddle and silver bells. Finally she chose as her daughter's companion for the journey a serving maid who was both quick-witted and fearless. Thus equipped, the good queen thought the princess would come to no harm.

When the hour for leave-taking drew near, the queen went to her bedroom and, taking a small silver knife, she cut her finger until it bled, and let three drops of her blood fall onto a white handkerchief. This she gave to the princess, saying:

"Dear child, take good care of this handkerchief. I have cast a spell on it, and while you have it you will come to no great harm."

So they said goodbye to each other, and the princess folded the handkerchief into her bodice, mounted the horse Falada, and set out to meet her bride-groom, with the serving maid following a short distance behind.

After they had ridden for a few hours the sun stood high in the sky, and the girls and their horses grew thirsty. The princess said to the serving maid:

"Please bring me some water from the stream; go, fill my silver cup with it."

To her surprise, the maid replied curtly, "If you are thirsty, dismount and lie down by the water and drink. I don't want to wait on you."

The princess, who had a gentle nature, dismounted from her horse and bent over the stream and drank. She had to cup the water in her hands, for the maid would not let her have the silver cup. As she drank, she murmured: "Oh, Heaven, what shall I do?" and the three drops of blood on her mother's handkerchief replied:

"Ah, if your mother only knew,
Her heart would surely break in two."

The princess quietly mounted her horse

again, and they rode on until the sun beat down on their heads and the princess became faint with thirst again. As they passed by a pool she called to her serving maid:

"Please bring me some clear water from the pool; go, fill my cup with it," for she was used to asking these things, and had forgotten the girl's rude words. But the maid replied:

"If you are thirsty, dismount and go and get a drink for yourself. I don't want to wait on you."

The princess was so thirsty that she dismounted and leaned out over the pool, and drank from it. Her tears fell into the water as she cried:

"Oh, Heaven, what will become of me?" And the three drops of blood replied:

"Ah, if your mother only knew;
Her heart would surely break in two."

The princess wept so bitterly that she did not notice that the handkerchief had fallen

out of her bodice and floated off into the pool. But the maid saw what had happened and was delighted because the queen's spell was now broken, and the bride was no more than a defenceless girl, weak and powerless against the world.

When she wished to mount Falada again, the waiting maid called out, "Take your hands off him; I mean to ride the magic horse now. You must take mine." So the princess was forced to hand over her horse with his golden saddle and silver bells. Then the maid ordered her to take off her royal robes and exchange them for her own common ones, right down to the princess's chemise of fine muslin and silk, which the serving girl slipped on in return for her own one of coarse linen. When this was done the maid took the gold and amber hairpins and silk ribbons out of the princess's hair, and placed the royal coronet of lace and pearls on her own head, while the princess's long golden hair fell loose around her shoulders.

Then the maid said: "Unless you solemnly swear that you will never tell a living soul of what happened on this journey, I will kill you." The princess saw that the maid meant what she said and was so terrified that she gave her word. Then the maid mounted Falada and the princess mounted the maid's pony and they rode on until they reached the king's palace. The prince hurried to meet them and at once mistook the serving girl for the princess. He led her up the steps to present her to the people as his bride, while the true princess stood waiting in the courtyard. The old king, however, saw her from the window and admired her beauty and gracefulness. He asked his son's bride who the slender, silent companion in servants' clothes was, and the false princess said quickly:

"That's just a simple girl I met wandering on the road and brought along with me for company. I have no need of her now; give her some work to keep her busy."

"In that case," said the king, "let her help the boy who minds the geese outside the city walls; it is simple work and will not tire her."

So the princess was sent to join Conrad, the gooseboy, on the green slopes outside the city walls.

Next the false princess said to the prince: "Before we celebrate our wedding I want you to grant me one favour. Please kill my horse Falada. He almost threw me several times on the way here, and is too dangerous to ride." The prince at once commanded that Falada be killed and his body thrown outside the walls.

When the true princess heard of the fate that had befallen her faithful horse, she wept. She begged the man who had killed him to nail his head over the city gate, through which she drove her geese every morning and every night, so that she could still see him sometimes. The slaughterer did as she wished, and nailed the head fast over the arched entrance to the city.

Early the next morning as she and Conrad drove their geese out of the city, they passed through the gate and under the horse's head. The princess sighed to herself and said:

"Falada, Falada, you hang there dead!" and the head replied:

"Alas! Princess, for the tears you shed!
Ah, if your mother only knew;
Her heart would surely break in two!"

The princess was so overcome at sight of the dead horse's head and at the sorrowing words it had spoken that she sank down to the ground beneath it, her eyes too misted by fresh tears to guide her way a step farther. The simple Conrad, as unaware as anyone of her true identity or the cause of her grief, hovered hesitant and somewhat curious by, until she was sufficiently collected to dab her tears away, to come unaided to her feet, and to fall in again beside him.

Then they went out of the city and drove the geese over to the green slopes and apple orchards where they could peck and wander all day long. The princess's golden hair was

caught by the wind and blown this way and that, because she had no pins nor clips to hold it down. In the past she had never dressed her own hair but had always had servant girls to arrange it for her, and now she found it hard to try to plait it together and tie it with a piece of string, which was all she had. She combed out the tangles and knots until her hair hung like a silk curtain down her back. But every time she tried to gather it together in her hands to plait it, the wind blew it high over her head and she had to begin all over again.

The gooseboy Conrad watched her with great interest. Her hair gleamed so brightly that he longed to pull out some of the strands for himself.

"Give me your hair!" he said, trying to snatch at it.

But the princess called out:

"Wind, wind, come today,
Come blow Conrad's hat away;
Let him chase past cows and swine
Till my hair so gold and fine
Is no longer hanging loose
But tightly plaited in a noose."

No sooner had she said these words than a gust of wind came and blew Conrad's hat away and he had to chase after it over the fields and through the orchards. While the geese pecked in the grass around her feet, the princess had all the time she needed to learn how to plait her golden hair. When at length Conrad came back with his hat in his hand she had one thick plait hanging down her back, and was able to laugh at him. That made Conrad angry, and he would not speak to her for the rest of the day. So they watched the geese in silence until the sun

went down, and then they drove them home.

The next morning, as they passed under the city gate, driving the geese before them, the girl said:

"Falada, Falada, you hang there dead!" and the horse's head replied:

"Alas! Princess, for the tears you shed!
Ah, if your mother only knew,
Her heart would surely break in two!"

Then she and Conrad went on their way until they reached the green slopes and orchards, where the geese wandered and fed. The wind was blowing again, and again the princess's hair slipped loose and the wind teased it over her head and around her face, until she had to sit down and comb it out. Conrad came running up to try to snatch at it, but again the princess called out:

"Wind, wind, come today,
Come blow Conrad's hat away;
Let him chase past cows and swine
Till my hair so gold and fine
Is no longer hanging loose
But tightly plaited in a noose."

No sooner had she said these words than a gust of wind came and blew Conrad's hat away. It tossed it up like a ball and threw it down again, always just out of reach of the boy.

By the time he had finally caught it and crammed it back on his head she had long finished plaiting her hair, and he had no chance of getting any of it for himself. This made Conrad so angry that he refused even to look at the girl, and sat poking a hole in the earth with his stick until it grew dark and time to return to the city.

That evening, when they came home, Conrad went to the king and said that he would not go herding geese with the girl any more. "She teases me all day, your majesty," he said, "and the wind obeys her command. She speaks to the dead horse's head and the head answers her with very strange words."

The old king listened with interest and then commanded Conrad to go out as usual the next day. Next morning he hid behind the city gate and heard the girl talking to Falada. Then he followed them to the orchard and watched while the girl let loose her glittering hair and the wind obeyed her and blew Conrad's hat away while she plaited it.

When she returned to the city that night, the king sent for her and questioned her about her strange behaviour. Weeping bitterly, she replied that she was under oath never to speak of it to a mortal soul. "Then tell your troubles to that iron stove," said the king, and he left the room.

The princess stood by the stove and, still weeping, told it everything that had happened since she left her mother's palace. The old king, meanwhile, had been standing beside the stovepipe outside the room, and heard everything she said. Then he commanded that royal clothes be brought to her and that her hair be dressed again as befitted a queen.

He sent for his son and told him about the serving maid's deceit and that this was his true bride. And the prince was glad, for he had begun to dislike and mistrust his intended bride and longed for a gentler and more loving wife. The maid was banished from the kingdom; the young prince married the true princess and they ruled the kingdom in peace and happiness.

Falada had meanwhile turned to stone above the city gate. But one morning as the princess looked up at the head, as always in passing, her astonished eyes saw it incline slightly to watch her go by. And the following morning, there the horse himself stood restored at the gate, golden saddle gleaming, silver bells jingling. For he was, after all, a magic horse, and had only feigned death against the day he could once more serve his rightful royal mistress. As he did, to her joy, from that day forth and for evermore.